Dooley Takes the Fall

Dooley Takes the Fall

by Norah McClintock

5 4 3 2

Published by Red Deer Press
A Fitzhenry & Whiteside Company

www.reddeerpress.com
www.fitzhenry.ca

Credits
Edited for the Press by Peter Carver
Cover design by Jacquie Morris
Text design by Dean Pickup
Printed and bound in Canada by Friesens for Red Deer Press

Acknowledgements
Red Deer Press acknowledges the support of the Canada Council for the Arts. We also acknowledge the financial support also provided by Government of Canada through the Book Publishing Industry Development Program (BPIDP).

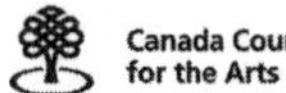

Canada Council for the Arts   Conseil des Arts du Canada

Library and Archives Canada Cataloguing in Publication

McClintock, Norah
Dooley takes the fall / Norah McClintock.

ISBN 978-0-88995-403-8

I. Title.
PS8575.C62D66 2007   jC813'.54   C2007-905343-2

Publisher Cataloging-in-Publication Data (U.S)

McClintock, Norah.
Dooley Takes the Fall / Norah McClintock
[320] p. : cm.
Summary: As a troubled teen struggles to free himself from his past and the implications of the present conspiracies that surround him, Dooley tries to prove his innocence in a suicide that looks like murder.
ISBN-13: 9780889954038 (pbk.)
1. Conduct of life — Fiction. 2. Self-acceptance — Fiction. I. Title.
[Fic] dc22   PZ7.M33656   2008

Nobody told me there'd be days like these.
– John Lennon

Hey, Mickey, I'm with you. F.Y.L.

One

Dooley was looking down at the kid sprawled on the asphalt path in the ravine when two things happened. First, Dooley's pager vibrated. Dooley knew without checking that it was his uncle trying to reach him. Second, a boy maybe twelve years old, on a bike, stopped next to Dooley, looked at the kid lying on the pavement and said, "Is he dead?"

"Yeah, I think so," Dooley said. In fact, he was sure of it. The moon was bright and the kid had landed in a half-circle of light cast on the ground by a lamp on one of the utility poles above him. Dooley squatted down. There was no air going into or coming out of the lungs of the kid on the pavement. Also, the kid's open eyes were staring at nothing, and his head was twisted, as if he had turned to look at something just before he made contact with the hard surface of the path. Plus there was blood and other stuff—Dooley didn't want to think about what it was—leaking out of the kid. He glanced up at the boy on the bike and wondered what, if anything, he had seen. "You have a phone on you?" Dooley said, standing up again.

The boy shook his head. So far he hadn't taken his eyes off the dead kid. Who could blame him? Dooley couldn't look away either. He still couldn't believe what had happened.

"You know where there's a pay phone?" Dooley said. The boy on the bike didn't answer. "There's one up there," Dooley said. He pointed to a bridge maybe half a kilometer south of where he and the boy were standing. There were pay phones on either end of it. Dooley saw them every time he crossed the bridge. Both of them had signs on them with the phone number of a distress center—the idea was that people should drop a quarter before they dropped themselves off the bridge. The phones were there even though no one could jump off that bridge anymore. The city had put up a suicide screen. If you were desperate to end it all, you had to move your action a little north or a little south to one of the other, smaller bridges and walkways over the ravine. There were plenty of them—like the one the dead kid had gone off. "Go and call 911," Dooley told the boy on the bike. "Tell them someone went off a bridge and it looks like he's dead. Okay?"

"Why don't you do it?" the boy on the bike said. Dooley had thought that he might.

"Because if he's really dead"—which he was, there was no doubt about it—"the cops are going to treat this as a crime scene," Dooley said.

That got the boy's attention. He looked away from the dead kid for the first time.

"You mean someone killed him?" he said, sounding impressed.

"I mean the cops are going to want to investigate, which means we should protect the scene from anyone disturbing it," Dooley said. The kid's eyes widened at the word "we." "The way we do that is I stay down here and make sure no one comes along and touches anything, and you go up there and call 911." The boy didn't seem to like the way Dooley had assigned responsibilities. "You have to come right back after you make the call," Dooley said. "The cops are going to want to talk to you. They're going to want a statement from you."

"Yeah?" the boy on the bike said, excited now.

"Yeah," Dooley said. "You think you can handle that?"

"You know it," the boy said. Dooley guessed he hadn't had much to do with cops. If he had, he wouldn't be so enthusiastic. The boy mounted his bike and started pedaling toward the path that led up the side of the ravine.

Dooley looked down at the kid on the asphalt. With his staring eyes and twisted head and all that blood, the kid looked pretty bad. Dooley could feel himself starting to shake. He'd seen a lot of things, but he'd never seen anything like this. He drew in a deep breath and told himself to get a grip. The kid wasn't a real person anymore. He didn't even look like a real person. He looked more like a wax dummy in a House of Horrors. Dooley wondered what the kid had been thinking on the way down. He knew he should feel sorry for the kid, but the truth was, he didn't. What goes around comes around, he thought.

Dooley felt like an idiot having to tell the first cop that showed up, "I gotta get to a phone and call home right away."

But he did it anyway because, if worst came to worst, the cop would be able to tell Dooley's uncle that Dooley had tried.

Dooley was pretty sure he recognized the cop and just as sure the cop recognized him, especially after the cop said, "First, you tell me what you know about this. Then we'll see about a phone call."

Dooley wished for the millionth time that he had a cell phone. But all he had was a dumb-ass, out-of-date pager that his uncle had given him with the following instruction: "I page you, I expect you to call me inside of ten minutes." He hadn't said, "Or else," but it was understood. Boy, was it understood. By the time the cops arrived, Dooley's uncle's first page was thirty minutes old, the second fifteen minutes old, and Dooley was picturing his uncle pacing up and down, maybe in the kitchen, maybe in the living room, definitely muttering under his breath.

Dooley looked at the cop, who walked with a swagger and who Dooley bet was one of those guys who go into policing just so he could carry a gun. He thought about his uncle, who was probably beyond pissed off that Dooley hadn't answered either of the pages by now. But what else could he have done? Left the boy on the bike alone to report a dead body after the boy had got a good look at Dooley standing over the corpse and could give the cops a description? Dooley could just imagine what the cops would make of that. Then there was the movement he had caught out of the corner of his eye: someone, it looked like, rounding the corner north of where Dooley was now. Who was that, and had that person seen anything? Besides, Dooley was about fifty percent sure that his uncle, who was a retired cop, would have approved of what Dooley was on the record as having done. Still, Dooley imagined his uncle saying, "If that kid could make one phone call, he could make two. It never occurred to you to get him to call me and tell me where you were?" Well, sure it had. But by then it was too late; the kid had already reached the edge of the ravine and was pushing his bike up, up, up to the bridge.

Dooley thought about asking the cop again, explaining the situation. But he decided, no, he didn't want to come off sounding like he was begging for a favor. He would take his chances with his uncle when the time came.

The cop told Dooley to stay put and not touch anything, and then he went to talk to his partner, who was with the kid on the bike. Dooley wondered what the kid had told the cops. The cop was back a few minutes later and pulled out a notebook.

"Okay," he said. "Name."

"Ryan Dooley."

"Age?" the cop said, wanting to find out where Dooley fit under the Criminal Code.

"Seventeen."

The cop looked annoyed. Dooley figured he'd been hoping to hear eighteen. Eighteen made it easy. Seventeen made it YCJA.

"Address," the cop said, and then asked him again a minute later, after Dooley had already told him, checking, Dooley knew, to see if Dooley was spinning him one. Dooley repeated what he had already said.

"ID?"

Right. That should have been maybe the second question the cop asked. He was watching closely now to see what Dooley would do or say, still probably hoping to catch Dooley out.

Dooley produced what he had, which was his school ID, his health card, his transit card, and, just for fun, his library card. Three out of four had his picture on them along with his name. One had his birth date on it. None had his address on it. The cop took a long time to make a note of everything. Then he handed the ID back to Dooley and said, "What can you tell me about what happened here?"

Cops just naturally made Dooley nervous. They made his mouth go dry and made him wish for something, anything, to take the edge off. But down here in the ravine in the middle of the night there was nothing he could do about that. He drew in a breath, long but shallow so that maybe the cop wouldn't notice, and answered the cop's question. ■

Two

Another cop showed up, this one in plainclothes, from the homicide squad. He spoke for a few minutes with the uniformed cop. Then he came over to Dooley and introduced himself: Detective Graff. He said the same thing the other cop had said: "What can you tell me about what happened here?"

Dooley repeated what he had told the patrol officer—that he had been on his way home from work, which was more or less true.

The homicide cop looked around the ravine before turning back to Dooley.

"Where do you work?" he said.

Dooley said, "At a video store." He told the homicide cop which one.

"When did you get off work?" the homicide cop said.

"Nine o'clock," Dooley said. He'd got off two hours earlier than he was supposed to because it was a slow night and because Kevin, the shift manager, was such a brown-noser that he always clocked someone off early when things were slow, to save the eight bucks an hour the store would otherwise have had to shell out in wages and to make himself look like up-and-coming management material. Dooley didn't care. Time off was time off.

The homicide cop looked at his notebook. He said, "It wouldn't take you more than fifteen minutes to walk from where you work to where you live. What did you do between the time you got off work and the time you found the body?"

"I took a walk," Dooley said. Because he had got off two hours early, and because his uncle wasn't expecting him home until eleven-thirty, and because he was tired—boy, was he tired—of having to be every place exactly on time just to prove to everyone that he wasn't a total fuck-up anymore, Dooley had decided not to go straight home. He'd taken a detour instead.

"Where'd you walk?"

"Down here," Dooley said. "In the ravine."

The homicide cop glanced around. "In the dark?" he said.

"There are some lights along the path," Dooley said, "and up there." He nodded to the bridge overhead. It used to be a railway bridge. Now it was a footpath and bike trail. "And it's a full moon." He thought about that for a moment. "Hey, maybe that's why it happened."

"What do you mean?" the homicide cop said.

Dooley was sorry he'd said that last part. He should have known better. When you're dealing with cops, the less you say, the better. The homicide cop was waiting for him to answer.

"I mean, people do weird shit when there's a full moon, right? That's where the word lunatic comes from. From the word for moon."

The homicide cop just looked at him.

"So you were walking along this path?" he said. "From which direction?"

"From there," Dooley said, pointing north. He told the homicide cop that he'd been on the path that ran through the ravine, alongside the river. He'd just been moseying along, enjoying the quiet and the solitude—well, except for the odd pedestrian, usually of the deranged variety. Like the old guy wearing a couple of overcoats one on top of the other and pushing a supermarket cart with a squeaky wheel and filled with what looked like bags of trash but was probably all of the guy's earthly possessions. Or like the woman who had big, rectangular painted-on Groucho Marx eyebrows—swear to God—so that Dooley did a double take when he saw her. There were a few other types down there, too, like that bunch of teenaged kids he'd passed who were smoking up under a tree. Dooley had sniffed the air hard as he went by. Talk about memories. But he didn't tell the homicide cop that.

He said he'd been maybe half a kilometer north of the old railroad bridge when he looked up.

"What made you look up?" the homicide cop said.

Dooley shrugged. "I don't know." And it was true. He hadn't looked up for any particular reason except that it was a nice night with a clear sky and a full moon and for once he had no worries. No pressing ones, anyway. "I just looked up and I saw someone take a header off the bridge."

He and the homicide cop both looked up at the bridge again.

"Go on," the homicide cop said.

Dooley said that from where he was, he couldn't tell if the person was male or female, let alone young or old or in between. He just saw that it was a person—at least, it looked like a person.

"It really surprised me," Dooley said. In fact, it had stopped him in his tracks. He'd shaken his head and thought to himself, Nah, it couldn't be. His eyes must be playing tricks on him. I mean, what are the chances, right? But even while he was thinking that, he was on the move again, not moseying anymore, but hurrying, walking fast, then jogging, then pushing it harder still, running toward the bridge, thinking about what he had seen, wondering if it was possible to survive a fall—a jump?—like that.

He told the homicide cop that it must have taken him a couple of minutes to reach the spot. He said that when he got there, he could see that the kid was dead. The homicide cop's eyes were hard on him.

"Did you touch him?" he said.

"Well, yeah," Dooley said. "I wanted to see, you know, if he was alive or dead or what, so I touched him here." He pressed a couple of fingers against the side of his own neck to show the homicide cop what he meant. "I felt for a pulse."

"Then what did you do?"

"I went up the path a little ways, to see if there was anyone else around, someone else who had seen what had happened or someone who had a cell phone and could call 911."

"And did you see anyone else?" the homicide cop said.

"Just the kid on the bike. He came along a few minutes later."

"And that's it?"

Instead of answering right away, Dooley hesitated. Big mistake. For sure the homicide cop would consider that suspicious. So Dooley said, "I think I might have seen someone up there." He pointed at a curve in the path about twenty meters north. "Maybe whoever it was passed by here. Did anyone else call it in?"

Of course the homicide cop didn't answer. Instead, he said, "This person you *think* you saw, can you describe him?"

Dooley said, "No." He said he only saw the person out of the corner of his eye because by then he was fixated on the body.

The homicide cop asked Dooley if he knew the dead kid.

Dooley hesitated again. He didn't like the way the homicide cop kept his eyes on him and never once looked away, like he thought that if he did, he might miss the one thing that would let him nail Dooley. That was the problem with cops—well, one of the problems. They were just naturally suspicious. They didn't trust anyone except maybe other cops.

"Do you know the kid?" the homicide cop said again.

Dooley wanted to say no. He wanted to tell the cop that there was absolutely no connection between the dead kid and himself. But then what would happen? So he said, "I think he goes to my school."

"You *think*?" the homicide cop said.

"Well, he looked pretty bad when I got to him," Dooley said. "And it's my first year at the school. It's only been a couple of weeks. But I think I've seen him around." What the hell. Dooley didn't have a high opinion of most cops, but these homicide guys had a reputation. They knew how to ask questions, and they knew who to ask. So Dooley added, "Yeah, I'm pretty sure I have." He wondered if he should say more, but decided against it for the time being. You can always add things, but you can never take them back.

The homicide cop took note of Dooley's shift from tentative hesitation to possible certainty.

"You know his name?"

Dooley shook his head. "I think it's Emerson," he said. "Or Everett. Something like that. He's not in any of my classes. I've just seen him around."

The homicide cop stared at Dooley for a few moments before he asked if Dooley had seen anyone on the bridge with the kid before the kid had gone over.

Dooley said he hadn't even noticed that the kid was on the bridge until he was already on his way down.

The homicide cop asked Dooley again if he had touched the kid, trying to trip Dooley up again.

"Like I said," Dooley said, trying to sound helpful even though all he wanted was to get the hell out of there, "I felt for a pulse."

The homicide cop asked Dooley if he would mind emptying his pockets.

"What for?" Dooley said.

The homicide cop didn't answer that directly. Instead, he said what Dooley already knew—that he couldn't force Dooley to empty his pockets and that Dooley didn't have to cooperate if he didn't want to. He said, "You've been in trouble before, is that right, Ryan?" as if there was some chance he might be wrong. When Dooley nodded—what was the point of denying it? The cop wouldn't have asked it that way if he didn't know the answer and exactly what kind of trouble Dooley had been in—the homicide cop asked if there was any particular reason Dooley didn't want to empty his pockets.

Dooley wanted to say, "You bet there is. It's called my Charter rights." But he knew why the cop was asking. Dooley was (supposedly) the only person who had seen the kid—a kid who went to his school—go off the bridge. Dooley had (supposedly) been alone with the body for five or maybe ten minutes before the boy on the bike came along. He'd been alone again when the boy went to make the phone call. So, fine, Dooley pulled his wallet out of his pocket and handed it to the homicide cop. He pulled out some coins, his house keys on a ring that was attached to a brass capital D—his uncle had given it to him along with the keys. He also pulled out his name tag from work, which he had unpinned from his shirt as he went out the door, and a pack of gum with half the pieces already gone. He pulled out his pager. The homicide cop took a good long look at it. Dooley bet he wanted to check what numbers had paged him. He asked if the homicide cop wanted to pat him down and said that if he did, he could go ahead.

So the homicide cop did, after a thorough examination of Dooley's wallet, which didn't contain anything except the four pieces of identification that Dooley had already showed the patrol officer and a five-dollar bill. The homicide cop should have been satisfied, but he still looked suspicious. He verified Dooley's information—again—and let Dooley go. ■

Three

Dooley could have headed for the nearest phone—after all, he knew where it was—and called his uncle. But he had a pretty good idea how that phone call would go. His uncle would interrupt him every two seconds to ask if Dooley had forgotten how to tell time, could he even count to ten, maybe making him do it just to prove he could, his uncle could be that harsh when he was pissed off, and nothing pissed him off more than someone who should know better breaking the rules.

Dooley was confident he could make the case that he was on the right side for a change—he had done his civic duty. But if he tried to argue that over the phone, his uncle would probably think it was some bullshit excuse Dooley was trying on to justify why he hadn't answered not just one but two of his uncle's pages. No, they were at the point now where his uncle would need to look Dooley in the eye to decide if he was telling the truth. Dooley wouldn't mind seeing his uncle's face, either, especially when Dooley told him, "You don't believe me, call the cops."

He wondered what the chances were that his uncle would apologize to him.

Dooley caught sight of his uncle when he was still nearly a block from the house. He was sitting on the porch almost directly under the porch light with the cordless phone in his hand, and he was scowling into the night. Dooley bet his uncle had spotted him the minute he'd turned the corner. He felt his uncle's eyes lock onto him but he didn't move, didn't stand up, didn't come down the porch steps. He just sat there and watched as Dooley came closer and closer. He didn't say anything either. He just waited.

Dooley climbed all the way up onto the porch, leaned against the railing, looked into his uncle's steel gray eyes, mostly because he believed that his uncle expected him to do the exact opposite, and said, "I got your pages. Both of them."

His uncle stared at him, still waiting. Dooley's uncle was good at waiting, good at making the other guy fill up the spaces and maybe even incriminate himself with the filler talk.

"I was going to call," Dooley said. Dooley was as good at paying out his words slowly—boy, could he be slow—as his uncle was at stretching out the silences. "But something came up." Actually, Dooley thought, it had come down.

"You worked until nine tonight," his uncle said. He hadn't taken his eyes off Dooley for a second. He hadn't even blinked. "Not eleven, like you told me."

His uncle must have called the store. If Dooley was supposed to be at work and his uncle wanted to check on him—or if he wanted him to bring home a movie, which he did sometimes when Jeannie was coming over—he called. When Dooley told him they didn't like employees taking personal calls, his uncle said, "Tell them I'm a customer." Dooley guessed he'd called the store and then, exactly one second later, had paged Dooley to find out where the hell he was.

"It was a slow night," Dooley said. "Kevin let me go early."

"Go where?" his uncle said, because the deal was that if Dooley wanted to continue living with his uncle, he was supposed to do certain things unfailingly. One of those things was coming straight home after work. Dooley's uncle was mad because Dooley hadn't lived up to his end of the bargain.

"I went for a walk," Dooley said. "I didn't think you'd mind." The truth was, he didn't think his uncle would ever find out. If that kid hadn't gone off the bridge, Dooley would have found a phone and answered the first page.

His uncle waited.

So did Dooley.

Then his uncle's impatience got the better of him and he said, "I paged you. Twice. Are you going to stand there and tell me you were—" he flicked out his wrist so that he could consult his watch—"an hour and fourteen minutes away from the nearest phone?"

"It was more like five minutes," Dooley said and waited until his uncle looked ready to yell at him again. That's when Dooley told his uncle exactly what he had been looking at when his pager had vibrated the first time.

A new look came onto his uncle's face. A curious look.

A cop look, even though his uncle had stopped being a cop before Dooley had got to know him. Now he owned a couple of dry-cleaning stores.

"The kid jumped?" Dooley's uncle said.

"Or was pushed or just fell," Dooley said. "I don't know. I didn't see that part."

"You did the right thing," Dooley's uncle said after Dooley told him about waiting until the kid on the bike came along and then getting the kid to call the cops while Dooley stayed put. Unlike the cop who had responded to the call, Dooley's uncle didn't seem to doubt Dooley. Dooley wasn't sure how he felt about that. Most of the time, his uncle kept him on a short leash and drove him crazy asking him where he'd been and what he'd been doing, checking mostly to make sure that he *hadn't* been doing things, which led Dooley to believe that his uncle didn't trust him. But every now and again—like now—he'd take what Dooley said at face value, and that made Dooley feel pretty good because it was as close to an apology as his uncle ever came. "But you should have called me before you left the store," his uncle said. "So I'd know." He meant, so he'd know where Dooley was. His uncle was religious about being on top of Dooley's whereabouts.

Dooley said, yeah, he should have.

Then Dooley's uncle said, "You finally took it in to get it sized, huh?"

Dooley looked at his uncle, wondering if maybe he was having an aneurysm or whatever it was that happened in older people's brains that made them say things that sounded like they were coming out of left field.

"Your grandfather's ring," his uncle said, nodding at Dooley's hand. "You finally took it in, like I said, to get it sized to fit properly."

"Yeah," Dooley said.

His uncle nodded his approval. He was never happier than when Dooley finally got around to doing something he'd told Dooley dozens, sometimes even hundreds, of times that he should do. Dooley nodded back, even though the only thought in his head was: what the hell had happened to his ring?

■ ■ ■

Dooley's uncle was the kind of guy who leapt out of bed wide awake and raring to go the minute the sun crested the horizon, and who either took a good long run or did an hour of weights and cardio (mostly jumping rope) before settling in for a high-fiber, whole-grain breakfast. Dooley was the kind of guy who mostly dragged himself out of bed at the last possible minute, chugged down two or three cups of coffee (black with a couple of sugars), and was in and out of the house a couple of times before he finally had (almost) everything he needed for school. There were, however, exceptions.

The exception for Dooley's uncle: when he had overnight company.

Dooley's uncle had been married once, way back before Dooley was born. He told Dooley it had lasted all of two minutes, his ex-wife bowled over by the uniform, the handcuffs, and the weapon but, it turned out, not too happy with the pay, the hours, and the work—and the fact that cops mostly talk to other cops and never tell their wives anything. Since then, his uncle had gone out with a lot of women—he was a good-looking guy, Dooley guessed, for his age. Most of them he just fooled around with, nothing serious. Once bitten, twice shy, was how his uncle put it. But lately he'd been seeing a woman named Jeannie who owned a chain of ladies' fashion stores in a few of the malls around town and who liked to have a good time. He'd been seeing her since before Dooley had come to live with him. Dooley never knew when he would come home and find her there, not that that was a problem. Jeannie was okay. Dooley liked her. He liked the way she put his uncle in a good mood. She had come over right after Dooley had finished explaining to his uncle what he had seen in the ravine, and she was still there when Dooley got up the next morning. He could tell because her purse was on the kitchen table, his uncle's bedroom door was closed (it was open when he was alone), and there was no smell of sweat and no sign of whole grain in the kitchen. All of this was good for Dooley because, although his uncle had retired, he was still one hundred percent cop, and if he were up when Dooley strolled through the kitchen fully dressed at seven-thirty on a Sunday morning, his eyes would narrow and he'd look at Dooley and want to know what in hell Dooley was doing up so early and where in hell he thought he was going.

Dooley had put on sweats and sneakers—not so much for going out as for coming back again, when he was sure to encounter his uncle. He even made a little show of it, jogging in place on the porch as if he were warming up, and tossing a jaunty wave to the old lady across the street who, if it came to it, could mention to Dooley's uncle that she'd seen Dooley. He jogged down the street, rounded the corner, slowed to a brisk walk, and headed for the ravine. He started jogging again before he was in sight of it, which was easy because it was downhill all the way. He connected with the path he'd been on the night before and ran (not too fast) along it, trying to keep his head up so it wouldn't look like he was scanning the path, even though he was. He had to force himself not to slow down when he got close to where it had happened and saw that the crime scene tape was still there and that a bunch of cops were there, too, combing through the surrounding grass and scrub. Boy, they were really working the kid's death. Dooley wondered if they'd have so many guys down there if it was the old guy with all the overcoats and the shopping cart or the woman with the Groucho Marx eyebrows who had gone splat. Theoretically they would say, yeah, you bet we would. But there had been a couple of homeless guys killed last winter. Dooley had read about it in the paper—he'd had to read the paper in civics class while he was in detention. He read that they'd been killed, but he never read that the cops had caught whoever had done it. Dooley jogged by, casting a glance in the cops' direction because who wouldn't, but being careful not to look overly interested. He thought he had pulled it off, too.

Until he saw the homicide cop who had questioned him the night before—Detective Graff.

Geeze, where had he come from?

Dooley realized that Graff must have been standing there the whole time, but he'd had his back to the path so Dooley hadn't noticed him. He turned as Dooley jogged past and looked right at Dooley, forcing Dooley to wonder what a normal person, an innocent person, would do in response. Look right back, Dooley decided. That would be a whole lot less suspicious than pretending he hadn't seen Graff. So Dooley looked and gave Graff a half-nod as he jogged past. He wondered if Graff or any of the other cops had found his ring. Or if they would. Or if it was even there. If it was, he figured he'd find out soon enough. If it wasn't . . . ■

Four

It turned out the dead kid's name was Mark Everley. Dooley found this out Monday morning when he walked into the kitchen and his uncle looked up from his newspaper and said something about school that Dooley didn't catch because he was worrying about the ring. His uncle had given it to him. He'd said, "Your grandfather always had the idea his grandson would wear it." He'd looked Dooley over that time and had shaken his head like he believed that the old man would have changed his mind fast if he'd ever got a good look at Dooley. "You're it," his uncle had said, and he'd set the ring onto the table in front of Dooley.

But the ring was too big. "Your grandfather was a hefty man," Dooley's uncle had said. "Take it to a jeweler. Get it sized." Which, of course, Dooley hadn't got around to doing. Every now and then he wrapped some tape around the back of the ring, where it wouldn't show. Every now and then the tape got black with dirt and ragged edged from sweat and grime, or it just plain wore out, so the ring slipped.

It could be that it had fallen right off his finger. Or it could be that he hadn't even been wearing it. He didn't wear it all the time. For example, he didn't wear it in the shower—water made the tape soggy and the ring uncomfortable. He didn't wear it to bed, either. So maybe he hadn't worn it to work on Saturday night. He couldn't remember. He'd tossed his room yesterday, looking for it. Now he was thinking: could it have fallen into the sink? It was possible. That would be too bad, of course—after all, it was his grandfather's ring, never mind that he had never met his grandfather. But falling down the sink was better than ending up in a few other places he could think of—and one place in particular.

His uncle was frowning at him now, his eyes sharp.

"What?" Dooley said.

His uncle studied him for another couple of seconds, probably wondering what was eating Dooley, probably thinking it was something to do with school, maybe some homework assignment he'd forgotten to do.

"Mark Everley," his uncle said at last. "The kid who went off the bridge." He shoved the newspaper across the table to Dooley. "You didn't tell me he went to your school."

"I thought I recognized him," Dooley said, which was true. "But his head was kind of smashed up, so I wasn't sure" which wasn't true, but it sounded a lot nicer than saying what he was actually thinking (*It couldn't have happened to a more deserving person*), which would only have annoyed his uncle. "Anyway, I didn't know that was his name and the cops didn't tell me," which was also true.

He glanced at the picture in the newspaper and this time recognized the face right away—Mark Everley, his longish hair combed back, posed in front of one of those gray-blue screens that school photographers use, smiling at the camera, looking like your average high school student, which was a whole lot different from looking like a broken doll. The newspaper picture of Everley triggered another one in Dooley's mind, but this one wasn't from school. Dooley's dominant impression: Mark Everley was an asshole.

■ ■ ■

There were more than two thousand students at the school Dooley went to. Dooley hadn't mixed much with any of them so far. He didn't know who was in, who was out, who was invisible, that kind of stuff. Didn't know and didn't care. His mission while he was there was tightly focused: get through this year and then get through next year, as promised, and get the hell out of there. But from the way girls were carrying on in the hall when he got to school on Monday morning—crying, mostly, and hugging each other—Dooley figured that Mark Everley must have been popular. His funeral, which was scheduled for the next day, was announced during homeroom. Anyone who wanted to attend had to get a special pass. At lunchtime, the office was jammed. Dooley thought about going to the funeral, decided not to—after all, he didn't know Mark Everley well (didn't know him at all, really) and, based on what little he did know (which wasn't much, really), didn't particularly like him—then decided, what the hell, he probably should go, seeing as he was the last person who had seen the guy alive (well, assuming he'd been alive when he went over the side of the bridge; the newspaper hadn't said anything about that). He went to the office after school and asked one of the school's administrative assistants for a pass.

Mr. Rektor, the A-to-L vice principal, looked over at him from the fax machine where he had been punching in a fax number.

"I didn't know you knew Mark," he said.

"I didn't," Dooley said.

Mr. Rektor came over to where Dooley was standing, folding his pass so he could put it in his pocket. Mr. Rektor snatched it out of his hand.

"Then you won't be needing this," he said. "And don't even think about skipping school tomorrow."

Mr. Rektor had been apprised, as he put it, of Dooley's past. Before Dooley was even allowed to enrol in the school, Mr. Rektor had made it clear to Dooley and his uncle that if Dooley caused any trouble, broke any school rules, or, God forbid, was seen anywhere in the vicinity of a baseball bat, he would be immediately suspended. Infraction number two would earn him an expulsion. Dooley's uncle said it was fine with him if that was how the school wanted to play it, but if Dooley messed up, Mr. Rektor was going to have to get in line because he, Dooley's uncle, had first dibs in the teach-Dooley-a-lesson department. After Dooley and his uncle left Mr. Rektor's office that time, Dooley's uncle had muttered, "Officious little prick. They're all the same. They must breed them that way."

Dooley looked at Mr. Rektor now and said, "I'll get my uncle to write a note."

Mr. Rektor said, "The only way I'm going to believe your uncle has excused you from school to go to the funeral of a boy you didn't know is if your uncle walks in here in person and tells me."

Right.

On the way home from school, Dooley stopped by his uncle's dry-cleaning store, the original one three blocks from his uncle's house, not the uptown store that his uncle had opened later. When he told his uncle what Mr. Rektor had said, his uncle reached for the phone.

"If you call him, he won't believe it's you," Dooley said. "He'll think it's me or one of my friends."

"You have friends now?" Dooley's uncle said, making a joke. "Tell you what, I'll go in tomorrow and give my permission to his boss, the principal. And while I'm at it—"

"I'm the one who has to be there every day," Dooley said. "I'm the one he's going see go by in the hall and try to find something wrong with."

"Fine," his uncle said, putting down the phone. He looked Dooley over. "You got something decent to wear to a funeral?"

Dooley said, sure, he had the pants and jacket that he had worn to court that last time. His uncle shook his head and asked him what was the matter with him, couldn't he see how much he had grown? He called to Carla, who managed the store for him, and said he was leaving and he'd check in with her later. He said, "Come on," and took Dooley to a menswear store where he picked out a pair of good pants, a dark jacket, a shirt, and a tie and told Dooley to try them on. When Dooley came out of the change room, his uncle said, "It always pays to look like you care." Dooley wasn't sure what he meant by that, but he had to admit that he looked pretty good in the mirror.

■ ■ ■

The church was packed. The girls who had been crying in school were crying again in their pews. So were some of the adults, including a girl that Dooley recognized from the video store. She'd been coming in maybe every other week and she always rented something interesting—not the latest Hollywood crap, but something British or from some other country. Subtitles didn't put her off the way they did most of the customers. On top of that, she was great to look at—lively brown eyes, like coffee with just a splash of milk, and hair the same color, only glossy. She had creamy white skin and full pink lips, and was nice and slim, but not flat-chested like some of the really skinny girls. She had kind of a husky voice for a girl. The name that came up on the computer when Dooley scanned her membership card was Helen Manson, but that was her mother—at least, that's what the girl had told him. So far she hadn't told him her name. He was pretty sure she didn't go to his school—he would have noticed if she did. But she must know Mark Everley, otherwise why would she be at his funeral? She walked past where he was sitting—which was at the back of the church—and took a place right up front, next to a woman who was sobbing. The girl put her arm around the woman. He heard someone behind him whisper, "That's Mark's mother and his sister."

Dooley saw her again when she and her mother, arm in arm, followed the casket down the center aisle of the church. He didn't go up to her and her mother afterward, like some people did, including some guys he recognized from school, one of whom was Eddy Gillette. He'd seen the other guys with Everley in the past and figured they must be his friends. One of them, a guy Dooley had heard referred to as Landers, was, in Dooley's limited experience, as much of an asshole as Everley had been.

Dooley didn't hang around outside the church when the funeral was over or go to the cemetery, either. Instead, he went back to school, handed in the note his uncle had written for him even though his uncle had spoken to the principal in person, and reported to English class. ■

Five

Dooley was walking past the school office on Wednesday after school, heading for the exit, when Mark Everley's sister appeared. She was pale and her eyes were glassed over, like she hadn't been sleeping well, if at all. She looked fragile but still beautiful. She glanced at Dooley, started to dismiss him, and then looked at him again.

"I'm sorry," she said. "But don't I know you? You work at the video store, right?" Dooley nodded. "It's funny to see people where you don't expect to see them," she said. "Do you go to school here?"

"Yeah," Dooley said. Then, because she looked so pale and because it seemed like the right thing, he said, "I'm sorry about your brother."

"Did you know him?"

"Not really," Dooley admitted. "I'm new here. But I heard what happened."

"Oh."

"You don't go to this school, do you?" Dooley said.

She shook her head. "I just came to drop this off." She held up an envelope. "Mark had a lot of friends. They've been great—coming to the funeral, dropping off cards for my mother. They filled the church with flowers. You should have seen it."

So she hadn't noticed him at the funeral. Well, why would she? She'd had other things on her mind. Now he didn't know what to say. He didn't want her to walk away, but he couldn't think of anything that would make her stay.

"Well," she said, "I'd better go. I guess I'll see you around the video store."

He realized, as she walked toward the office, that he still didn't know her name. He considered going after her, but abandoned the idea when he saw Mr. Rektor, the A-to-L vice principal, come out of his office and stride to the counter to greet her. As he did, he glanced out at Dooley with the same distaste that he always had on his face when he saw Dooley, as if he were telling Dooley: I know you, and I know it's only a matter of time before you screw up and I can get your ass out of here. When he turned back to the girl, though, he was all smiles. Well, why not? Then someone else went into the office. It was a guy Dooley had seen at the funeral. His name was Rhodes. He was tall with blond hair—a good cut—blue eyes behind sharp-looking glasses, and jeans that looked like they'd been pressed if they hadn't been dry-cleaned. Rhodes laid a hand on Mark Everley's sister's shoulder, which told Dooley that he must know her pretty well. Dooley wished he knew her well, too.

■ ■ ■

Dooley saw Everley's sister again a lot sooner than he'd expected and not at the video store, either. She was in his face the next afternoon when he started down the front steps after school. Yesterday, she had looked tired and sad. Today she looked pissed off.

"You're Ryan Dooley," she said, turning his name into an accusation that Dooley wanted to deny.

"Yeah," Dooley said cautiously. It sounded like she was mad at him for something.

"Why didn't you tell me that you were the one who called the police?" she said. She was definitely mad at him, and shaky too. Dooley detected a tremble in her voice. "You spoke to me yesterday. Why didn't you mention that you're the one who saw what happened?"

"I didn't exactly see it," Dooley said. He heard the door open behind him and stepped a little to one side so that whoever was coming out could get by him.

"But you were there," she said, still worked up, as if she suspected that he had committed the crime of the century and she was angry that she couldn't prove it. "You found him."

"Yeah, I guess," Dooley said.

Her coffee-brown eyes were hard on him. "I want you to tell me what you saw. Everything."

Everything? Dooley thought about Mark Everley's glassy doll eyes. He thought about the way his neck was twisted and the stuff that had been leaking out of him.

"There's really nothing to tell," he said, talking softly even though she had been practically yelling at him. After all, she had just lost her brother.

She glanced over his shoulder now, and Dooley remembered that he had heard the door open behind him, but so far no one had come down the steps past him. He turned. Vice principal Rektor was standing two steps above him, his face pinched as if a bad smell was coming off Dooley. Dooley met his eyes.

"You getting all this?" he said to Rektor.

Rektor didn't budge.

Dooley touched Everley's sister's and nudged her down the steps away from the vice principal. She didn't resist. Instead, she glanced around.

"There's a place over there," she said, nodding across the street. "I'll buy you a coffee." She had calmed down a little and sounded businesslike instead of hostile, so Dooley said okay. He would have said okay even if she was still worked up. He'd never had coffee with a girl like her.

He sat across the table from her in a booth at a place opposite the school that was jammed with kids at lunchtime and was pretty much deserted the rest of the time. A bored-looking waitress with fake two-inch fingernails slid a mug of coffee in front of each of them and a little bowl filled with plastic containers of cream and milk between them. Dooley dumped two packets of sugar into his coffee. The girl—Dooley, embarrassed, finally asked her name; it was Beth—didn't put anything in hers. She didn't even touch it.

"So?" she said. "Can you tell me what you saw?"

"How did you know I was there?" Dooley said.

"The detective who's investigating Mark's death," — her voice caught a little when she said that word — "asked me if I knew you or if Mark had ever mentioned you. When I asked him why, he said because you're the person who found him."

He wondered if Graff had told her anything else about him. "And?" he said.

"And what?" she said.

"Did you say you knew me?"

She shook her head. "He asked me if I knew Ryan Dooley. I said no. I didn't make the connection until last night. I went to the video store to return some DVDs and I heard a girl—she works there, too—talking to some other girl, and she said the name Dooley." Dooley wondered if she meant Linelle. "So I asked her if she meant Ryan Dooley. And she said yes. Then I described you, and she said, yeah, that was you, and she told me what school you went to. Mark's school. That's when I figured out it was you."

"Everyone just calls me Dooley," Dooley said.

"You were there," she said. "Tell me what happened, what you saw." She stared across the table at him with those dark coffee eyes until he had no choice.

He told her where he had been (strolling down the path in the ravine), what he had seen (her brother, going over, only the way he said it was, "I saw him fall"), what he hadn't seen (anyone or anything else up there on the bridge) . . .

"What?" she said, leaning forward a little, peering at him, frowning.

"What?" he said. Why was she looking at him like that?

"There's something you're not telling me. I can see it in your eyes. It's okay. I can handle it."

"There's nothing," he said, careful to keep his eyes blank and his face neutral. But it wasn't easy because no sooner had he said he hadn't seen anyone else on the bridge than he wasn't sure that was true. He couldn't *remember* seeing anyone, but something niggled at him and he wondered if maybe there hadn't been someone or something else up there, someone or something that he hadn't fully registered because he had been focused on the body falling off the bridge.

No, he decided. No, he'd been straight and sober. If he'd seen something else, he would have remembered it. He was just second-guessing himself now because he wished there was something he could tell this girl, something that might make her feel better or, at least, not so bad.

"I told you everything," he said. "Like I said, I just happened to glance up, that's all." She was still peering at him, her head tilted to one side now, her lips tight. She wasn't satisfied, but Dooley didn't know what he could do about that. "I'm sorry," he said.

"They think he jumped," she said. "Either that or he was on drugs or maybe he'd been drinking and he did something stupid and he fell. But they won't know that for sure until they get results from toxicology, and they told me that could take a while. They won't even tell me what that means, how long a while is. What do you think?"

At first he thought she was asking him how long he thought it would take to find out what her brother was doing before he went off the bridge, if he'd been doing anything at all. But, no, that didn't seem to be it.

"I can't say," Dooley said. "I didn't know him, so I have no idea what he might have been thinking or doing." He looked across the table at her. According to the newspaper, Mark Everley had been two weeks shy of his eighteenth birthday. Dooley wondered, was she his older sister or younger sister? You couldn't tell with some girls. They looked eighteen or nineteen and then they turned out to be fourteen or fifteen.

"When you got to him," she said, meaning her brother, "was he wearing a backpack?"

"Backpack?" Dooley said. Finally, a question he could answer without thinking about how to put it. "No."

"You're sure?" she said. "Because he always had it with him. Always. But the police said it wasn't there when they got there."

"I'm sure," Dooley said. She kept right on staring at him. "Maybe he left it up top," he said.

"They looked up there when they were trying to find out what happened. They didn't find it."

"Did he have valuable stuff in it?"

"His digital camera," she said. "I guess that's valuable. He was always taking pictures. Always. He had some notebooks in there, too. He writes stories." Dooley wondered if she even noticed that she was saying it like he was still alive. "Some of them are pretty good. So are his pictures."

"Maybe he didn't have the backpack with him that night."

She shook her head impatiently. Right. She'd just said that he always had it with him.

"Maybe he took it off before," Dooley said, careful not to say before what. "And maybe someone came along before the cops got there and took it."

"I could see him taking it off if he jumped," she said. "You know, so the camera wouldn't get broken. But I can't see Mark jumping. It wasn't suicide. He wasn't sick or depressed. He had no reason to kill himself."

"So it must have been an accident," Dooley said. He could see why the cops were thinking drugs or alcohol. Everley would have had to be leaning pretty far over the guardrail to fall accidentally, and why would he do that unless he wanted to fall or he was completely out of it?

"If it was an accident," she said, "he would have had his backpack on him when you found him."

"If you don't think it was an accident and you don't think he did it on purpose—" What did that leave? "You think he was pushed?"

"I know he didn't jump. I also know that if it was an accident, he would have had his backpack on him when you found him."

Dooley chose his words carefully when he said, "Maybe someone took the backpack off him afterwards."

"You were the first person there," she said, her eyes steady on him, reminding him of the way his uncle sometimes looked at him, wondering what he'd been up to, probably thinking the worst. "You said you saw him fall. You said you ran right to where he was and you kept an eye on everything while a kid went and called the police. You said that, right?" She even sounded like his uncle. He wondered again what, if anything, she had heard about him. Did she really think he would strip a dead guy of his possessions?

"Yeah," he said. "I saw him go over." She flinched. "But I didn't see him the whole time he was lying there. I couldn't. I was too far away. I didn't see him again until I got close a couple of minutes later."

She digested this.

"So," she said, "you're saying that someone else could have seen him fall and could have got to him before you did and that person could have seen him lying there either dead or dying and, instead of doing anything to help him, that person could have stolen his backpack?"

He was amazed how calm she was—angry, sure, her jaw twitching with indignation, but overall composed—when she said this.

"It's possible," Dooley said. "There are some strange people who hang out down in that ravine."

She leaned back in the booth now. She hadn't taken her eyes off him for even a second. She was giving him the same look he got from every social worker, court worker, youth worker, corrections officer, judge, prosecutor, and probation officer who had ever read his file, like it was all his fault.

"You said he had a digital camera," he said. "There's plenty of people who'd steal something like that."

She cocked her head to one side and studied him, as if she were wondering if he were one of those people.

"The camera, okay," she said finally. "But the whole

backpack?" Her eyes drilled into him. "A person who would steal from someone who was lying there like that, that person is no better than an animal," she said.

Dooley said he agreed. He said he understood how she felt. But what he was thinking was, it wasn't as if Mark Everley was going to need his backpack or his camera or his stories anymore. ■

Six

By the end of the week, things at school were back to normal. Kids were carrying on, outwardly at least, as if Mark Everley had never existed, and Dooley was back to remembering why he had never liked school. Reason number one was standing right up there at the front of the class—Dooley's math teacher, droning out the rudiments of calculus, sounding like he one hundred percent didn't gave a crap if anyone was listening or understood what he was saying. Reason number two: having to cram your head full of shit you knew for a fact you were never going to use, like, say, calculus. But the blue-ribbon winner, reason number three, was all the assholes. In Dooley's experience, your average high school had a higher asshole-to-solid-citizen ratio than your average youth detention center. The only difference was, most of the high school assholes weren't violent.

But some of them sure were.

Look, for example, at what was going in the yard on the school's blind side, the side that faced a brick wall with no windows, the place where all the shit went down because no one in authority could see it unless they ventured out of their offices. It reminded Dooley of the Roman Coliseum he'd seen in some cheesy movie that for some reason had stuck in his memory. In the middle, two gladiators. Around the edges, the bored and bloodthirsty citizens. And somewhere, Dooley was willing to bet on it, there was an emperor ready to give thumbs-up or thumbs-down. Dooley told himself it was none of his business. What he should do was just walk on by. But what he actually did: he turned his head to take in the scene. He didn't know what it was all about, but one thing was for sure, one of the guys in the middle was going to be fucked pretty soon. Two gladiators? Make that one stringy little Christian about to be eaten alive by one nasty looking old lion in the shape of a man. Well, a man-sized teenaged boy. The Christian was being played by a scrawny kid who obviously didn't know a thing about fighting. He had his hands up, but they weren't even curled into fists. Also, he looked scared, which was a big mistake because it only added to the confidence of the big guy with hands like mallets who was standing opposite him, staring him down, his mouth working, probably telling the guy how he was going to pound him into the ground like a tent peg.

The big guy was Mark Everley's friend, a guy named Landers. He was taunting the scrawny kid. One of the spectators, standing close to Landers, but not in the middle of the semi-circle with him, was the only person in the whole school whom Dooley actually knew: Eddy Gillette. The first day Dooley had started school, he had been surprised to see

Gillette there. He'd figured that first day was also going to be the last day he saw Gillette because Gillette wasn't much of a regular school attender. But Dooley kept seeing him around, not every day but often enough to get the idea that Gillette was showing up more than he was skipping.

Dooley slowed his pace when he saw Gillette, but then he picked it up again. He had an appointment. Right after that he had to get to work. But before he did, he had to go home and grab his stupid video store T-shirt and his stupid video store name badge.

Gillette was saying something to Landers when he spotted Dooley. His expression changed and he turned away from the action in the semicircle to look directly at Dooley. After that it got weird. As soon as Gillette turned to look at Dooley, Landers turned to look at what Gillette was looking at. Then one of the people in the semi-circle turned to look. The person next to him turned to look at what *he* was looking at—and so on and so on and so on, until all of a sudden Dooley was the main attraction. Dooley glanced at the scrawny kid with his hands in the air. If the kid were smart, he'd cut out of there while everyone was looking at Dooley. But, it figured, the kid wasn't that smart. He just stood there, waiting almost patiently for Landers to turn back to him, as if he knew, like the Borg, that resistance was futile. While Dooley was looking at the scrawny kid, Gillette turned and looked at him too. It took a moment, but Dooley finally understood. Gillette was wondering if the scrawny kid was a friend of Dooley's. If he was, maybe Gillette would tell his pal Landers to leave the kid alone, at least while Dooley was standing there. Maybe he'd even get Landers to back off altogether.

Dooley glanced around at all the faces looking at him. Some of them he sort of recognized from some of his classes. A couple he was pretty sure he had seen at the funeral. But most were just faces, people he didn't know, people he was pretty sure he didn't want to know, people who had obviously all heard something about him. They were watching him and exchanging nervous glances, like they were wondering what he was going to do, probably wondering if he was going to produce a baseball bat out of thin air and let 'er rip.

Dooley kept moving.

Someone came around the side of the school. Principal? Vice principal? Teacher? Someone who could break things up?

No.

It was Beth. She was carrying a handful of paper and a tape gun, and she frowned as she took in what was happening. She started toward the semicircle, a determined look on her face. Dooley wished now that he'd been a hero, but it was too late. Someone else had stepped into that role—Rhodes. Dooley wondered where he had come from. He hadn't noticed him and didn't think he'd been standing there the whole time. Rhodes waded through the crowd until he was standing between Landers and the scrawny kid. He looked a little nervous, or maybe it was the way the sun caught the lenses of his glasses that accounted for the way he dropped his head a little and seemed to be looking up at Landers, even though he was as tall as Landers.

"Why don't you leave him alone?" Rhodes said, his voice

quiet, quavering just a little. He must have been sweating, too, because he reached up and pushed his glasses up his nose. Everyone strained forward, even Dooley, to see what Landers was going to do.

Landers was breathing hard. He glowered at Rhodes, clearly unhappy that his fun was being interrupted.

Rhodes turned to the scrawny kid and said, "Go on, get out of here."

A buzz went through the crowd. Beth was staring at Rhodes. Dooley could just imagine what she was thinking—who knew they actually made guys like that outside of the movies?

Landers glanced at the guy he'd been ready to pulverize. He pivoted to look at Rhodes. He took in all the kids who were crowded around in a semicircle, his audience and his screen. Rhodes leaned in close to Landers and said something. A warning maybe? A threat?

Landers threw up his hands in a gesture of frustration and disgust. He did a slow one-eighty, checking all those faces. Then he curled his hands into fists and thumped Rhodes hard on the chest with them. Rhodes recoiled with the impact, like one of those bottom-weighted punching toys—you can whack them so that they look like they're going to fall over, and then they do what Rhodes did: they rebounded. Rhodes didn't back off or down. He stood with his own hands clenched, determined in his clean, pressed jeans, his light leather jacket, his kick-ass boots, and watched as Landers turned and elbowed his way through the spectators.

Rhodes reached out and touched the scrawny kid who seemed to be having trouble understanding what had just happened. He looked like Dooley had always imagined that dead guy Lazarus in the Bible must have looked like when Jesus brought him back to life. Think about it. You died—Dooley believed, he *feared*, there was a moment when you knew it was going to happen, what he called the aw-shit moment, the same as when you knew the cops had you good, only about a million times worse. That guy Lazarus, he must have known it was permanent lights out. Then the next thing he knows, he's up and walking around again. Dooley had never figured out if that was a good thing or a bad thing. And anyway, why Lazarus? A better question: why *only* Lazarus? If you were that good, if you could raise the dead, why stop at just one?

"Go on," Rhodes said. He nudged the scrawny kid to get him started. The kid blinked and stumbled toward the semicircle of spectators. Two girls reluctantly moved aside to let him through. Then the kid took off, and there it was, the sound Dooley hated, the sound of forty, maybe fifty, kids laughing at the kid, look at him go, sprinting for the side of the building like he believed his life depended on it.

Rhodes turned. His eyes widened in surprise when he saw Beth. He smiled at her and started toward her. Dooley walked away.

He spotted the first notice on a utility pole outside the school. Then he saw that notices just like it had been taped on every third or fourth pole for at least a block in all directions. He was sure Beth had put them there. He took a detour on the way home and saw them taped to the utility poles near the ravine, too. *Lost: Red backpack with black trim. Net pockets on both sides. REWARD OFFERED. If found, please call . . .* He ripped one off a pole mostly because it had her phone number on it, but he couldn't imagine himself calling her. The thing about his life so far: it hadn't allowed for many girls.■

Seven

Kingston had one of those old-fashioned clocks, the kind that ticked and tocked, measuring out the seconds and the minutes of nothingness every time Dooley stopped talking, the kind that bonged on the hour. Dooley shifted in the hard plastic chair and chanced a look at Kingston who, of course, was staring steadily at him. What a gig. Dooley wondered if all his patients were court-mandated like Dooley was. Dooley had to see Kingston once a week to discuss his progress. Kingston would look up when Dooley took a seat. He would toss out a question about some aspect of Dooley's life. Dooley was supposed to spend his time answering it.

The problem, though: Dooley didn't like talking about himself. He didn't like talking about his fucked-up past, hated talking about his soul-sucking present—which in his opinion was being wasted in high school and at a part-time job that everyone assumed could be done just as effectively by a lobotomized orangutan—and hated reflecting on his nonexistent social life. But that's what he was here to do:

talk about how screwed up his life had been so far and strategize (Kingston's word, not his) about how he could change it for the better.

The question of the day: "How is school going, Ryan?"

So far today Dooley had said nothing.

Nor had Kingston.

Dooley glanced at the clock. Twenty minutes down—it felt like ninety—and forty to go.

Kingston, his chin resting on one hand, his elbow propped up on the desk, looked impassively at Dooley through the round lenses of his rimless glasses. For all Dooley knew, the guy was composing a grocery list. Or maybe he was thinking about his wife. Kingston never talked about her—the one time Dooley had asked, Kingston had made it clear that he wasn't there to talk, let alone to talk about himself. No, he was there to listen. To Dooley, Kingston always looked mildly bored. Dooley couldn't blame him.

Once, at the beginning when Dooley was still pissed off that he had to attend these sessions, he'd kept his mouth shut and waited to see how long it would take for Kingston to break down and say something. It took sixty minutes. What Kingston said was, "Time's up." Then he said, "You have to come. You sit there and don't say a word, I still get paid. But it works better if you say what's on your mind."

Works better for who? Dooley wondered.

Sometimes Dooley talked, usually fitfully, with long silences, usually about stuff that didn't matter, like what a dork Kevin was, how dumb most school assignments were, why it was that teachers, even the younger ones, couldn't seem to remember what it was like to be in high school (Dooley's theory: all teachers, especially the younger ones, were people who had actually *liked* their high school years), and, once (and only once) what a hard-ass Dooley's uncle was. Dooley had been mad that time. The situation: Dooley had just come off a long shift at work, all the customers with problems ("How many times do I have to tell you, I returned that movie on time?" "Yeah, I watched the whole thing, that's how I know it sucks, I can't believe I spent good money on that piece of shit, I want a refund." "So what if my son has a membership card, I told you people, I said, put it in your computer, that kid is not to rent any more movies." Blah-freakin'-blah). Dooley had arrived home, sweaty from the July humidity that had hung on long after the sun went down, pissed off at all the stupid customers, pissed off at Kevin who kept telling him to "smile, for Christ's sake, make people think there's half a chance you give a shit" (which Dooley didn't), pissed off that he had to get up at seven-thirty the next morning to go to summer school—and there it was, an open bottle of beer sitting on the kitchen table beside a pair of big sunglasses and a silk scarf, which is how he knew that it was Jeannie's bottle of beer. He listened for a moment, but didn't hear anything, not a sound. So he picked up the bottle and tasted the contents.

Big mistake.

His uncle appeared the minute Dooley put the bottle to his lips, which made Dooley wonder if he'd been set up.

"We had a deal," his uncle said.

"It was one sip," Dooley said.

"One sip, one toke, one snort, one tab—I see it or smell it or hear about it and you're out of here for good. You got that?"

Yeah, Dooley got it. Got it and told Kingston, Jesus, you'd think he'd rolled in smashed the way his uncle had reacted.

Kingston had peered at him through his rimless glasses.

"It was one sip," Dooley said, and, boy, had it tasted fine. The beer hadn't been long out of the fridge. It was still cold. Droplets of water had beaded up on the outside of the bottle. Jeannie must have set it down just before Dooley walked through the door; maybe she'd gone to the can. If Dooley had stood there long enough and listened hard enough and still hadn't heard anything, he would have been sorely tempted to take another sip. And, okay, maybe another one after that. So what? It wasn't even a whole bottle of beer. Geeze, on a good day, back before he'd come to live with his uncle, he could put away a twelve-pack without either passing out or puking. What was half a bottle?

Dooley glanced at Kingston's old-fashioned clock again now. Thirty-five minutes to go.

"You go with a lot of girls when you were in high school, Doc?" Dooley said.

Kingston surprised Dooley—he answered—and then didn't surprise him at all when he said, "No."

Well, what do you know? Dooley and Kingston had something in common, even though Dooley bet it was for different reasons. He bet Kingston was one of those nerdy looking brainiacs who get picked on a lot but who don't get much action. Dooley hadn't got much either, so far. But mostly that was because he'd spent most of his time being otherwise occupied. So when he'd seen Beth in the video store back before he knew who she was or even knew her name and when he'd chatted with her—at her initiative—he was never sure where to take it. He'd thought: she probably has a boyfriend. He'd thought: what are the chances a girl like that would be interested in a guy who works in a video store? And before he could work his way up to maybe asking her out, there was her brother, dead. Then today she'd seen Rhodes play the white knight while Dooley played See No Evil.

Big deal. It's not like anything was ever going to come of it.

She sure was pretty, though. And he enjoyed what she had to say about the movies she rented. A lot of times Dooley ended up taking them out and watching them himself after she returned them and, at first, was surprised at how much he liked them. Now he just took it as given that if she'd liked it, he'd like it too. So they had that in common, right?

Kingston sighed, the closest he'd ever coming to expressing what he was feeling, even if what he was feeling was boredom.

It turned out that wasn't what was on Kingston's mind.

Kingston put down the heavy fountain pen that he liked to write with and said, "You're wasting your time and mine, Ryan, not to mention your uncle's money."

"What?" Dooley said.

"I'm going to recommend to your uncle that you stop coming here."

"But I have to come here," Dooley said. "It's part of my plan." He had to report regularly to a court-appointed youth worker. He had to go to counseling. He had to attend school. He had to stay away from alcohol and drugs. He had to stay away from certain people. He was supposed to hold down a part-time job.

"You have to attend counseling," Kingston said. He had a dry way of talking, as if he were describing beige wallpaper or old asphalt. "It was initially recommended that you go to group counseling. Your uncle thought you would benefit from a more individualized approach."

"My uncle?"

"He's paying for this," Kingston said.

Jesus. Dooley hadn't given any thought to who was paying. He'd assumed it was just covered, that the court picked up the cost, or the system. It had never occurred to him that his uncle was footing the bill. Why would he do that?

"You report to my uncle what goes on here?"

Kingston shook his head. "What we talk about is between you and me."

"What are you going to tell him about this?"

"That we've made all the progress we're going to make."

"I still have to go to counseling."

"I can refer you to some excellent group counseling programs if you'd like. So can your youth worker."

Dooley's uncle was not going to like this.

"I guess other people you see talk more than me, huh?"

"Most of them do, yes."

"They fill out those papers too, huh?"

"The ones who are serious about making progress, yes," Kingston said.

"Do you think I've made any progress?"

"Do you?"

Dooley had been coming to Kingston's office in a small uptown medical building once a week for more than three months now. Kingston would ask him a question and most of the time Dooley would spend his time either talking about bullshit stuff or, if he didn't feel up to that, just waiting Kingston out. Kingston was always giving him worksheets to fill out between sessions, exercises that were supposed to help Dooley reflect on his life, his attitudes, his behavior. They reminded Dooley of homework. He didn't fill them out, didn't even look at them. A couple of times Kingston asked about them. Dooley just said he forgot. And now here was Kingston basically firing him, which Dooley wouldn't have minded so much if his uncle hadn't been paying the bill all these months.

"How much?" Dooley said.

"How much what?"

"How much do you charge my uncle?"

It was one of those questions that, once he heard the answer, he wished he'd never asked.

"That much?"

Kingston nodded.

Multiply that by, say, twelve weeks . . . Jesus.

"Other people, they just sit here and talk to you?"

Kingston nodded.

"And that makes a difference?"

"It does, yes."

Dooley didn't see how.

Kingston looked at the clock. "Time's up," he said.

"Maybe you could hold off on talking to my uncle," Dooley said. "Maybe we could give it another try."

To be honest, Dooley couldn't figure out which was worse—having wasted all of his uncle's money by sitting here like a slab of stone for the past three months, or wasting any more of it by taking a shot at what he should have been doing all along but, to be honest, he still didn't think would do any good.

Kingston just stared at him.

"You never know, right?" Dooley said.

Kingston stood up, about to move to the door to let Dooley out.

"I'll put you in for next week at the same time," he said. "After that, we can re-evaluate."

Dooley was surprised at how relieved he felt.

■ ■ ■

Two hours later, Dooley was antsy and wishing he could have a drink or smoke some weed, anything to take the edge off. He'd been inside eighteen months with only a couple of slips and outside three months with nothing except that one sip of beer. You'd think he'd be over it by now. But he wasn't. He wasn't even sure half the time what made him so jangled, which, of course, was the whole point of seeing Kingston. He was supposed to develop self-awareness. He was supposed to understand what made him tick. He was supposed to identify his danger areas and his flash points and then learn coping mechanisms that would help him get through the day. When he thought about it, the same question always popped up, namely: was that the best he could expect from life—being hyper-aware of all his problems as he trudged through one mind-fucking day after another?

Today everything was putting him on edge: school, what had happened after school, Kingston, work. Beth.

When Dooley was in detention, he'd had regular sessions with a psychologist named Dr. Calvin. Unlike Kingston, Dr. Calvin actually talked. A lot. He also gave advice such as, when your past starts sneaking up on you, when it starts calling your name, trying to get you to do something that deep down inside you knew you shouldn't, just tune it out. It's what his uncle told him, too: You don't like it? Let it go. Tune it out. Well, gentlemen, there is no better way to tune out life—all life, past, present, and future—than by clerking in a video store. You step in behind the counter and in five seconds flat your brain switches from active mode to screen-saver mode, because there's nothing going on in the central processing unit that is your brain. It turns out that everyone is right—the same picture scrolls past your eyeballs over and over. You really don't need a brain to do Dooley's job, which consists of, one, emptying the drop box; two, checking that the DVDs are (a) inside the cases that are being returned and (b) not scratched beyond redemption; three, scanning the barcodes so that the titles are registered in the computer as being returned; and, big finish, four, re-shelving everything. It's all about turn-around, get the product back out there on the shelves where the customers can find it so they don't go *across the street*—Kevin was always yelling those words at Dooley and the rest of the clerks . . . er . . . customer service associates—to Blockbuster where they have entire walls of the same title. Dooley wanted to strangle Kevin sometimes—well, okay, so he wanted to strangle him most of the time. When Dooley felt like that, he knew (from Dr. Calvin, not from Kingston) that it was time to come up with an alternative scenario.

Dr. Calvin: Instead of strangling Kevin, what could you do?

Dooley: Homer him with my baseball bat?

Dr. Calvin: What could you *constructively* do?

Dooley: Ignore him?

Dr. Calvin: Splendid! Yes. Ignore him.

Right. Except that Dr. Calvin didn't have to spend four times six hours a week plus eight hours on the weekend—a total of thirty-two hours a week, *every* week—with a dork like Kevin who was always telling you do this, do that, all of the things he wanted you to do, trained monkey shit that you didn't have to be told to do, you already knew. Geeze, as if Dooley was going to let the DVDs pile up on the front counter where no one could find them and rent them. As if he couldn't remember to put them in alphabetical order. As if he couldn't remember to check the computer if he wasn't sure if the Bruce Willis movie some middle-aged customer was for some reason desperate to rent but couldn't find was in the action section, the thriller section, or the sci-fi section. As if he couldn't remember that he wasn't supposed to argue with the customers, which Kevin had made clear to him right after Dooley told some fifty-something action junkie that, no, as a matter of fact, he didn't buy into the theory that movies in which Bruce sported a bad toupee were bad Bruce whereas movies that featured Bruce with his natural hairline, which is to say a hairline that began and ended at the back of Bruce's neck, were high-quality Bruce. In fact, if the customer wanted Dooley's opinion, which, it turned out, he didn't, there was no such thing as high-quality Bruce. What Kevin didn't understand: it wasn't that Dooley couldn't remember not to argue. It was just that sometimes, with some customers, he couldn't resist.

After his appointment with Kingston, Dooley had taken the subway back downtown, pushed open the door to the store, and walked in past the front desk, down between the aisles that ran the length of the store, and into the back where he shucked his sweatshirt and put on a red golf shirt with the store logo over his heart and, above that, a badge with his name spelled out using one of those tape machines. Dooley's badge read: *Hi, my name is Dooley*. Kevin had had a fit when Dooley made the label: "Look at *my* badge," he'd said. "It says *Kevin*, not Sanders. Get it, Dooley? See what Linelle's says? It says *Linelle*. *Your* badge is supposed to say Ryan. Hi, my name is Ryan. You get it, Dooley?" Dooley had glanced at Linelle, who was turning pink from trying not to laugh out loud. He bet she was thinking the same thing he was. They were both thinking: Did Kevin ever listen to himself? "We're a friendly place," Kevin said. "People call us by our first names. That way they feel like we're their friends."

Right.

In Dooley's experience, people weren't interested in being friends with video store clerks. They thought video store clerks were brain-dead, going-nowhere semi-human beings who if they had any potential at all, even a dribble of it, would be working at a real job, which is to say, not retail, not part-time, and not for minimum wage.

"People call me Dooley," Dooley had explained to Kevin that time. "It's my name."

"You going to tell me your mother calls you Dooley?" Kevin said.

Not that it was any of Kevin's business, but, yeah, that was exactly what Lorraine called him, usually giving it a bitter little spin when she said it. Dooley's father's name was Dooley. Dooley didn't remember him—he'd gone missing, Lorraine said, when Dooley was just a couple of months old. Lorraine must have had high hopes for the guy; she'd registered Dooley under his name instead of her own, which was McCormack. Once in a blue moon, if she was in one of her nostalgic moods, she used to smile at him and tell him he reminded her of his father. Most of the time, though, especially when she was loaded or when she was coming down, she'd look at him like he *was* his father, that no-good asshole who had knocked her up, made some promises, and then blown her off. Like it was Dooley's fault.

"It's Dooley," Dooley had told Kevin. Sure, his teachers insisted on calling him Ryan. And, sure, he was called Ryan whenever he went to court. His uncle called him Ryan, too. Dooley never even tried to argue that one. What was the point? Apart from that, well, listen to Kevin—even he called him Dooley. And because he knew that Kevin knew where he had been the previous eighteen months (even though Kevin wasn't supposed to know), he had stood up as tall as he could (which was a minimum of two inches taller than Kevin) and stepped into Kevin's personal space, close enough that he could smell the Listermint strip melting onto Kevin's tongue.

Kevin smiled a twitchy smile and said, "Whatever," like he didn't care but, boy, it was obvious that he did. He cared in the worst way. He wanted to fire Dooley—which he (a) couldn't do without passing it by the store manager (Kevin was only a shift manager), who, go figure, got a kick out of Dooley and (b) was afraid to do because he was scared shitless that if he did, Dooley would meet him out back with, say, a lead pipe or a tire iron or his personal favorite, a baseball bat, and beat his brains in. Dooley did nothing to soothe Kevin's fear. He couldn't control what people thought, he'd developed that much self-awareness. Besides, if people were going to think something and it turned out it was to your advantage, well, whose fault was that?

Friday night was the busiest night at the store. Saturday was bad, too, but a lot of people went out on Saturday, whereas on Friday most people were exhausted from work or school or whatever and all they wanted to do was pop something in their DVD players and sprawl in front of the tube. So there was Dooley, emptying the drop box up front, stacking DVDs, and wondering what to do about Kingston, when the sensor over the door bonged and in walked Beth. Rhodes was with her. They walked down the far aisle. Neither of them looked at him, but Dooley sure looked at her. He finished stacking the DVDs from the drop box, picked up the scanner, and started scanning bar codes, watching her the whole time. She was over in the far corner, in the foreign film section, which, as far as Dooley could tell, was her favorite. He wondered who was picking the movie—her or Rhodes. She moved along the aisle, bending down now and again to look at some of the cases on the bottom shelves. Rhodes just stood there, waiting, so that answered Dooley's question. He ducked his head when she turned and headed for the cash so she wouldn't know he'd been watching her, Rhodes right at her side.

"Hey, Linelle," Dooley said, putting down the scanner. "Why don't you take a break? I'll handle cash for a while."

Linelle gave him a look. "You hate cash, Dooley."

She was right. Scanning, shelving, even vacuuming and mopping at end of shift, those were tolerable, primarily because they didn't involve interacting with customers. But cash? Cash was always a pain. People were always surprised by something, but never pleasantly. "Two movies, a large Coke, and a package of microwave popcorn cost *how* much?" "Restocking fee? What the hell is that? You telling me you hire special people and pay them extra to put movies back on the shelf when they're returned late?" "But I returned that movie last week, I know I did." "What do you mean, my credit card is rejected?" Shit like that.

Beth and Rhodes were halfway to the front of the store.

"Give me a break, huh, Linelle?" Dooley said.

Linelle glanced at Beth. She shook her head and stepped aside. "You owe me, Dooley."

"You sound like an American tourist," Beth was saying to Rhodes as she approached the counter. "They travel the world and expect everyone to speak English to them."

"You miss half the movie when you have to read subtitles," Rhodes said. "Dubbing, okay, at least you can concentrate on what's happening. But you can't read and watch the movie at the same time. That's all I'm saying."

Beth put the DVD on the counter and started to rummage in her purse.

"Hey, my treat," Rhodes said, reaching in his pocket for his wallet.

"You're not even going to watch it," Beth said. "Why should you pay for it?"

"Who says I'm not going to watch it?"

"It's *my* homework assignment."

"I'm a great tutor."

She laughed. "I don't need a tutor. I'm at the top of my class." Most people, when they said something like that, it came across as boasting. But not her. When she said it, it sounded right.

She pulled out her wallet and looked across the counter at Dooley, noticing him for the first time. Her smile slipped, but just a little.

"Hi," she said.

"Hi." He picked up the DVD and scanned it. "Did you find everything you were looking for today?" It was what they were supposed to ask, but Dooley never did. Well, almost never. He heard Linelle gag and shot her a look over his shoulder.

"Yes, thank you," Beth said.

He glanced at the DVD cover. *Roshomon.*

"It's a good story," he said.

Rhodes looked surprised that Dooley had watched it. Beth didn't.

"I'm writing an essay on it for my media class," she said.

Media class? He wondered what school she went to. There were no media classes at Dooley's school.

"You're lucky," Dooley said, "getting to write about movies. I have to write an essay on *Hamlet.*"

"I like that play," she said.

Dooley didn't think much of it himself. What do you make of a guy who's sure his uncle murdered his father, but he doesn't do anything about it? Okay, Dooley could see maybe if Hamlet didn't like his old man. But that wasn't the case, was it? So what was his problem—other than he was a wuss?

He scanned her movie. She handed him some money. She said, "So, did you remember anything else yet?"

"Remember anything about what?" Rhodes said.

She didn't answer. Her brown eyes were fixed intently on Dooley. He wished he could tell her what she wanted to hear.

He shook his head.

"Remember about what?" Rhodes said again.

"Nothing," she said, still watching Dooley.

Dooley slipped her DVD into a plastic bag along with her receipt.

"It's due back next Friday by eleven," he said. As she walked away, he heard Rhodes say, "Remember about what? How do you even know him?" Then they were out the door, gone.

"Don't tell me, let me guess, I've had enough of a break, I can go back on cash now," Linelle said dryly. She slid back in front of the register. "She was in here the other night asking about you."

Dooley was watching her through the window. She was walking down the street with Rhodes, but she wasn't holding his hand or anything.

"I saw her on TV, too," she said. "On the news. She's the one whose brother died, right?" Dooley nodded. "Is she going out with The Winner?"

"The Winner?"

"The guy she was with. Rhodes. Winston Rhodes."

"You know him?" Dooley said, surprised. Linelle didn't go to his school.

"I went with a guy who used to know him. You should see his place." She shook her head. "Him and that girl, I guess they have a lot in common." Before Dooley could ask her what she meant, she said, "They showed a picture of her brother on TV, too. Isn't he that guy you—"

"You finished scanning the returns, Dooley?" Kevin said, popping up, it seemed, out of nowhere. "Yes? So would it be too much to expect you to re-shelve them?"

Yeah, it was mostly Beth who had him thinking about the good old days when there was always something he could reach for, something to smooth out the rough parts of the day, take the sharp edges off. But it was Kevin, too. He dumped the returns onto a trolley and headed for the back of the store.

Isn't he the guy . . .

■ ■ ■

The store closed at midnight. By then it was just Dooley and Kevin in the store. Linelle's shift had ended at ten. While Kevin did the cash, Dooley vacuumed the carpeted part of the floor and wet-mopped the tiled part. Then he perched on the counter while Kevin, who was in the back room, counted the cash, reconciled the accounts, and got the deposit ready. It was company policy that there always had to be two people in the store, so Dooley had no choice. He had to wait for Kevin, who didn't emerge from the back room until nearly quarter to one.

It was one-fifteen by the time Dooley got home. The first thing he saw: Jeannie's purse sitting on the little table in the front hall. He went into the kitchen, pulled a box of Cheerios from the cupboard and a carton of milk from the fridge and poured himself a bowl of cereal. He was halfway through it when his uncle appeared in nothing but boxers, which, ordinarily, Dooley didn't mind. His uncle was in pretty good shape for a guy his age. He ran regularly and lifted weights at the gym a couple of times a week. But, geeze, when he turned up in his boxers and Dooley knew that Jeannie was in the house, Dooley couldn't help but think about one thing—and it wasn't something he wanted to think about, especially not involving his uncle.

His uncle grabbed a glass from the cupboard and filled it with ice cubes from the freezer. He took a bottle of vodka from the cupboard next to the fridge and poured a good three fingers over the ice. It was for Jeannie. Dooley's uncle was a scotch drinker.

"How was work?" his uncle said.

"It was work," Dooley said.

His uncle looked at the bowl of cereal. "That your dinner?"

"I had a slice of pizza before I went on shift," Dooley said.

His uncle shook his head. "You're like a kid. Unless I make you a decent meal, you eat garbage."

"Technically," Dooley said, "I am a kid."

"Right," his uncle said. "Seventeen going on seventy." He looked at the cereal spoon in Dooley's hand. "You forget to pick up your ring from the jeweler?"

Shit.

"No, I got it," Dooley said.

"You're not wearing it."

Dooley shrugged, looked down into his cereal bowl, and ransacked his brain for something to say. "It's just—I've been thinking about Lorraine."

"Jesus," his uncle said. "What's she got to do with anything?"

"Where do you think she is?"

"Probably shacked up with some loser. Why? Don't tell me you're nostalgic."

That was the part Dooley never understood. His uncle didn't think much of his own baby sister. He held her in complete contempt, as far as Dooley could figure. Yet he'd come to see Dooley when they locked him up the last time. And he'd kept on coming, even when Dooley didn't give a shit because, face it, when you're locked up, pretty much the last person you want coming around is some hard-ass ex-cop who keeps telling you how fucked up you are and how it's no surprise, your mother is even more fucked up, always was, probably always will be, and, by the way, you ever consider doing something constructive like, say, reading a book? *You* ever considered not being such an asshole, Dooley used to think. But still, he showed up regularly and when the time came he told Dooley, you do it right, you can stay with me. So here Dooley was—straight, sober, in school, in a bed with clean sheets once a week (Dooley changed them Saturday morning—his uncle insisted on it), with vegetables on his plate (the only vegetable Lorraine ever served was fries from McDonald's or KFC), dishes that matched, place mats and coasters on the table, and floors that got mopped (mostly by Dooley, mostly operating under orders). Dooley didn't know exactly why his uncle was doing it or even what he thought about Dooley and his prospects. To be honest, Dooley wasn't sure he wanted to know.

"I was just thinking about her," Dooley said, which was true now but hadn't been when he'd first said it.

His uncle looked at him. "She is what she is," he said. "It has nothing to do with your grandfather, if that's what you're thinking. He tried. So did your grandmother. Saint Peter himself could have raised her, she would have turned out the same."

Dooley was what he was, too. But his uncle was giving him a chance. Dooley looked down at his cereal going soggy in the bowl. He wondered if he should say something about Kingston but decided not to. Then his uncle changed the subject.

"That kid you saw go off the bridge," he said. "What I heard is, he'd been drinking." Dooley looked at him. "A guy who works downtown came in today to pick up his shirts." A lot of cops and ex-cops brought their dry-cleaning to Dooley's uncle. He gave them a special cops-only discount. "He mentioned it. He said the kid was loaded."

"What? Did they find a bottle?"

Dooley's uncle shook his head. "Toxicology," he said. "He had a blood-alcohol level that would have made him pretty near incoherent. If he was that drunk and fooling around up there on that bridge . . . there's a lesson in that, Ryan."

Right, Dooley thought. As if bridges had ever figured into his problems.

His uncle stood up with Jeannie's glass of vodka. "It's late. Finish your cereal. Go to bed." ■

Eight

hat girl was here looking for you," Linelle said when Dooley showed up for work the next day. She had a cart of returns and was putting them back on the shelves.

"What girl?" Dooley said.

"What girl?" Linelle said, echoing him. "The girl you were making puppy eyes at yesterday. The one who was in here with The Winner."

"She was looking for me?" He tried to sound casual about it.

"Isn't that what I just said?" Linelle said.

"What did you tell her?"

Linelle rolled her eyes. "What happened, Dooley? Did your brains leak out of your head while you were sleeping? What do you think I told her?"

"Did she say if she'd be back?"

"Yeah," Linelle said. "She said she'd check back later."

"When later?"

"She just said later."

Dooley headed for the back room to sign in.

"She doesn't know, does she?" Linelle called after him.

"Know what?"

"About you and her brother."

"There's nothing to know. It wasn't personal. I didn't know who he was. I didn't even know his name."

"I'm guessing that's a no," Linelle said. She started to wheel her cart over to the next aisle.

"Hey, Linelle? You said she had a lot in common with Rhodes." He hesitated. He liked Linelle, but he wasn't sure who she talked to and what she said. "Is she rich?" That would just about clinch it. He couldn't imagine a rich girl ever being interested in a video store clerk.

"How would I know?" Linelle said. "I don't know her except she comes in here to rent movies. Based on her picks, though, you know, all that foreign shit she rents, I'd say she has brains. She dresses preppy, too, so, yeah, she's upscale or a serious wannabe. But is she in the same league as The Winner? I don't have a clue."

Now Dooley was baffled. "But you said—"

"I meant the dead sib thing," Linelle said.

Dead sib thing? What the hell?

"Her brother died. His sister died."

"Geeze," Dooley said.

"It was years ago," Linelle said. "But it means that he can do the I-know-exactly-what-you're-going-through routine and come off as totally sincere. Girls like sincerity, Dooley."

What did that mean?

"You think I'm not sincere?"

Linelle rolled her eyes.

"Girls also like guys who don't come across as totally pathetic," she said. "If you see her again, try to keep your eyes in their sockets and your tongue in your mouth, you know what I mean?" She pushed her cart into the Action/Adventure aisle and started to re-shelve DVDs.

■ ■ ■

Dooley waited all afternoon. Beth didn't show. He had a supper break at seven, but he hung around instead of going, still waiting, until Kevin told him, "Use it or lose it, Dooley." Linelle was gone by then. Kevin was up front. A new guy named Stefan took over the cash so that Dooley could take his break. Dooley said to him, "If a girl comes in looking for me, I'm across the street at the Greek place. Okay?"

Stefan shrugged. "Whatever."

"I'm saying, *tell* her that's where I am," Dooley said.

"Yeah," Stefan said, sounding as bored as he looked. "And I'm saying, whatever."

She walked into the restaurant just as Dooley was taking a giant bite of his souvlaki sandwich. He wiped the tzatziki off his mouth and swallowed as fast as he could.

"Sit down," he said. "You hungry? You want something to eat?"

She shook her head. She looked tired. He wondered if that was because of her brother. He wondered if the two of them had been really close. Some siblings were—at least, that's what Dooley had heard.

"How was the movie?" he said.

"It was good," she said. "They don't make them like that in Hollywood. The really interesting movies all come from somewhere else."

"What kind of school do you go to where you get to watch movies and write essays about them?"

"It's a private school."

Private schools cost a lot of money. That had to mean her parents were loaded. But if that were true, how come her brother had gone to a regular school? Why hadn't they sent him to a private school, too?

At the exact same time that she said, "Would you consent to being hypnotized?" Dooley's pager vibrated, startling him. He glanced down at it. She looked questioningly at him.

"It's nothing," he said. "It can wait." For another nine minutes and fifty seconds, anyway. "What were you saying?"

Geeze, where had that question even come from?

"Maybe you saw something you don't even realize you saw," she said. "Something that could help the police."

"The police?" Dooley said. "But I thought—" He shut up fast. Just because some cop friend of his uncle's had said something in passing, that didn't mean they had got around to saying anything to the family.

"You thought what?" she said.

"Nothing." It wasn't his place to break the news to her. Besides, no one had said he'd been drinking alone. Maybe he'd been with someone, maybe someone who had panicked when he went over. It was possible.

"People who witness traumatic events sometimes go into shock. Sometimes their mind blocks out what they saw and they don't even realize it. It's like a coping mechanism, you know?"

Dooley nodded. He knew all about coping mechanisms. He didn't tell her that seeing her brother take a header off the bridge hadn't even come close to traumatizing him. Seeing him lying there on the ground, that was something else. But even that wasn't what Dooley would call traumatic.

"Sometimes, under hypnosis, people remember things that their conscious minds have been shutting out," she said.

What Dooley knew about hypnosis: not much, other than you were talking in your sleep to a complete stranger and when it was over, you couldn't remember what you had said. No way did Dooley want to be involved in anything like that. There was no telling what he might say. Geeze, look at some of the stupid things he'd said when he was drunk or stoned. Look at the trouble that had got him into.

"I'm pretty sure I remember what I saw," he said. "You want me to get the waitress for you? You want to order something?" He felt bad eating a sandwich in front of her.

She shook her head, so he pushed his plate aside, even though he was still hungry.

"See, that's the thing," she said. "You're *pretty* sure. But you're not positive, right?"

"I saw what I saw," Dooley said.

"Maybe you only *think* you saw what you saw," she said. She looked right at him with those coffee-colored eyes.

"Okay, maybe what you say you saw is really all there is to it. I'm not saying it isn't. But what if it was your brother who died? Wouldn't you want to know for sure what had happened to him?"

"Yeah, I guess," Dooley said. He wondered if she'd say the same thing if the cops had already told her that her brother had been drinking and that it was his own stupid fault he'd gone off that bridge.

"So you'll do it?" she said. "You'll agree to be hypnotized?" She sat forward in her chair now, her eyes sparkling.

"I didn't say that," Dooley said. "No offence, but I'm not into that whole hypnosis thing."

Her expression hardened. "You don't know me," she said. "And I don't know you. But you know what? If I'd seen your brother go off that bridge, I'd do whatever you asked me if it would help you figure out what really happened."

Boy, she was intense. Her eyes were glistening now, like maybe she was going to cry. But she didn't. She stared at him fiercely.

"Okay," Dooley said. "How about this? How about you let me look into this hypnosis thing a little, you know, ask a few questions, find out what's involved? Then, if it seems okay, maybe . . ."

"I can give you the name of a police officer I spoke to," she said, all eager now.

"It's okay," he said. There were enough cops in his life. "I know a few people I can ask. I'll get back to you. Okay?"

She pulled out a notebook and a pen and wrote something down—her name and phone number, it turned out.

"Call me," she said. "If you can't get me, leave a message."

He nodded.

She smiled at him, reminding him of a little kid. Dooley knew the way most little kids were; you tell them maybe, and they automatically think it means yes. But for Dooley, it was different. When Dooley was growing up and Lorraine had said maybe, it always meant no, so that's what it meant when Dooley said it. He knew he should have come right out and said it. But he couldn't make himself do it. Not to her. Not right away.

"Thank you," she said. "Thank you."

As soon as she left the restaurant, he fumbled in his pocket for a quarter and dashed to the pay phone near the door.

"I called the store," his uncle said when he answered the phone. "They said you're on your break."

"Yeah," Dooley said. "I'm across the street at that Greek place." Then, partly kidding around and partly wondering if his uncle was making any progress on trusting him, he added, "You want me to put the waitress on?"

There was silence on the other end of the line, and Dooley imagined his uncle thinking it over. But all he said was, "Jeannie wants to know if you can bring home a movie for her. There's this new one she's interested in—I never heard of it."

Dooley grinned when his uncle told him the name of the movie. "Yeah," he said. "I think we've got that one. Tell Jeannie okay." He wished he could be in the room when Jeannie popped that one in the DVD player. It was pure chick flick. His uncle was going to hate it. ■

Nine

Dooley knew exactly what Gillette thought of him. Fill a room full of serial killers, whack jobs, perverts, mass murderers—hell, throw in Hitler and Stalin and Saddam Hussein, add those other guys, too, that guy in Cambodia and the one in Africa who got his people to hack the competition to death with machetes—and then put Dooley in the same room and tell Gillette he had to invite any one of them to dinner, his choice, and the very last person he would pick, no matter what, would be Dooley. Those other people, they were all hearsay to Gillette, all he had to go on were other people's accounts of what they had done and why they had done it (they were insane, that's why). Dooley, though—Dooley was first-hand. Gillette knew what Dooley was capable of. He'd seen him in action.

So what the hell was he doing leaning against Dooley's locker and glancing down the hall now at Dooley, looking like he'd been waiting for him?

Dooley stopped in front of Gillette and locked eyes with him. Gillette stared right back at him—see, you don't scare me—before standing aside, *casually*, as if to say, hey, look at Joe Student, what a loser, the guy is desperate to get to his locker, so, fine, be my guest. Dooley wished Gillette would get lost. He grabbed the lock with one hand and spun the combination with the other.

"Hey, how's it going?" Gillette said.

Jesus, Dooley thought, *does he realize how phoney he sounds*?

Dooley pulled on the lock, opened his locker, and started to fill his backpack with textbooks and binders. When he'd finished, he zipped it shut, locked his locker, and spun away from Gillette, heading for the stairs. Gillette scampered after him like a three-year-old trying to keep up with his long-legged daddy.

"Hey, what's the rush?" Gillette said, catching Dooley on the main floor and grabbing him by the arm to make him stop.

Dooley looked at Gillette's hand. You didn't need more than one brain cell to know what he was thinking: take your hands off me or else. That was the thing that Gillette knew better than anyone—the "or else." He dropped his hand.

"I was just wanted to talk, see how things are going, that's all," he said.

"Yeah?" Dooley said. He had a pretty good idea what it was Gillette wanted to say, but was surprised that he still wanted to say it. "Why's that?"

"Old time's sake," Gillette said.

"Right," Dooley said. He turned and walked out the door. He glanced over his shoulder as he went through it and saw Gillette just standing there, as if he couldn't decide what to do—let it go or chase after Dooley. In the end, he chose the latter and caught Dooley this time on the street, heading away from school.

"I heard you saw that kid go over," he said, getting right to the point this time. It wasn't the point Dooley had expected.

"*That kid*?" Dooley said. "Like you don't know his name? What's the matter with you? You think I'm some kind of idiot?"

"No," Gillette said, startled. "No, it's just a way of speaking, that's all. Yeah, I knew him. A lot of people knew him. But so far as I know, you're the only person who saw what happened to him."

Dooley gave Gillette a look he knew Gillette would recognize, one that said you can kick me, you can kill me, it's all the same to me, but whatever you're going to do, do it now, before I take you out.

"What's it to you?" he said.

"I was just wondering, that's all."

"So it's, like, idle curiosity," Dooley said. "Kinda like those videos, huh, the ones where you see animals rip other animals to shreds."

Gillette stepped back a little, like Dooley was making him even more nervous, but he didn't back off altogether. Dooley wondered why not.

"A lot of people are saying he jumped," Gillette said. "But there's some people wondering if he was pushed."

Dooley just stood there, dead-eyed, but also patient—his

hands crossed over each other, one knee bent a little—waiting for Gillette to continue. Anyone looking at him would think he looked pretty casual. Well, anyone except Gillette. He knew better.

"So, what do you think?" Gillette said. He kept glancing around, like he wished he were somewhere else. Anywhere else. "You were there."

Dooley looked at him a little longer before he said, "Why? Are you worried?"

He enjoyed the look of alarm that appeared on Gillette's face.

"What do you mean?" Gillette said.

"You knew the guy," Dooley said. "You worried the cops'll think you had something to do with it?"

"Fuck, no," Gillette said. He stiffened and now Dooley could see a little of the old Gillette. "What about you?" he said, an edge to his voice. "Did you tell the cops about you and Everley?"

Dooley tried to keep his face blank, but he saw a look of triumph in Gillette's eyes. Gillette knew he'd hit something, and he liked the feeling.

"You know what I thought when I saw you there at my locker?" Dooley said. He let Gillette wonder for a few moments. "I thought maybe you were going to finally come clean with me—to my face. Who knows, maybe you were even going to apologize."

Gillette frowned. He looked wary now.

"I know what happened," Dooley said. "I know exactly what happened and what a fuck-up you are. But, funny thing, I didn't hear it from you."

"Hey, look—"

"Stay away from me, Gillette. Don't make trouble for me, and I won't make trouble for you."

Dooley watched Gillette's eyes go cold. He wondered if Gillette was sorry he'd approached him. He still couldn't figure out why he had. What difference did it make to Gillette what Dooley had seen out there in the ravine? ■

Ten

Dooley couldn't get Beth out of his mind and not just because she was beautiful—although she was that. It was also the way she was so direct. She just came right out with whatever was on her mind. Dooley was no expert on girls. He'd never had a girlfriend—he'd never had the time, he got locked up when he was fifteen. But he'd known a few girls who'd hung around with some of the older guys he used to hang with, and they were nothing like Beth. Even the pretty ones looked somehow harder than her. Their hair was stiffer or they fooled with it more. They wore more makeup. They dressed in a fuck-me way. Beth, though—she just looked good. Her hair was long and always shone and always hung a certain way over her shoulders. She probably had stuff on her lips and on her eyes, but not so you'd notice. She dressed nice—pants and sweaters, nothing too fancy, but you could tell it was good stuff. He wondered if she had a boyfriend. He wondered if it was Rhodes.

He felt in his pocket for the piece of paper with her phone number on it. She wanted so badly for him to get hypnotized and he wanted just as badly to avoid the whole thing. Besides, what was the point if all that had happened was that Everley had been drinking? Maybe there was something else he could do for her, something that might make her feel a little better about what had happened to her brother—or at least not so bad.

For example, there was Everley's backpack, which was missing and which he supposedly had with him all the time. Beth seemed to attach a lot of importance to that backpack. Maybe the things he had in it—his camera and his stories—meant something to her. He wondered what had happened to it. It could have been any one of a number of things. For example, maybe Everley had taken it with him when he left his house that day, but maybe he didn't have it with him when he was up on that bridge. Maybe he'd left it wherever he was before he got to the bridge. The cops said he'd been drinking. If he'd had enough to start fooling around on a bridge so recklessly that he'd fallen off it, then he'd probably also had enough to forget his backpack somewhere. Maybe he'd forgotten it wherever he'd been drinking. Maybe nobody had noticed it. Maybe it was still wherever he'd left it. He wondered if Beth had thought about that. If that wasn't it, then it had to be one of the other possibilities he had already mentioned to her. Either Everley had taken it off when he was fooling around up there on the bridge just before he went over and someone had come along (before the police got there) and had taken it. Or someone had got to Everley before Dooley and had seen he was dead and had taken the backpack off him. It wasn't pleasant to think about, but it was possible. There were a lot of homeless people down there in the ravine.

■ ■ ■

Dooley's uncle came into the kitchen a little before six. He was carrying five plastic grocery store bags. Dooley, who had been sitting at the kitchen table working on his math homework (which he hated) and his history homework (which was not so bad), got up to help him put everything away.

"The mushrooms and the salad stuff stay here," his uncle said. "And the steaks. The dips, the cheese, and the cold cuts you can put in the fridge. The rest of the stuff goes on the dining room table."

The rest of the stuff was a couple of bags of potato chips, a bag of pretzels, a couple of boxes of crackers, a loaf of rye bread, and a couple of large plastic bottles of soda water. Poker night. Most guys played poker on a Friday or Saturday night. Not his uncle. At least, not necessarily. Because of the shifts of the regulars, he played whenever everyone could get together. Sometimes it was a Friday night. Other times, like now, it turned out to be a Monday night. But it didn't matter when it was; Dooley hated poker night.

The first time Dooley experienced poker night was two weeks after he moved in with his uncle. He came home from work and found eight cops and ex-cops in the living room, haloed by a cloud of cigar smoke, fueled by plenty of beer, playing cards to the accompaniment of a symphony of pissing and moaning. Dooley took one look at the gathering, gave a little nod of acknowledgement when his uncle introduced him—"my nephew Ryan, likes to be called Dooley"—and detoured into the kitchen, planning to grab a soda from the fridge and then go upstairs to his room, out of the way of so much blue muscle. One of the cops came into the kitchen while Dooley had his head in the fridge. The cop was scowling when Dooley straightened up after closing the fridge.

"Yeah," he said. "I thought that was you. So you're the nephew Gary's always talking about, huh?"

The scowling cop turned out to be the same one who had arrested Dooley that last time, before Dooley even knew his uncle. He looked at Dooley and said, "What'd you get for that?"

Dooley didn't answer. He figured the cop already knew.

"And now you're walking around without a care in the world," he said. He shook his head. "And they say there's justice in the world."

Dooley wondered how long the cop was going to go on. Then, over the cop's shoulder, he saw his uncle, who had appeared in the doorway. The cop glanced at him.

"What's going on?" Dooley's uncle said. He was looking at the cop, not at Dooley.

"Just getting a beer," the cop said. Fucking coward, wouldn't even own up to what he was doing. He grabbed a Molson's out of the fridge and headed back to the game in the other room. Dooley's uncle looked at Dooley. Dooley just shrugged.

Later, after all his cop and ex-cop friends had gone home, Dooley's uncle knocked on Dooley's door.

"I didn't know Dennis knew you. He's not a regular. Art brought him. I doubt he'll be back." His uncle's way of apologizing—maybe. "Did he give you a hard time?"

"No," Dooley said.

"Because Art says he's a good guy," his uncle said. "He just takes his job seriously, that's all."

"Right," Dooley said.

Ever since that first time, if Dooley happened to be home on poker night, he stayed up in his room. If he was at work, he came in through the side door and slipped up the stairs unseen. His uncle never asked him to meet the guys, and Dooley had the impression he did it as a favor, not because he was embarrassed.

"Wash the mushrooms and slice them, will you?" Dooley's uncle said now. "And make them nice and thin."

While Dooley got to work, his uncle took a beer out of the fridge, twisted off the cap, and sat down at the table to drink it. He looked tired, glad to be home, gladder still to be pulling on a cold one. Dooley purposefully kept his eyes on the mushrooms when he asked the question he'd been saving up all day: "The guy who told you that Mark Everley going off that bridge was an accident, did he tell you where Everley was before he fell?"

Silence.

Followed by the sound of a beer bottle being set down onto a tabletop.

Followed by more silence; in other words, the sound of his uncle thinking. Probably staring at the back of Dooley's head, too, like he wished he could see clear through it into

Dooley's brain.

"No, he did not," his uncle said finally. "Why?"

"I was just wondering."

"I thought you didn't know that boy," his uncle said. Dooley was glad he was standing at the sink with his back to his uncle, washing mushrooms.

"I met his sister," he said. "She's real upset by what happened. So I was just wondering, that's all." He dumped the washed mushrooms onto a cutting board and reached for a knife. "This guy, this friend of yours, you think he would tell you if you asked him?" He tried to make it sound casual, like it was just a question, like it was no big deal.

"Why would I do that?" his uncle said. "Turn around, Ryan."

Dooley set the knife down. He turned and let his uncle look at him. He even met his uncle's eyes.

"What's going on?" his uncle said.

"I already told you. I met his sister. She's upset."

"Right. Now pull the other one."

Dooley was sorry he'd asked. Now he was going to have to explain.

"She says her brother always had this backpack with him. But the cops didn't find it. She thinks someone stole it from him. But if he'd been drinking . . ."

"You think maybe he forgot it wherever he was," his uncle said. He must have been some cop, Dooley thought, the way he picked up on things. "And what? And you want to find it for this girl, maybe impress her a little, is that it?" He sounded as casual as Dooley had tried to be. But he didn't look it. His eyes were hard on Dooley.

Dooley shrugged.

"Is she pretty?" his uncle said.

"Yeah," Dooley said. As soon as he said it, he had a picture of her in his mind as clear as if she were standing right there in the kitchen with him. He could smell her, too. Maybe she wore perfume, but he didn't think so. He thought the way she smelled was shampoo and soap, all sweet and fresh.

His uncle was still watching him, but something changed in his face.

"The guy who told me is Joe DeLucci. I don't think you've met him yet. He's a staff sergeant. He'll be here tonight," his uncle said. "Now, how about washing some lettuce?"

■ ■ ■

After supper—steak with fried mushrooms and a green salad with homemade salad dressing (mixed by Dooley, following instructions from his uncle), Dooley helped his uncle set up for poker. Then he went up to his room to do his homework.

He woke up at one in the morning when his uncle knocked on his door and then pushed it open so that the light from the hall hit Dooley right in the eyes. Dooley sat up.

"Is everything okay?" he said.

"Made out like a bandit," his uncle said, grinning. Must have drunk like a fish, too, Dooley thought. He was swaying a little on his feet. "They don't know where the kid was."

"What?"

"According to DeLucci, the dead kid—what's his name? Everley?—he left home around four-thirty that afternoon. Didn't tell his mother where he was going. She didn't even know when he left the house, which, according to DeLucci, the mother said was standard. Apparently he didn't feel he should have to keep her apprised of his whereabouts." Dooley knew exactly how he must have felt. "None of his friends saw him. Nobody knows where he was between the time he left home and the time he went off that bridge." His uncle stood in the doorway, one hand on the frame to steady himself. Finally he said, "I'm going to bed." ■

Eleven

r. Calvin poked his head out into the small waiting room and seemed surprised to see Dooley sitting there, leafing through an old copy of *Time* magazine.

"Dooley, long time, no see," he said.

"Hey, Doc," Dooley said. "I was hoping you could spare a few minutes."

Dr. Calvin checked his watch. "I can spare thirty," he said. "But only if you don't mind coming downstairs with me. I haven't had lunch yet."

It was four o'clock in the afternoon. Dooley said he didn't mind.

Unlike Kingston, who always wore a suit and tie, Dr. Calvin was dressed in jeans, sneakers, and a navy blue pullover sweater. He locked his office door behind him and took the stairs, not the elevator, down three floors to the lobby. Just off it was a coffee-and-sandwich place.

"Can I get you anything?" Dr. Calvin said.

"No, I'm fine," Dooley said. He sat down at a table and

waited while Dr. Calvin ordered a sandwich and a coffee, which he brought over to the table.

"So," Dr. Calvin said, sitting opposite Dooley and spreading a paper napkin on his lap, "how are you doing? Keeping out of trouble, I hope."

Dooley nodded. He filled Dr. Calvin in on school (it sucks), his job (it sucks), and his uncle (he's tough, but he's fair) before he got to the point.

"Hypnosis, huh?" Dr. Calvin said. He finished off the first half of his sandwich—ham and Swiss. "Sure, it works. Why? Is there something you're trying to remember?"

Mainly there were things Dooley was trying to forget.

"How do you know the person who's hypnotizing you isn't going to ask you a bunch of stuff you don't want to talk about?" Dooley said.

Dr. Calvin munched on the second half of his sandwich. "It doesn't work the way you think it does, Dooley," he said after a swallow. "It's not like you're unconscious and totally out of control. It's more like intense daydreaming. The way a lot of people approach it, they tell you your mind works like a VCR, that you can see a replay of an event, you can slow it down, stop it, rewind it, enlarge it, anything. The person doing the hypnosis controls the subject's mental viewing with his questions."

"But how do you know that while you're daydreaming or whatever that you're not going to say something you'd maybe rather not say?" Dooley said. "You know, say you were walking along and you were thinking about something and then all of a sudden you saw something, but maybe you saw more than you remember. When you get hypnotized, how do you know that you won't say something about what you were thinking about at the time?" That was the thing that was bothering him. After all, the point wasn't what he'd been thinking—that was personal and had nothing to do with anything. The point was what he had seen but maybe hadn't realized he'd seen or maybe had forgotten. "How do you know that what you were thinking and what you saw aren't so stuck together in your brain that remembering the one makes you talk about the other?"

Dr. Calvin polished off the rest of his sandwich and washed it down with a couple of gulps of coffee.

"That's a good question," he said. "The answer is, I guess you don't. But you could discuss it in advance with whoever is doing the hypnosis, you know, so that he or she can focus the questions on what you saw. But if, as you say, your thoughts and actions are intertwined—which, by the way, they are for most people—well, then, I suppose it's possible that you might say something about it. So when you come right down to it, I guess there's no guarantee that you wouldn't say something that perhaps you'd prefer not to say."

And there it was in a nutshell—the reason Dooley had come to Dr. Calvin with his question instead of going to, say, Kingston. Dr. Calvin was always straight. Always. Plus, he didn't mind talking. In fact, he seemed to enjoy it.

"They're making me go to counseling," Dooley said. "My uncle says he called you, but you said you were too busy to take me."

"That's true," Dr. Calvin said.

"Are you still too busy?"

"I'm afraid so." He finished his coffee. "I see private patients in addition to the patients I see at the detention centre. I see them for forty-five minutes at a time, eight sessions a day, three days a week. Then there's all the paperwork—files and notes and reports. There's only one of me, Dooley."

Shit.

"And I'm getting married in a couple of months."

"Hey, congratulations," Dooley said.

"Thanks." Dr. Calvin glanced at his watch. "I'm afraid I have to go. It was good seeing you again, Dooley."

As Dooley walked to the bus stop, he thought about what Dr. Calvin had said: there was no guarantee. Dooley didn't like that. He also didn't like not being able to do anything for Beth. Nor did he like the idea of telling her, sorry, that's a big nope on the hypnosis and, what's more, there's not a damned thing I can do to help you get over the death of your brother. He told himself it didn't matter. So she'd be mad at him? So what? There was no way a girl like her was ever going to be interested in him anyway. ■

Twelve

A typical school-day lunch period: Dooley walked six blocks from his school to a hole-in-the-wall Chinese restaurant frequented, during the daytime anyway, mainly by Chinese seniors, slid into a booth, ordered one of the cheap lunch specials—he was partial to spicy chicken with cashews—and read, usually something he had to read for school, but sometimes something he actually wanted to read (he was making his way through Irvine Welsh) while he ate. No one ever bothered him. So it was a big surprise when, halfway through his lunch on Tuesday, Rhodes appeared and stood beside his booth.

Dooley checked him out. Behind his glasses, which Dooley bet had designer frames, he was a good-looking guy. It was easy to see why the girls were always giving him looks, maybe giving him a whole lot more besides. The guy dressed like a magazine ad—leather jacket that looked as soft as butter, golf shirt with one of those little labels sewn into one side of the collar to let you know it cost a bundle, jeans that were clean and looked like they had been pressed, boots, not sneakers, straight white teeth that had probably cost him a couple of years in braces, and eyes that were blue like the sky in summer. Dooley bet the girls were as crazy about those eyes as they were about the fact that Rhodes' parents were (according to Linelle) loaded. The thing Dooley wondered was, how come Rhodes didn't go to a private school? Dooley was pretty sure Rhodes was checking him out, too—taking in the beat-up denim jacket that Dooley had scored at a secondhand store a few years back, way too big for him then, perfect now, also jeans, but a little frayed at the bottoms and one of the back pockets showing the wear from his wallet, black T-shirt, one of maybe a dozen he owned, none of them new.

"How's it going?" Rhodes said, smiling at him, but looking shy at the same time. "Do you mind if I sit down for a minute?"

Dooley shrugged and forked some fried rice into his mouth.

"We haven't really met," Rhodes said. "I'm Winston." He thrust a hand across the table at Dooley, which told Dooley, as if he didn't already know, how different Rhodes was from him. It had never occurred to Dooley to shake anyone's hand—well, except for a couple of times when his uncle was introducing him to people, and then it still hadn't occurred to him. His uncle had nudged him and given him a look: *Shake the man's hand, Ryan.* But Dooley's uncle wasn't here and Dooley didn't know much about Rhodes and was inclined not to like him purely on the basis that he seemed to know Beth much better than Dooley did. Dooley speared a piece of chicken with his fork. Before he popped it into his mouth, he said. "I'm Dooley."

"So I heard," Rhodes said. He smiled at Dooley as he withdrew his hand. If he was offended, he didn't show it.

Rhodes dipped into the pocket of his jacket, pulled out what looked like a business card, and set it on the table near Dooley's plate of food. Dooley glanced at it without picking it up.

"I'm having some people over on Friday," Rhodes said. He peered at Dooley, and Dooley wondered how much he could see without his glasses. "It's a thing for Mark."

"You mean, the dead guy?" Dooley said.

Rhodes recoiled a little when Dooley said that, as if he didn't want to think about Everley that way. But he nodded. "I'm having a get-together for him. Well, in his memory." He tapped the business card. "Those are my coordinates. You're invited."

Dooley glanced at the address on the card as he chewed another mouthful of fried rice. He looked across the table at Rhodes.

"You're inviting me to your house?"

"Everyone who knew Mark is going to be there. Beth is going to be there. Mostly I'm doing it for her. You know Beth, right?" Dooley nodded. "Mark was a photography freak. Beth wants to set up a scholarship in his name for a kid to get into a photography program at university. She wants to call it the Mark Everley Memorial Scholarship. So I'm having a sort of fundraiser—I supply the food and drink and everyone who comes makes a donation to the scholarship. Beth is having a hard time dealing with Mark's death. I thought maybe this would help her, you know?"

Dooley had been wishing he could do something to help her—besides hypnosis—and here Rhodes had come up with the perfect thing. He obviously knew more about what girls liked than Dooley did. For sure he knew more about what Beth would like. Dooley glanced at the card again. Rhodes was asking him to make a donation to a scholarship in the name of a guy who, from what Dooley knew, was a class-A jerk. Dooley thought about how hard he worked for his spending money and the allowance a guy like Rhodes probably got from his parents.

"I didn't really know the guy," Dooley said.

"I know. But you were the last person to see him alive," Rhodes said. "And I know it would mean a lot to Beth if you were there."

It would? Dooley was so surprised that it was a few seconds before he wondered how Rhodes would know a thing like that. Had Beth said something to him?

"You should come," Rhodes said. "You're new at school. It wouldn't hurt for you to meet a few people." He scanned the quiet and nearly deserted restaurant. "And don't worry. It doesn't have to be a big donation. Whatever you feel like giving is fine. It all adds up. That's the main thing." He smiled pleasantly at Dooley again. Dooley glanced down at the card again. "I hope you can make it," Rhodes said as he started to slide out of the booth.

"Hey," Dooley said.

Rhodes looked at him.

"You were the guy's friend, right?" Dooley said.

"I was one of them, yeah."

"What do you think happened to him?"

"I don't know," Rhodes said. "You were there. What do you think?"

"The cops say he was drinking. You have any idea where he'd do that?"

"Where?" Rhodes looked surprised by the question. Dooley was kind of surprised, too. It had just popped out. He hadn't planned to ask Rhodes anything—well, he hadn't planned to until Rhodes told him what he was doing for Beth. "What do you mean, where?"

"He wasn't at home. He wasn't with any of his friends—at least, that's what the cops say."

Rhodes looked intrigued now. "How do you know what the cops say?"

Dooley didn't want to get into his home situation, so he said, "It was on the news," and left it at that. "So if he wasn't at home and he wasn't with any of his friends and he'd been drinking, where do you think he'd do that?"

"Why does it matter?" Rhodes said.

"It doesn't," Dooley said. "I'm invited to a party to raise money in the memory of a guy I don't even know. I guess I'm just curious about him."

"Mark liked to party," Rhodes said. "Sometimes maybe a little too much."

"Where did he like to party?"

"Here and there," Rhodes said. "Everywhere. Maybe up on the bridge."

"Where did he get his booze?"

"Bought it, probably," Rhodes said. "Why?"

Everley wasn't even eighteen when he died. That meant he'd have needed fake ID if he was going to buy alcohol. Dooley wondered if the cops had found any in Everley's wallet. Or maybe it was in the missing backpack. Maybe the bottle was in there, too; they hadn't found one on the bridge or near the body. But where was the backpack?

"You didn't see him that day?"

"No," Rhodes said. He sounded sorry about that, like, maybe if he had, things would have turned out differently. "Friday," he said. "You should come." ■

Thirteen

That afternoon, Dooley unfolded the slip of paper Beth had given him and looked at it instead of at the blackboard where his history teacher was chalking a time line. Beth had printed her name and her phone number in black felt pen. Her letters and numbers were nice and tight and easy to read. He thought about calling her. But what would he say? *Hi, listen, I know you really want me to get hypnotized, but I've decided not to . . . Any chance you'd want to go to a movie with me*?

Whoa, where did that last part come from? Boy, one more reason to stay away from a hypnotist.

How about: *I've gone over it and over it and I am one hundred percent positive that there was no one up there on the bridge with your brother. He was drunk. The cops think he was fooling around and he fell. They're pretty thorough.* If there was one thing Dooley knew for a fact, it was that cops could be thorough. *You have to face the facts. You have to accept it. You can get angry about it—that's normal. You can put your fist through a wall over it—people have been known to do that. But no matter what you do, you can't make it go away. It is what it is and sooner or later you'll have to face it and accept it.*

Right. Like she was going to want to hear that from an almost complete stranger. And that was the thing, too, wasn't it? He was a stranger, but he didn't want to be. He didn't want her to be mad at him, either. He wanted to make her happy—as much as he could under the circumstances.

He looked at her phone number again. If he wasn't going to do the hypnosis, then maybe he could do something else. Maybe he could find Everley's backpack. There were only three possibilities that Dooley could think of on that one. One, Everley had left it on the bridge when he went over and someone had found it and taken it before the cops got a chance to get up there and look around. Two, he was wearing his backpack when he went over and someone had got to him before Dooley and had taken it. Or, three, he'd left it wherever he'd been drinking.

Dooley tried to imagine what kind of people would take a backpack from a guy who was lying motionless on the ground a couple of dozen meters below them or, for that matter, from a guy who was lying motionless on the ground right at their feet? The only answer he could come up with: people who needed or wanted that backpack bad enough and were pragmatic about the situation (the dead guy didn't need it anymore). If Dooley had to guess, he'd say it was one of the crazy people down in the ravine or one of the homeless ones. So that was one place to start.

The other possibility: Everley had left the pack where

he'd been drinking. According to Rhodes, that could be just about anywhere. Still, someone must know where he liked to hang out. It was possible Beth knew, but he sure didn't want to ask her. He already had the feeling that there were things about her brother that she didn't know. She probably had a picture of him in her mind that Dooley couldn't begin to imagine. He didn't want to start asking her questions that might upset her. He didn't want to do *anything* that might upset her.

So who else would know where he might have been? Dooley half wished he'd been paying more attention to what was going on at school, but he hadn't. He'd kept his head down, kept to himself, hadn't wanted to get involved in high school bullshit. The deal was do the work, graduate, and then get the hell out and get on with life, not that Dooley had a clue what *that* was going to be. The only thing he knew for sure: Gillette and Landers were friends with Everley, and Gillette was acting kind of antsy about him. Geeze, what had that conversation been all about anyway? Why had Gillette come up to him like that and asked him those questions? It made Dooley wonder. What had Gillette been up to the night Everley died? Did *he* know something? If he did, Dooley was willing to bet that he hadn't told the cops (who couldn't possibly be so stupid that they hadn't figured out who Everley hung around with). And if he hadn't said anything to the cops, what were the chances that Gillette would say anything to Dooley if Dooley asked? Mind you, Dooley had a little leverage.

Rhodes had known Everley, too, or maybe he was just

trying to catch Beth if he hadn't already. But he'd already told Dooley that he didn't know where Everley was that night.

Landers and Everley seemed to be tight, but if Landers knew what his buddy had been up to the night he died, he obviously wasn't saying anything or the cops wouldn't know as little as his uncle had said they did. Not that it mattered. Dooley couldn't imagine that Landers would talk to him under any circumstances.

So who did that leave? Who else knew Mark Everley? Who else might have an idea where he was that night? If there was anyone, they obviously hadn't told the cops. Why not? Or maybe it would turn out that Mark Everley was a lot like Dooley. Maybe it would turn out that he liked to drink alone. Wouldn't that be something? But if there was one thing Dooley knew, it was that you could tell yourself that no one knew what you were doing. You could even make yourself believe it. But that didn't make it true. Someone always knew. Someone always found out. Who would know about Everley? Why hadn't that person—or those people—told the cops? Or maybe they had. Maybe they'd said, Mark's one of those guys who like to sneak off somewhere and have a private party. His uncle had said the cops didn't know *where* Everley was between the time he left his house and the time he left the bridge. But they did have some idea what he'd been doing.

Dooley rounded a corner on his way out of school that afternoon and saw two guys leaning hard on a locker door, straining to close it. They were having trouble with it, and no wonder. There was a kid inside and they were trying to close the door on him. Jesus, some people.

The two guys cooled it for a moment when they realized someone was coming. When they saw it was Dooley, they looked uncertain. Sometimes Dooley wished he were invisible. He hated when people looked at him like that, like he was a hungry tiger that had escaped from the zoo and was prowling the school looking for something—some*one*—to eat. Dooley's intention: just walk on by. But he made a mistake. He looked and saw that the kid who was mostly jammed in the locker was the same scrawny kid he'd seen out in the schoolyard, the one that didn't know how to fight, the one Landers had been taking on while Gillette stood by and watched. By now, the two guys who were trying to shut the locker door on the kid had gained confidence from Dooley's initial indifference. They both leaned hard on the door and finally got it closed. One of them started to loop the lock through the door while the other one grinned over his shoulder at Dooley. Dooley reached out and plucked the lock from the guy who was holding it. The guy looked so surprised that he came away from the locker door. The second guy, the one who had grinned at Dooley, puffed himself up so he'd look tough. He said, "Hey, that's my lock."

Dooley looked at him and said, "It's my lock now. You got a problem with that?"

The first guy whispered something to the second guy. The second guy's tough look slipped.

"No," he said. "You want it so bad, it's yours."

"Good," Dooley said. "Beat it."

They beat it. If Dooley'd been wondering what kind of

reputation he had around school (and, truly, he hadn't wanted to think about it), he had his answer.

He opened the locker door. The kid was wedged in tight. It took him a few moments to work himself free. When he did, he said, "Great. Next time they see me, they'll kick the shit out of me for sure."

"You're welcome," Dooley said. He handed the kid the lock.

The kid closed and secured the locker. He started down the hall away from Dooley.

"Hey," Dooley said.

The kid turned. He looked pissed off and not even remotely intimidated.

"How come they were doing that?" Dooley said.

"They're Neanderthals," the kid said.

"What about the other day, out back?"

"More Neanderthals," the kid said. "They're thick on the ground around here. You hadn't noticed?"

He said it matter-of-factly. Dooley didn't get it.

"It doesn't bother you?" he said.

"No," the kid said, the tone of his voice telling Dooley that he really meant yes. "No, I love being stuffed into my locker where, if I'm lucky, the janitor might eventually find me and I can get home before my mom freaks and calls the cops. I love being shoved around by guys who only feel good about themselves if they're giving guys like me a hard time. I love walking down the hall and wondering who's going to trip me or slam me into a wall or grab my books and dump them in the garbage."

Geeze, what a loser. He had a kind of whiny voice that could get on your nerves real fast. Dooley bet kids made fun of it behind his back. Maybe to his face, too.

"You ever thought of transferring schools?" Dooley said.

"I did. Last year. Those two guys? They transferred, too, for other reasons. As soon as they saw I was here, they started in again." The kid scowled at Dooley. "What's it to you, anyway?"

"You shouldn't take shit from people," Dooley said.

"Right," the kid said. "I should maybe go to the office and complain about them and have Rektor say something to them so that then they'll get really motivated to beat the crap out of me. Or maybe I should fight back, you know, me against the two of them—and let them beat the crap out of me. Or, hey, here's a good idea: maybe I should get myself a baseball bat and let them take it off me so they can use *it* to beat the crap out of me."

Dooley shook his head. Yeah, it was everywhere.

"Whatever," he said. He was going to move on, but here he was having an actual conversation with someone who probably paid a *lot* of attention to what went on around him. "You know that kid that died? Everley?"

The kid looked warily at Dooley like he was trying to scope out where the question had come from and why Dooley was asking. Then he must have decided, what the hell, because he put on attitude and said, "You mean, was he a friend of mine? Are you kidding? The guy was an asshole."

Which Dooley already knew.

"Who'd he hang with?"

The kid frowned. "Why?"

Boy, he was full of surprises. He had victim practically tattooed on his forehead, but here he was talking to Dooley, of all people, like it was no big deal.

"Just curious."

"He hung around with Rhodes and Landers and Bracey, that bunch."

Bracey. The name was a new one to Dooley. But if this kid knew those three names, then the cops must know them, too. The cops must have checked with them.

"You said Everley was an asshole. Did he give you a hard time, too?"

"All those guys give me a hard time," the kid said. He sounded resigned. "But Everley? He's real scum. He harassed my sister. He made her cry."

"Harassed her?"

"Made fun of her. In a store. She's got Down's, okay?" The kid was angry now, like he was daring Dooley to make a crack about it. "What kind of guy makes fun of a kid with Down's? You know what kind? The ignorant kind. The guy was a major asshole. I'm not sorry he's dead."

"I'm Dooley," Dooley said.

"I know," the kid said. Dooley waited. "Warren," the kid said. "I'm Warren." His eyes skipped beyond Dooley's shoulder. Dooley turned and saw Gillette and Landers standing half a dozen paces away, maybe close enough to be listening although he was pretty sure that if they'd been there for more than a few seconds, the kid, Warren, would have noticed sooner.

"I'm walking out now," Dooley said to Warren in a low

voice. "You want to walk with me?"

Warren didn't answer, but he stuck beside Dooley as they passed Gillette and Landers and went down the stairs.

After they parted company, Dooley found a phone, made a call, and then headed for the ravine.

■ ■ ■

Dooley's uncle was getting ready to dish out supper—chicken in mushroom sauce, rice, and green beans—when Dooley got home. He said, "I thought I was going to have to send out a search party."

"I left you a message," Dooley said. "I said I'd be home by six. I took a walk, that's all." He added, "You could have paged me."

"I was just about to," his uncle said. Dooley could tell he was steamed. He handed Dooley a couple of plates of food to put on the table.

"You know the deal. You're supposed to come right home after school."

"It was just a walk," Dooley said. "You been in a high school lately? Some days, you need to unwind. Walking's about all I have left."

They sat down. His uncle took a bite of chicken and said, "Dr. Kingston called me at the store today."

Dooley swallowed hard.

"You have any idea why he called, Ryan?"

The question told Dooley his uncle was pissed off. Whenever his uncle was angry with Dooley for something, he asked questions he already knew the answers to, and he got even angrier if Dooley didn't answer them.

"He wanted to tell you about my progress, I guess."

"He cancelled what he called your last appointment. He said he had to fit in a new patient. What it came down to, Ryan, is he fired you. He says he told you last Friday that he feels he's made all the progress he's going to make with you, given your demeanor." His uncle set his fork down on the side of his plate and looked across the table at Dooley. "He's supposed to be good. That's why I sent you to him. But, when I pushed him—and I did push him, Ryan—he finally told me that you weren't cooperative and that you failed to do the work you were assigned between sessions." Yeah, he was pissed off all right. "You know you're supposed to be in therapy, right, Ryan?"

"He said he'd refer me to group counseling."

"Yeah," his uncle said in a flat voice. "He gave me some names."

"I don't think he was the right person for me."

"He said the same thing."

"I'm sorry," Dooley said.

"I don't want sorry, Ryan. Sorry is bullshit. I want you to do what you're supposed to do. Grow up, for Christ's sake. This is no joke."

The rest of the meal passed in silence. Dooley was glad when it was time to clear the table. He was gladder still when his uncle turned on the sports channel in the living room while Dooley cleaned up the kitchen. ■

Fourteen

Dooley rolled out of bed the next morning with every intention of doing the right thing. He was scheduled to work that night. Schedules were posted every Saturday for the coming week and once they were set, they were carved in stone. Dooley had started at the video store right after he moved in with his uncle, so that made three months he'd been working there. He'd never missed a shift. He'd gone in a bunch of times when other people called in sick, but he'd never called in sick himself. Rhodes's get-together was tonight. If Dooley wanted to go, he had two choices: switch with someone or call in sick. The only person he knew well enough to ask to switch was Linelle, and she was already working tonight, which meant he'd have to call in sick. He would also have to tell his uncle. At least, he *should* tell him. He could imagine how well that would go. His uncle would want to know why he was telling the store he was sick when, in fact, he was perfectly healthy. Then Dooley would have to make another decision—tell the truth: I've been invited to this party; or lie: maybe something like, I asked this girl out. If he lied, his uncle would want to know why the hell he had asked a girl out when he knew full well he was scheduled to work. He'd also want to know who the girl was. Then he'd tell Dooley, take her out some night when you're not working. If he told the truth, his uncle would want to know why the hell he had accepted a party invitation when he knew full well he was scheduled to work (in other words, tough shit, Ryan, obligation and responsibility trump party time). He'd also want to know who was having the party and, tell me the truth, Ryan, are we talking booze, maybe a little smoke? Because if we are . . . no party time for Dooley.

And that was just too bad, right?

Then Dooley's uncle came into the kitchen, fully dressed, a mug in his hand, which he refilled from the coffee machine, and said, "You working tonight?"

"Yeah," Dooley said. "Until closing. Why?"

"Jeannie has some charity event she's been working on. One of those fancy dress things at a hotel downtown. We'll be late. Later than you."

"No problem," Dooley said.

And there, just like that, he had an opening. Still, he might not have taken it if he hadn't run into Rhodes in one of the school bathrooms that morning and if Rhodes hadn't said to him, "So, you're going to be there tonight, right? Because the more people who show up, the more money we raise, and I guess I don't have to tell you what that would mean to Beth." And, just like that, her face appeared in Dooley's head and the opening his uncle had given him became the door that he just had to walk through.

The rest of the day unfolded like every other mind-numbing weekday: class, lunch, class, class. Then home—which was deserted—where he called the store and prayed that Linelle would answer. When she did, sounding bored as she rattled off the name of the store, its location, and, "How may I help you?"—all of it delivered in the same prairie-flat tone—he told her, "I'm calling in sick."

Linelle perked up immediately. "Kevin's gonna be pissed," she said with delight. "He's gonna go all spluttery and red in the face. Thanks, Dooley. You made my day."

"Do me one more favor?"

"I'm going to expect payback."

"If my uncle calls the store—he probably won't, but if he does—tell him I'm on a break. Ask him, does he want to leave a number where he can be reached. He'll probably say I can get him on his cell. If he does, call my pager, okay?"

"This is getting complicated, Dooley."

"He probably won't call. He's going out tonight. But just in case. Okay?"

"You owe me big time."

"Goes without saying," Dooley said. He didn't know why, but he felt comfortable talking to Linelle. He knew she knew all about him, but she didn't seem to care. The thing about Linelle, though: she didn't seem to care about anything.

Next: Shower and get dressed. Put on something nice but not too fancy. Or should it be fancy? Shit. He didn't know. He finally decided on clean black jeans, shoes (not sneakers), and a black shirt he had bought with his first paycheck from the store. All nice, but casual, comfortable. Ready to go.

■ ■ ■

He stopped at a bank machine on his way to Rhodes's place. Rhodes had said the party was to raise money for a scholarship in Everley's name. Dooley wondered how much he should give and how much other people would be giving. The kids who were going to be at the party had actually known Everley. They were his friends. Dooley hadn't really known the guy and, anyway, he hadn't liked him. He withdrew two twenties, broke one of them buying a pack of gum, and set aside the other twenty and a five-dollar bill to put toward the scholarship.

When he got to Rhodes' house, he stood outside on the sidewalk for a few minutes, looking at the house and thinking: Wow! The place looked like a castle. It was made of stone and even had a turret on one end. Dooley bet it would be cool to have a room in that turret, with windows all the way around. The house stood on a property that was flanked on both sides by wide lawns edged with flowerbeds. Tucked away behind the house, but still visible from the sidewalk, was a six-car garage. All the garage doors were closed, so Dooley couldn't see if there actually were six cars inside. However many there were, he bet they were high-end. All the other houses that Dooley had walked past on Rhodes's street were as big as Rhodes's. Some were even bigger. Dooley wondered how come a guy who lived in a house like this in a neighborhood like this went to a regular school instead of some exclusive private school.

It wasn't Rhodes who answered the door when Dooley rang—of course not. It was a small, brown-skinned young woman in—a maid's uniform! Dooley had never seen anything like it outside of the movies and TV.

"I'm here for the party," Dooley said.

The young woman stepped aside so that Dooley could enter. She was pretty but seemed shy and didn't look him in the eyes. She gestured to her left, where Dooley heard the babble of voices underlaid by the pulse of music. He followed the noise and found Rhodes in what looked like a gigantic games room filled with people and all the big-ticket toys money could buy—a pool table, a pinball machine, a couple of arcade-style video games, a flat screen TV—plus a wet bar and a table spread with snack food. He stood in the doorway and scanned the room. There was a large photograph of Mark Everley trimmed in black sitting on an easel near the bar. In front of the easel, on a small table, was a glass ball with an opening at the top—it reminded Dooley of a goldfish bowl. It was half-filled with money—olive green and pink, which meant twenties and, Jesus, fifties—as well as what looked like checks. Rhodes was sitting on a couch near the easel, a skinny blonde beside him. He had a bottle of beer in his hand. Everyone in the place had a drink of some kind. Rhodes spotted Dooley and waved him over.

"Glad you could make it," he said. He introduced Dooley to the people around him, including the guy Landers, whose first name turned out to be Peter and who obviously remembered Dooley (he stared at him as if he were a stain on the carpet before leaning over and whispering something in Rhodes's ear) and another guy, Marcus Bracey. Both of them, judging from their clothes and accessories—check the shoes, check the watch—looked to be out of Rhodes's league financially. Dooley glanced around to see if he recognized anyone else and saw Gillette on the other side of the room, watching him. He wondered how Gillette had got himself in with this crowd.

Rhodes smiled pleasantly as he listened to something Landers was saying—Dooley wasn't paying attention; he was looking at Gillette. Then Rhodes said to Dooley, "What can I get you to drink? We got beer—domestic and imported. Also the hard stuff. If you're into smoke . . ."

"Ginger ale would be fine," Dooley said.

Rhodes laughed. "Come on," he said. "It's a party. People are supposed to have fun remembering Mark. Like a wake, you know?"

"Ginger ale would be fine," Dooley said again.

Rhodes shrugged. "Then ginger ale it is," he said. He turned to the skinny blonde beside him on the couch, who was, in Dooley's opinion, wearing too much makeup, and said, "Be an angel, Jen, and get the man a ginger ale."

"Why can't Esperanza get it?" Jen said, her voice whiny.

"Esperanza is on the door," Rhodes said. He had a soft way of speaking that didn't have much effect on the blonde. When she didn't move, he leaned over, whispered something in her ear, and kissed her on the cheek. That got some action. She giggled and staggered to her high-heeled feet. She was back a few minutes later with Dooley's drink.

Dooley sipped his ginger ale and listened while Rhodes told Bracey, yeah, it was true his dad had paid what sounded to Dooley like a fortune for the latest addition to his Fender Stratocaster collection, which was a Fender that had belonged to Eric Clapton for about five seconds. He told Dooley that his dad also had Fenders that had belonged to Muddy Waters, Jeff Beck, Stevie Ray Vaughan, Richie Sambora, and Tommy Castro, whoever the hell he was. Dooley just nodded. He also had (the information provided by Bracey) a gun collection that included a Colt six-shooter that had supposedly once belonged to Wyatt Earp and a decommissioned automatic weapon that had been featured in a Schwarzenegger movie—all of it, like the Fenders, under lock and key.

Dooley looked around while Bracey and the others talked. He wondered where Beth was and if she was really going to show up.

"Hey, Dooley," Rhodes said. "You shoot pool?" He nodded to the pool table that dominated the far end of the room.

"Not in a long time," Dooley said. And, boy, hardly ever sober.

"Come on." Rhodes stood up. As Dooley got to his feet, he saw Gillette across the room again, still staring at him. Rhodes noticed, too.

"Eddy mentioned that he knows you," Rhodes said. "He wasn't big on details, but I get the impression you and he aren't exactly best buddies anymore."

It would surprise Dooley if everyone in the room didn't

come to that conclusion. Gillette was glaring at him like he wished he could take a chainsaw to him, or a baseball bat.

"How did you two hook up?" Dooley said.

"Well, he *is* part of our school community," Rhodes said. It took Dooley a moment to get that he was trying to be funny. The principal at their school always referred to the place as a community and was always reminding them that in a healthy community, people make allowances and accommodations and everyone tries to get along.

"There's all kinds of geeks and losers that go to that place," Dooley said. "I don't see all of them here."

"Eddy got off on the right foot with me," Rhodes said with a smile. "He trashed a car of this guy I know, a guy who lives right across the street."

Dooley could think of a lot of ways to get a friendship off to a good start, but that one sure hadn't come to mind.

"It was over some girl," Rhodes said. "And the guy is a total prick. So I—" He ducked his head a little, just like he had out in the schoolyard when he'd stopped Landers from hammering Warren. It made him look modest and kind of shy. Dooley bet the girls liked that look. "I kind of alibi'd him," he said. "I know it was wrong. God, my parents would kill me if they found out I'd lied to them—*and* to the police. But it served the guy right. He's one of those guys who thinks that just because his parents are loaded, he can be a dickhead and no one will call him on it."

Dooley guessed that Rhodes had a different view on what it meant to have rich parents.

"Eddy's nothing like most of the people I know," Rhodes

conceded. "But he's okay. He can be a lot of fun."

That had been Dooley's experience, too, once upon a time.

Rhodes nudged Dooley toward the pool table, and Dooley let himself get roped into a game, which he lost and which Rhodes seemed to have a good time winning, although he was a gentleman about it. Dooley started to relax a little and even let himself think, Jesus, it must be nice, living in a place like this, being able to entertain so many people—he couldn't begin to figure how much all the booze and food and what-have-you was costing. Rhodes played Landers next, while Dooley and Bracey watched. Landers turned out to be a better pool player than Rhodes, but Rhodes didn't seem to mind. He leaned on his cue and watched Landers sink three balls in a row. Landers was lining up another shot when all of a sudden he straightened up, glowering. Rhodes and Bracey both turned to where Landers was looking. Landers thrust his cue at Bracey and strode across the room, muscling a few people aside.

"Here we go," Rhodes said. He handed his pool cue to Dooley and went after Landers, who by this time was shoving a guy who had been making it with a stick-thin girl in a tiny black skirt. The guy Landers had shoved staggered backward, but he recovered fast and came back, ready to deal with the situation. The stick-thin girl was tugging on Landers' arm, trying to pull him back. Landers yelled something at her. Rhodes stepped in between Landers and the other guy. He had his arms out, keeping Landers and the other guy away from each other, and was talking mostly to

Landers. Dooley remembered the scene in the schoolyard. He had the impression that Rhodes was used to breaking up fights between Landers and whoever Landers was pissed at for whatever reason. He wondered if things might have been different if Rhodes had been there with Everley and Landers that time. The stick-thin girl was still hanging onto Landers. Landers shook her off, like a horse flicking off a fly. Rhodes leaned into Landers and said something else. Landers grabbed the girl by the wrist and dragged her away from Rhodes and the other guy. Rhodes turned then and said something to the other guy, who was shaking his head and shrugging. You didn't have to be a lip reader to get what he was saying: *It wasn't my fault.* Rhodes waved Jen over. Jen guided the other guy to the bar and popped a beer for him.

"Problem?" Dooley said when Rhodes joined him and Bracey again at the pool table.

"Girls," Rhodes said. "They can fuck you up, right?"

"I guess," Dooley said. He started to hand one of the pool cues to Rhodes, but Rhodes was already walking away from him again. No wonder. Beth had entered the room.

"She is definitely not as advertised," Bracey said, eying her appreciatively. "Not even remotely."

Dooley had no idea what he meant and didn't care. He watched as she hovered near the door, scanning the room. She was wearing a pink sweater and a black skirt with high, black boots. Her hair hung loosely over her shoulders. When she spotted the photograph of her brother, she went still. Even from where he was standing, clear across the room, Dooley could see the color in her cheeks fade. It was clear she loved her brother. He thought, even if she knew what an asshole he could be, it probably didn't matter to her. She'd probably forgive him. There were guys he knew, guys who had gone out of their way to put other people into the hospital with serious injuries, whose mothers used to come to visit them and hug them and kiss them and tell them over and over, "I love you," not that it made much difference.

Rhodes greeted her, taking both of her hands in his and holding them, talking to her and nodding at the glass bowl with all the money in it. Dooley had to hand it to him, the guy was always on the mark. He knew exactly what to do and his timing was impeccable. He was smooth, too. Maybe that was bred into him. Or maybe he learned it from his old man. Dooley admired the easy way that he introduced Beth around to the people she didn't know. After that, he stopped the music and clinked a knife against a glass until everyone settled down. When the room grew quiet, he began to talk about Mark Everley—what a great guy he was, what a cut-up he was, the guy could have been a comedian, what a fantastic photographer he was, even better than he was a comedian, how he maybe could have been the next Richard Avedon or the next Yousuf Karsh (Dooley thought, *Who*?) and, finally, how much everyone was going to miss him—in other words, the kind of stuff people said about somebody who had died, no matter how much of a jerk the guy had been. Beth wiped a few tears from her eyes, but she didn't start bawling. Rhodes talked next about the scholarship Beth wanted to establish in her brother's name and pulled something from his pocket—a check, Dooley guessed—and made a big deal of showing it to Beth, enjoying how her eyes widened, before putting it in the glass bowl.

Dooley was wondering how much Rhodes's check was for when he noticed Beth looking across the room at him. He started to smile at her, but something in her eyes stopped him. She looked angry about something—probably the fact that he hadn't called her about the hypnosis thing. Now he wasn't sure what to do. He'd only come to the party so that he'd have a chance to see her, maybe talk to her, and here she was looking at him like he was something a dog had deposited on her front lawn. The hard look that she was giving him threw him.

■ ■ ■

Someone—Bracey—thrust a glass into Dooley's hand.

"Champagne," he said when Dooley began to protest. "We're gonna do a toast."

It turned out to be a toast to the memory of Mark Everley. The toast was done not by Rhodes but by Landers, who referred to Everley as the best friend he'd ever had and then knocked back his glass of champagne. Everyone else did the same. Dooley saw Beth looking at him from across the room, so he raised his glass to his lips—he didn't want to make her any angrier than it looked like she already was by being the only person in the room not to toast her dead brother—but he didn't take a sip. Bracey went around refilling glasses before another guy—a guy Dooley recognized but didn't know by name—made a second toast. Beth crossed the room and stopped in front of him.

"What are you doing here?" she said. He couldn't believe

how hard her eyes were, like iced pebbles. "You didn't even know my brother."

What was she so mad about?

"Rhodes invited me," he said. "Look, I was going to call you."

"Right," she said, like she didn't believe that for a minute, like he was one of *those* guys, the kind that slept with girls (Jesus, he wished he could sleep with her) but never called them afterwards, and then bumped into them, say, at a party.

"You know," he said. "About the hypnosis thing."

"You're not going to do it, right?" she said, snapping the words at him. What was going on? Why was she so pissed off? "I talked to that homicide cop again, the one who they called when Mark . . . when he died." Her eyes were burning into him. "When I told him I'd talked to you about getting hypnotized, he told me about you."

Oh.

"I bet some people think you're pretty cool," she said.

It was true. A certain kind of person found him very cool. A certain kind of girl, too.

"Well, I don't," she said, confirming what Dooley had already figured out. "Not even remotely. I think what you did is despicable."

Geeze, the cop told her *that*?

"So you don't want to help me, fine, don't help me. Just stay away from me, okay? Stay away from me." Tears glistened in her eyes, but they weren't sad tears. No way. They were mad tears, like what she really wanted to do was hit him. She looked hard at him for a minute longer. Then she spun around and walked back to Rhodes, who frowned as he listened to whatever she was saying and slipped an arm around her. That's when Dooley walked through a second door.

He looked at the champagne in his hand and at the big photograph of Mark Everley up there on the easel. What the hell? Here's to you, asshole. He downed the whole glass in one long swallow and turned to leave, but there was Bracey, refilling glasses again. Refilling Dooley's glass.

Dr. Calvin: Say you find yourself in a situation where your peers are drinking or doing drugs. What do you do, Ryan?

Dooley: Join the fuck in.

Dr. Calvin: Let me rephrase that, Ryan. What *should* you do?

Dooley: Why is it a guy's always supposed to do what he *should* do? Why can't he once in a while do whatever the hell he *wants* to do?

He knocked back the second glass of champagne and headed for the door. At least, he started to head for the door, but then he detoured, weaving through people until he reached the other side of the room where Beth was standing, her head bowed a little, saying something in a soft voice to Rhodes, who was looking at her, all blue eyes and sympathy.

"Hey," Dooley said. Rhodes looked at him, but Beth didn't. Dooley poked her in the arm. "Hey," he said, angry now. "You think you know me, is that it? You really think you know me?"

"Hey, Dooley, are you okay?" Rhodes said.

Beth looked at him. What he saw in her eyes was what he used to see in the mirror some mornings.

"You don't know me," he said. "You don't know anything about me."

A hand fell lightly on his shoulder. It was Rhodes. He steered Dooley gently but firmly away from Beth.

"You don't know me," Dooley yelled over his shoulder at her. He was thinking maybe he should have eaten something because, boy, that champagne had gone right to his head.

"Hey, take it easy," Rhodes said, his voice soft and soothing. "Come over here." He led Dooley to the bar and sat him down. Dooley saw Beth across the room. A couple of girls were pressed in around her, talking to her, looking like they were comforting her. "Hey, how about something to take the edge off?"

Dooley said no. He said he had to go. Across the room Beth had turned her back to him. So what? What did he care? The only thing he knew for sure about her, other than she was pretty, was that her brother was an asshole. Maybe she was one, too. Maybe behind those coffee-colored eyes, she was some kind of bitch. She heard a cop tell it and she thought she knew everything about him. Maybe she was telling all those girls, "Hey, that guy Dooley over there, what a loser. You know what he did?" Well, so what if she was?

Rhodes was handing him a glass. Coke. With a kick.

He took it but thought he should go home.

"Bracey's looking for someone to play," Rhodes said. "He's a good match for you, Dooley. Come on, you're not going to run off because of that, are you? She's just upset. She loved her brother. You know how that is."

Dooley didn't know.

Rhodes steered him to the pool table, where Bracey was shooting by himself. A girl wandered over. It was the same stick-thin girl Landers had dragged from the room earlier. Rhodes introduced her: Megan.

"Hi," Megan said. She had one of those little-girl voices that Dooley couldn't decide, was it natural or was it put on? "I'll keep score," she said. Dooley couldn't help staring at her skirt. It didn't cover much. She had big lips that were bright red. Her eyes were spacey.

"You break," Bracey said.

Dooley set down his glass and picked up a pool cue. It turned out to be a long game, and Bracey turned out to be a funny guy, the one-liners spinning out of him one after another, keeping Dooley laughing, which was something he didn't do a lot of. Megan got Dooley a refill on his Coke. He glanced across the room at Beth, who was sitting with Rhodes and the blonde, Jen. He wanted her to notice him—*See, I'm still here and you know what? I'm having a great time*. But she didn't even glance in his direction.

He missed his shot. Bracey walked down one side of the table, sizing up his play. Megan stood so close to Dooley that he could feel the heat coming off her body.

"You like to party, Dooley?" she said.

"Depends." Party was such a fun-sounding word, but Dooley had learned that it meant different things to different people.

"I bet you do," she said. "I bet you're a party central." She pressed against him, wriggling and smiling.

Bracey sank the last ball on the table and grinned.

"Let's go again," he said. "Hey, Megan? Get lost."

She stuck out her tongue at him and snuggled closer to Dooley. Dooley wondered if Beth was watching. He hoped she was.

"Hey, Dooley?" Bracey said. "Trust me, you don't want the grief." He nodded to his left. Dooley looked and saw Landers scowling at him from the other side of the room. He glanced at Megan.

"He's your boyfriend, right?" he said.

"He thinks he is," Megan said. She turned her back to Landers, concentrating everything she had on Dooley, moving when he moved, staying with him for the whole game, which Bracey won. He whooped and jumped up and down.

"Let's go again," he said, pumped with victory.

Dooley glanced around, looking for Beth. She was still over there with Rhodes. He didn't see Landers anywhere.

"Sure," he said to Bracey. "Let's go again."

Then his pager vibrated. He checked the readout. It was the store.

"You know where there's a phone I can use?"

Bracey pointed to the bar. "There's one behind there."

Beth was over by the bar.

"Some place quiet," Dooley said.

"There's a phone in the kitchen," Bracey said. "Out that door, hang a right."

Dooley took his drink with him and set it down on the

counter while he made the call, praying it would be Linelle who picked up, not Kevin.

It was.

"Your uncle called," she said. "I told him you were in the can. He said for you to call him."

Dooley was thinking, shit. If he called from here, his uncle would see on his display on his cell phone that he wasn't calling from the store. Shit, shit, shit.

"He gave me a number," Linelle said.

"He's not on his cell?"

"He gave me the number of some hotel, Dooley. You want it or not?"

Dooley listened closely, repeated it to himself as he punched it in, and came up with what he thought was a pretty good plan B. (*I'm on a cell. Someone at work is letting me use theirs. I don't know why you won't let me have one . . .* His uncle would get impatient then, wanting to get to the reason he'd called Dooley in the first place. Yeah, that could work.)

One problem: Bracey was only partly right about the kitchen. It was quieter, but it wasn't quiet enough that his uncle wouldn't catch the party sounds. Dooley left the kitchen and moved through the house farther from the party, looking for a quiet place with a phone in it. He passed one room. The door was partly open. Through it he saw Landers with the maid, Esperanza. Landers had her by one arm and he was muscling her, pulling her toward him even though it was clear she didn't want to go.

"Please," she said, her voice soft and Spanish-accented.

"Leave me go or I will tell Mr. Winston."

Mister Winston? The maid looked like she might be a year or two older than Rhodes. Dooley wondered how she could bring herself to call him *mister*. He wondered how she felt when she said it. He wondered, too, if she called Rhodes that to his face and, if she did, he wondered how it made Rhodes feel.

"You sure about you want to do that, Esperanza?" Landers said. He yanked her close to him and held onto her with both hands. "You sure you want to tell *Mr.* Winston? Because if you do, I'll have a talk with *Mr.* Ray. You want me to do that, sweetheart? You want Mr. Ray to fire your ass and send you back home?"

Dooley guessed that Mr. Ray was Rhodes' father.

Landers backed Esperanza up against the wall and pinned her hands to her sides. She squirmed and twisted her head to one side, as he moved in toward her.

"Hey," Dooley said.

Landers turned his head around to look at him, but he kept his grip firm on the girl.

"I don't think she's interested," Dooley said.

"Who asked you?" Landers said. He reached out with one leg to kick the door shut in Dooley's face. Dooley put out a foot to stop it closing all the way, then pushed it open again.

"Why don't you go see what your girlfriend is up to?" Dooley said, stepping in close to Landers, crowding him. In a soft voice meant just for Landers, he said, "Gillette told you about me, right?"

Landers hesitated. Dooley could see he didn't want to back down, but he also didn't want to take Dooley on, not one-on-one. He released Esperanza but gave her a menacing look, the kind that suggested that he'd be back when she was alone and that, boy, she'd be in for it then. He shoved his way past Dooley.

"You okay?" Dooley asked her.

She nodded, but she looked scared.

"Esperanza," someone called. A girl. Dooley didn't recognize the voice. "Esperanza, Win said to tell you they need more potato chips."

Esperanza straightened up. She rubbed her fingers under her eyes to dry her tears, and went back out into the kitchen.

Dooley continued his hunt for a phone in a quiet place.

He found another room, wood-paneled, with a desk over by the window and a phone on it. He dialed the number his uncle had given Linelle. A man answered and gave the name of the hotel. Dooley asked for his uncle. He glanced around while he waited for his uncle to come on the line. All the furniture—a couch, a couple of armchairs, the big chair behind the desk—was black leather. The desk was neat—nothing on it but the phone and some framed photos, not even a speck of dust. One of the photos was a woman. Rhodes's mother, Dooley guessed. Another was a family shot—a man, the same woman, a kid who looked like Rhodes, only younger, and a girl who had to be Rhodes's sister. Two more: single shots of the same two kids.

"Ryan?" It was his uncle, shouting into the phone, it sounded like, but his voice still almost drowned out by music and voices. "Ryan, you there?" he said. It turned out Jeannie had left her cell some place, she couldn't remember where, and she had been using his all day checking last-minute arrangements, and now it was out of juice. "Jeannie took a room at the hotel," his uncle said, getting to the point. "We're going to stay over. I'll be home some time tomorrow. Okay?"

"Yeah," Dooley said. "You want me to call you when I get home?"

"What time's that going to be?"

"I'm on until closing. Then mop and vacuum and get home, so maybe quarter to one."

"Hell no, don't call me," Dooley's uncle said. "Just be good, okay?"

"Okay," Dooley said.

He went back through the house to the kitchen. Gillette was in there now, perched on the counter, an open beer bottle in one hand, talking to someone. At first Dooley didn't see who it was. Then, as he entered the room, he saw that Esperanza was there, too, pouring potato chips into a couple of bowls, talking softly to Gillette, even smiling at him. She didn't look nervous around Gillette the way she had around Landers.

Dooley glanced around.

"Looking for this?" Gillette said. He picked up a glass from the counter next to him—Dooley's glass, with Dooley's drink in it—and handed it to Dooley. Dooley took it with him back to the party room where Bracey was waiting for him.

"Everything okay?" Bracey said.

Dooley looked around the room. He didn't see Beth anywhere and wondered if she had left. He scanned the room again. Rhodes wasn't there, either. What did that mean? Jesus, figure it out. A guy like Rhodes, living in a place like this, the guy probably had his pick. Dooley walked over to the easel with the picture of Mark Everley on it and looked down into the glass ball. Rhodes's cheque, unfolded, was lying right on top. Five hundred dollars. Right. Dooley knocked back half his drink and headed back to the pool table where Bracey was waiting. He picked up his pool cue again. It was early. If he wanted, he had all night. ■

Fifteen

Dream shards, sharp and spacey. Pool table. Megan, hanging on him, her body hot in that tiny skirt and clingy top. Bracey laughing. Gillette, crooked in the doorway, like he was standing on an angle. Esperanza crying somewhere—not in the party room, in another room. Gillette, holding her again, his arms wrapped right around her. The floor, rising and falling like the ocean, and the walls, rippling like hot air over black asphalt on a hot July day. Laughter, echoing in wave after wave. Megan's lips pressed against his. Landers, scowling. Beth, watching. Rhodes, watching, his arm around Beth. Shouting. Gillette, leaning into Beth, telling her something, then both of them staring at Dooley. Landers, his face twisted and close to Dooley's, so close it blurred. Then outside. Black sky. Gillette. A few half-hearted stars peeking through what looked like cloud cover. A car sliding by. Footsteps echoing on pavement. Loud ringing.

Then nothing.

Someone poking at him.

"Come on, pal, wake up."

Rough hands on him, hauling him to his feet.

Nausea. Throwing up.

"Jesus Christ, they don't pay me enough! Call an ambulance. Let them handle it."

Nothing.

Nothing.

Nothing.

Pounding headache.

Lights stabbing through his eyelids like the blades of a knife, slashing them, gashing them.

Reaching with his right hand to shade his eyes and hearing: "Ryan!"

Sounding familiar.

His uncle. Shaking him.

"Wake the fuck up, Ryan."

Shaking him again, majorly pissed.

Shielding his eyes with one hand and opening them and finding himself in a room he didn't recognize on a bed with side rails—a hospital bed, he realized blearily—and seeing a uniformed cop sitting on a chair near the door. Standing over him, looking pretty sharp in a tuxedo, was his uncle.

"What time is it?"

"Five-thirty in the morning. You have any idea where I'm supposed to be right now, Ryan? I'm supposed to be sleeping in a bed with a mattress you wouldn't believe anything that firm could be that soft in the swankiest hotel in town."

Dooley had never heard his uncle sound so disgusted.

He tried to sit up. His head throbbed. The light blinded

him. He had to squint to look at his uncle.

"What happened?" he said.

"Jesus," his uncle said. "Were you that far gone you don't even remember? Is that what you're telling me? I trust you to live up to the conditions, and what do you do? You go out and get yourself high. What the hell's the matter with you? Are you aching to go back or are you just stupid?"

Dooley felt sick inside. Not throw-up sick this time, but the other kind, the kind of sick you get when the cops show up at your door and you're pretty sure they have you good this time. But worse than that because, contrary to what his uncle probably thought, no, he did not want to go back. He wanted things to get better, not worse. Why else had he spent the last couple of months doing everything they told him to do? He'd been working on it. He'd been trying, for Christ's sake. But looking at his uncle now, he realized that it was all gone. None of it counted. He'd burned it up good. It was ashes. But he knew he had to offer something.

"There was this girl," he began.

"Don't," his uncle said.

"I just want to expl—"

"Don't you dare try to tell me that some girl *made* you get high," his uncle said, spacing the words out, talking slowly so he didn't start yelling, he was that mad.

Dooley glanced at the cop who was sitting just a couple of feet away and who could hear everything. He wondered what he was doing here. His uncle looked at the cop, too, then he looked back at Dooley, waiting, making it clear that if Dooley was in the position where he had to explain himself in front of a cop—and apparently he was—it was his own damned fault.

"This guy invited me to a party," he said.

"A party," his uncle said. "You said you were working tonight. You didn't say anything about a party."

"I thought if I told you about the party, you'd tell me I couldn't go."

His uncle gave him that smart-ass know-it-all cop look of his. "And that didn't tell you anything?" he said. "When was this party? After work?"

"I called in sick."

His uncle digested this. "So when you called me from the store . . .?"

"I was at the party."

"You lied to me. Good one, Ryan."

Dooley felt ashamed.

"There was this girl," he said. "She's not an excuse. She's just the reason." After more than a year with Dr. Calvin, he knew the difference between the two. "It didn't go the way I wanted. I got mad. I took a drink." It wasn't good enough. Even he knew it. "I took a couple of drinks."

"A couple?" his uncle said. "You were out cold when they picked you up."

"Two glasses of champagne. A Coke with something in it." He hadn't asked for it, but he hadn't refused it, either. "That's it. I swear."

His uncle shook his head. "You ask me what happened like you don't have a clue and all of a sudden you're one hundred percent positive all you had was three drinks?

Or maybe you're bullshitting me, because something sure doesn't add up. The least you could do is be straight with me."

"I am being straight," Dooley said. "Three drinks, which, yeah, I know I shouldn't have had."

"You could go back for that."

As if Dooley didn't know.

"I don't remember what happened after that," he said. "I don't even know what I'm doing here."

His uncle peered hard at him. He turned to the cop and said, "You want to wait outside?" The cop didn't budge. "He's not under arrest," Dooley's uncle said.

"He's a suspect," the cop said.

Suspect? Jesus, in what?

"He's also seventeen years old. He has rights. He has a right to consult with a parent or guardian—that's me—in private. You want me to call your sergeant and ask *him* to ask remind you of that?" Dooley's uncle said. The cop got up.

"I'll be right outside," he said.

Dooley's uncle watched the cop go. Then he turned back to Dooley. "There was a smash-and-grab at an electronics store a couple of blocks from the house," he said. "They think you had something to do with it."

"*What*? No way. I was at a party. I wasn't anywhere near any electronics store. Why do they think *I* had something to do with it?"

"Well, for one thing," his uncle said, "they found your wallet at the scene."

"What?" Dooley reached automatically for his pants

pocket and realized that he wasn't wearing pants. His head was pounding. He closed his eyes against the light. "My wallet," he said slowly. He didn't want to ask the next question—he was embarrassed and ashamed that he had to—but he needed to know. "What about me? Where was I?"

"You they found passed out in the backyard."

"Backyard? You mean, at home?"

"At my place, yeah."

My place. Not *home.* That didn't sound good.

"They also found a length of pipe they think was used to smash the store window. They're going to see if there are any prints on it. The good news, so far, is that they didn't find any of the stolen property on you. They want to search the house and I'm going to let them. They won't find anything, right, Ryan?"

Jesus, Dooley sure hoped not.

"The theory they're working on is that you're a real bonehead. They think you took the stuff to sell so you could buy drugs, but that you were so blasted when you did it, you dropped your wallet with your address in it and then passed out before you even got in the house."

He could imagine the cops all having a good laugh at that.

"I don't think I'd do anything like that," he said.

"*I* didn't think you'd lie to me," his uncle said. "Goes to show, huh?" Dooley wondered if he was ever going to get over being pissed off.

"I don't remember doing it," Dooley said.

His uncle was looking at him hard. Finally he said, "This

party you went to—whose was it?"

"A guy from school."

"You know him well?"

Dooley shook his head and then wished he hadn't. Just that little movement made his head pound even harder.

"He's just a guy."

"What, is he The Man With No Name?" For some reason that Dooley couldn't fathom, his uncle was very big on old Clint Eastwood westerns, what he called spaghetti westerns.

Dooley told him Rhodes's name.

"So this kid Rhodes who you don't really know, did he invite you to the party, or did you just decide to show up?"

Dooley's first thought: geeze, on top of everything else, now he thinks I'm a party crasher? His second thought: he probably deserved whatever his uncle thought.

"He invited me. And I went—"

"Because of this girl?"

"Yeah."

"And what? She blew you off and you got mad and took a drink? Three drinks?"

"Something like that. Look, I know it was dumb."

"Damn straight it was dumb. Then what?"

"Then I don't know. Everything just went weird."

"What do you mean weird? You mean you were drunk?"

"Not like that," Dooley said. "Not after three drinks." It would take a lot more than three drinks to get Dooley drunk.

"You remember leaving the party?"

"No."

"What about the other guy?"

"What other guy?"

"The responding officer says he has someone who saw two people in front of that store maybe fifteen minutes before the alarm went off. Who were you with?"

All Dooley could do was shake his head. He still wasn't sure that he'd been there.

His uncle was staring at him, like if he looked hard enough, he could see the truth.

Then the cop came back with a second cop, and they quizzed Dooley about what had happened. They pressed him on what exactly he had done and who he had been with. Dooley had to tell them, "I don't know." They didn't like that. He was pretty sure they didn't believe him.

After the cops left, Dooley's uncle glanced at his watch and said, "You get some rest. I'm going back to the hotel to apologize to Jeannie on your behalf. Then I'm going home. I'll be back with some clean clothes after they've searched the place."

"I'm sorry," Dooley said.

"Save it," his uncle said.

■ ■ ■

A doctor showed up later in the morning and asked Dooley what he had taken. Dooley told him about the three drinks. The doctor asked him, was he allergic to alcohol? Dooley said, not that he knew. The doctor asked if maybe he'd taken some drugs. Dooley said, not that he knew of. After a while, a nurse came in with an orderly and told Dooley they needed a urine sample, his uncle had requested it. She asked him if he could get to the bathroom. Dooley said he thought he could, but as soon as he tried to stand, his knees buckled. The orderly grabbed him and steadied him. Then he walked Dooley to the bathroom. Dooley started to close the door. The orderly said, "Sorry, kid." Dooley wanted to argue—there was no one else in there, what did they think he was going to do?—but didn't think it would help. At least the orderly didn't stare at him while he filled the specimen bottle. After that, Dooley went back to sleep. He woke up when his uncle shook him.

"Did they search the house?" Dooley said.

"House and property."

"Did they find anything?"

His uncle shook his head. Dooley couldn't tell if he was relieved or disappointed.

"Get dressed," his uncle said. He had brought the new clothes he'd bought Dooley for Mark Everley's funeral. "It might help if you don't look like a fuck-up," he said.

It turned out they were going to see Al Szabo, Dooley's youth worker. Dooley's uncle sat grim-faced beside Dooley while Dooley explained that he had called in sick to work when he hadn't been sick, that he had gone to a party even though he had told his uncle he was going to work, that he had taken a couple of drinks even though he knew that under his supervision order he wasn't supposed to touch alcohol, and that he was suspected of involvement in a smash-and-grab at an electronics store, but that he was pretty sure he hadn't done it, even though he had no memory of what had happened. He had been hoping that Al Szabo would be at least a little surprised. After all, for the past couple of months, right up until last night, Dooley had been a model citizen—he'd gone to school regularly, he'd held down a job, he was seeing a therapist, he hadn't touched drugs or alcohol, he hadn't been in any trouble.

The whole time Dooley was talking, Al Szabo sat behind his desk looking as stern-faced as Dooley's uncle. The only difference was that every now and then he jotted something down on a pad of paper. After Dooley finished talking, Al Szabo made a few more notes and leaned back in his chair so he could get a good look at Dooley. He said, "Well, Ryan, what do you think we should do about that?"

It was a question Dooley had hoped he would never hear again. He'd always hated the question because always what the person who was asking it was really saying was, "Pick your poison. You want the gas chamber, or do you prefer lethal injection?" But, what the hell, since he was asking . . .

"I think we should give me another chance."

His uncle must have thought Dooley was being sarcastic, because he gave him a sharp look. Then he surprised Dooley by saying, "It's the first trouble he's been in since he came to live with me. He's come a long way, considering." *Considering the shit pile I pulled him out of*, he meant. "He messes up again and he knows you're the least of his problems." He was all gruff, maybe trying to scare Dooley, possibly trying to impress Al Szabo. Dooley thought it was most likely the former.

Al Szabo fiddled with his pen and stared across his chipped metal desk at Dooley.

"How are your grades?" he said.

"Okay, I guess," Dooley said. He always did his homework. Always. Even when he suspected that the teacher didn't like him or didn't expect much from him. "We have midterms in a couple of weeks."

"Attendance?"

"He hasn't missed a day," Dooley's uncle said.

Al Szabo's eyes flicked from Dooley to Dooley's uncle and back to Dooley again.

"I haven't missed a day," Dooley said. "Haven't skipped, either. You can call the school and ask them."

"How's the job?"

"It's boring and it pays minimum wage," Dooley said. There was no point in trying to bullshit Al Szabo. "But I get free rentals."

'The manager there seems to like you," Al Szabo said.

"Kevin?" That didn't sound right.

Al Szabo glanced down at the file that was open on his desk. "Guy Fielding," he said.

Mr. Fielding. The store manager. He managed three stores in the chain. He was the one who had hired Dooley. For some reason Dooley didn't understand, he and Mr. Fielding had hit it off during the interview. Dooley had been up-front with him. He'd told him the trouble he'd been in. Mr. Fielding had said, "So, I'm guessing you're not a big fan of cop movies. I'm guessing you're more of a Tarantino guy." Dooley had said, well, he thought Tarantino was one smart guy, but, to tell the truth, he was too blood-happy. Dooley said he liked some of the British stuff better. "You mean, Guy Ritchie and what's-his-name, the guy who did *The Limey*?" Mr. Fielding had said. No, Dooley said. Some of the quieter stuff, the stuff they showed on TV there but that you could rent here. He said he liked Robbie Coltrane, the character he played, he drank too much, he ate too much, but he always figured out the case without breaking a sweat, and you know what? The guy didn't even own a gun. Yeah, Dooley liked him a lot. That's when Mr. Fielding had said, "Welcome aboard, Dooley," making him the first adult ever who had gone along just like that with calling Dooley by the name he preferred.

Al Szabo looked across the desk at Dooley for a moment before he said, "Why don't we see what happens on these smash-and-grab allegations? They nail you for that, Ryan, and it's out of my hands. You understand that, right?"

Dooley said he did.

After Dooley and his uncle left the office, Dooley's uncle said, "You realize I just stuck my neck out for you."

Dooley said he did. He said, "Thanks." When he finally got home with his uncle, he took off his tie and said, "Now what?"

"You tell me," his uncle said.

"You going to ground me or something?"

"You're being investigated for a crime that, if it turns out you did it, they're going to lock you up again, and you want to know if I'm going to ground you?" His uncle shook his head.

Dooley went up to his room, crawled into bed, and slept

until his uncle woke him up at four-thirty.

"You're working tonight, right?" his uncle said.

Dooley had a monster headache. He felt queasy, like he was going to throw up, only he didn't see how he could because there was nothing in his stomach. He wished he could call in sick, but he knew that wouldn't fly, not today.

"Get dressed," his uncle said. "Come downstairs. I made you breakfast."

"I'm not hungry."

"You have to eat something. Come on."

When he got downstairs, his uncle put a plate in front of him—scrambled eggs and dry toast. Also, a mug of coffee.

"I know you don't believe it, but it'll make you feel better," his uncle said.

Dooley almost gagged on his first mouthful, but he choked it all down, mainly so his uncle wouldn't have an excuse to get pissed off again. His uncle sat opposite him at the table.

"You know what Rohypnol is, Ryan?"

"Roofies? Sure," Dooley said, and then wished he hadn't answered so fast. Boy, the things he knew and the things he didn't. "Why?"

"You ingested some." The urine specimen. His uncle must have some connections to get the results do fast. "Either you knew what you were doing or you didn't."

Dooley stared at his uncle.

"Are you saying someone put something in my drink?"

"So you're saying you didn't know?"

"That's the date rape drug. Why would I take that?"

His uncle rolled his eyes. "Give me a break. I've been around the block more than a few times, Ryan."

Okay, so some guys slipped roofies into girls' drinks so they could score on them. But there were other people who took them because they gave that extra kick to a drink, made you float, made you oblivious. And, okay, so there were plenty of times, including now, when Dooley wished he could be oblivious.

"If you say I ingested it, I ingested it," Dooley said. "But I didn't know." Roofies—odorless, colorless, tasteless.

His uncle studied him for a few moments.

"I'm going to pass this information on," he said. "I don't know what kind of difference it's going to make on the smash-and-grab, especially with your record. But we'll see. And, Ryan? These new friends of yours? How about you stay away from them, okay?" ■

Sixteen

"You look like shit," Linelle said. "And here I thought you were malingering last night."

Malingering? If Dooley's head didn't feel as if there was a road crew inside it, jack-hammering what was left of his brains, he might have asked her where she'd got that one. The bright lights in the store were like a thousand needles piercing and re-piercing his eyeballs. He wished he could wear sunglasses but knew Kevin would never go for it. Eggs and toast and coffee were churning like dirty laundry in his stomach (his uncle had been wrong about them making him feel better). He wished he wasn't working straight through to midnight.

Rhodes came in around nine while Dooley was alone at cash. He was wearing a different leather jacket this time and jeans that looked worn and crisp all at the same time.

"Dooley, geeze, are you okay?" he said, peering at Dooley, which told Dooley that Linelle was right, he looked like shit. "The cops came by my house this afternoon. They wanted to know if you were at my place last night. After they left, I realized I didn't know how to get in touch with you. You aren't in the book. I was hoping you'd be here. What happened?"

Dooley just shrugged. He didn't want to get into it, not here.

But Rhodes did. At least he kept his voice low.

"The cops, they were really pressing me about the party," he said. He looked worried. "My dad nearly lost it. You should have heard him. He gets pissy with cops. Doesn't like them. He told them, yeah, there was a party. And, yeah, whenever there's a big party like that, there's always kids who bring stuff and do stuff." His voice was pitched lower now, doing what Dooley guessed was an imitation of his father. "What can you do, right? But there was no damage done in the house. No damage done to the property or to any of the neighbors'. No neighbors complaining."

Dooley spotted Kevin at the back of the store, watching him, trying to figure out if Rhodes was a customer, which would be good, or a friend on a social visit, which was against store policy.

"He said to the cop, this kid who robbed that store—he meant you, Dooley. Geeze, you robbed a store? What was that like?"

"I didn't do it," Dooley said.

Rhodes looked a little disappointed. He got that a lot—kids who had never been in trouble always wanting to know what it was *really* like and always disappointed when what he told them didn't live up to what they had seen on TV or in some movie or, more often, when Dooley said nothing at all.

"Yeah, well, my dad said to the cop, this kid who robbed that store, nobody twisted his arm to take a drink," Rhodes said. "He said, there were dozens of kids there who saw him knock them back, isn't that right? Then he looked at me, and what could I do? I mean, it's true, right?" He sounded sorry about it.

"Yeah, I guess," Dooley said.

"Then my dad said, when it comes right down to it, who's to say this kid didn't do most of his drinking after he left the house?" Rhodes shook his head. "That's my dad. He didn't want to get involved. He never wants to get involved, not when there's cops around. He doesn't like me getting involved, either. That's just the way he is. After the cops left, he told me if anything like that ever happens again, cops coming to the house, he meant, he's cutting me out of his will." He showed Dooley a crooked little smile, the expression suggesting to Dooley that this was probably something Rhodes's father said all the time. "You're sure you're okay?" Rhodes said again.

"I'll live," Dooley said.

"The cops sure seem to think you robbed that store. That's why they came by my house. Because you said you'd been at my party. They wanted to know what time you left, what kind of shape you were in, who went with you, stuff like that."

"And?" Dooley said. He'd been wondering about that himself. When had he left the party? He didn't remember. Who had he left with, or had he left alone? He didn't remember that, either.

Two kids came up to the cash with a couple of horror movies. Dooley used to watch stuff like that all the time, but he'd stopped since the last time he was in lockup. Now he wondered what people saw in movies where people got hacked up and ripped open and tortured. He scanned the DVD cases and took the kids' cash.

"And what did I tell them, you mean?" Rhodes said after the kids left. "I told them what I knew, which wasn't much. I don't know exactly when you left. I didn't see you go. One minute you were there, the next you were gone. I figured you slipped out, you know, on account of Beth and then because of Landers."

"Landers?"

"You know, because he was ready to tear into you."

Dooley had no memory of that.

"Because of Megan," Rhodes said, looking at him closely now. "You know, because Megan was coming onto you and Landers didn't appreciate it. What's the matter, Dooley? You're acting like you don't remember."

"What about Esperanza?" Dooley said.

Rhodes looked completely baffled. "Esperanza? What do you mean?"

It sounded like Esperanza hadn't told Rhodes what Landers had done. Landers had tried to scare her, and it looked like he had succeeded. She'd kept her mouth shut because she didn't want Landers talking to Rhodes' father. Dooley wondered what that was all about. He wondered if he should say something to Rhodes but decided not to. Things were hard enough for her. She was a maid, for

Christ's sake. He didn't want to mess her up if he didn't have to. So he said, "The blonde girl. That's her name, right?"

Rhodes laughed. "The blonde girl is Jen. Esperanza is our maid. Geeze, Dooley, you were really wasted, huh?"

"Yeah, I guess," Dooley said.

He wondered if he should ask Rhodes about the roofies, did he know if anyone there was doing them or did he notice if anyone had slipped him anything. Landers could have done it. He had sure been pissed off enough. Or it could have been Gillette.

"What about Gillette?" he said to Rhodes.

"Eddy? What about him?"

"When did he leave?"

Rhodes shook his head. "I'm not sure. Late. You two got into it, too. You really have a temper when you get going, don't you, Dooley? But you calm down again, which is good."

"So you don't remember when he left?"

"I saw the two of you talking, then I kind of lost track."

A middle-aged woman came up to the counter with a sullen-looking teenaged girl. As Dooley reached out to take the DVDs she had in her hand, Rhodes said, "I just wanted to make sure you were okay. Look, I gotta run. I got someone waiting for me out in the car." He nodded over toward the store window. Dooley turned and saw Beth sitting in the passenger seat of a black Mustang. That figured.

■ ■ ■

Dooley made it through his shift. He also made it through cleanup and Kevin's non-stop mouth-running about up-selling—"So they rent a DVD, maybe a couple of DVDs. It's obvious they're going to be planted in front of the tube all night. So you're doing them a favor by asking, you want snacks with that? You're doing them a favor by checking their record, looking up their rental pattern. You say, I notice you rent two movies a week every week, or whatever it says. You tell them, you know, you should be a gold-card member. Nine-ninety-nine and you'll save a dollar off every new rental for the next year—you have two movies tonight, that's like getting the gold card for seven-ninety-nine and you'll end up saving a hundred dollars . . ." Blah blah blah. Dooley's headache came back.

■ ■ ■

What Dooley wanted to do the next morning: find Gillette and Landers and ask them a few questions. The stuff in his drink—there were different ways that could have happened. Some kids who party want everyone else to party, too. Anyone who was there could have done it. Or he could have picked up the wrong glass. Or, true, someone could have slipped him something. Someone who thought it would be funny. Or someone who wanted to get back at him for something. But his wallet at the electronics store? If he was brutally honest with himself, he'd have to admit that it was possible he'd done what the cops suspected—if he'd been blasted enough and angry enough, and all the evidence suggested that he'd been both. But if he hadn't done it—and, boy, did he ever want to believe that he hadn't—then how had his wallet ended up in front of that store? The cops had someone who had seen two people near the store. Who were they? Say he was one of those two people—who was the other person? Had those people or that person taken Dooley's wallet and planted it at the store? It was possible. The shape he'd been in, someone could have lifted him upside down and shaken everything out of his pockets and he wouldn't remember. Why would someone do something like that? To make him look bad, maybe, or maybe to get even with him for something. Once upon a time, there would have been a long list of people out to get him, but given the life Dooley had been leading lately, he felt he could whittle it down to just a couple of names: Gillette or Landers. Or maybe both of them.

So what he wanted to do was find them and talk to them. See if one or other of them had fucked him up.

What he didn't trust himself to do: stay calm if it turned out one of them had. It was a real Dr. Calvin moment.

■ ■ ■

Dr. Calvin: So you think someone maybe drugged you and then framed you for a smash-and-grab. What's the smart thing to do about that, Dooley?

Dooley: Kick the guy's teeth in?

Dr. Calvin: I believe I said *smart* thing.

Dooley: Let the police handle it?

Dr. Calvin: Very good.

■ ■ ■

People like Dr. Calvin always thought that you should leave things to the experts because people like Dr. Calvin *were* experts, and experts always thought they knew everything—it's what made them experts.

Dooley wasn't so sure. Not when it came to the cops and for sure not when someone had handed the cops a *gimme*. I mean, come on, there's a smash-and-grab and what do you find at the scene? Something that screams the name of a person who is not only known to the police but who is known for crimes that are similar in nature. You gotta check it out, right? And what do you find? Said guy, passed out in his own backyard—where have we heard that one before, my fellow officers? And the guy claims that he doesn't remember a damned thing. Right.

No, Dooley didn't like the odds on that one.

But—and here, he believed, was where there was some wisdom in what Dr. Calvin always said—if he went and found Gillette and Landers, and if he came to believe that one (or both) of them had framed him, he wasn't sure he would be able to hold it together. And that would jam him up even worse. So instead of doing what he wanted to do—find Gillette and Landers—he went down into the ravine. He spent the morning there, walking, looking, talking to anyone he could find. On the way home, he circled around and climbed up onto the old railway bridge, the one Everley had gone off, and got a big surprise. Beth was sitting there, her arms on her knees, her head on her hands. He hesitated—

should he advance or retreat? Before he could decide, she raised her head, and he saw that she had been crying. She had a fierce expression on her face as she wiped the tears off her cheeks.

"What are you doing here?" she said, as if he were on private property instead of on a public walking path.

He didn't answer. He wasn't sure himself why he had come up here.

She stood up. "Get off this bridge," she said.

"Look, I'm sorry about your brother," he said. "I really am."

"Right." Boy, was she bitter. Was she still mad about his reluctance—okay, his refusal—to be hypnotized? "You expect me to believe that after what you did?"

"Look, about the hypnosis this—"

"The hypnosis thing?" She shook her head in disgust. "You're going to pretend you don't know what I'm talking about?"

He stared helplessly at her.

"Right," she said again. He was getting the idea that she was one of those girls who always said the opposite of what she meant. "Mark came home a couple of months ago with one eye swollen shut and a big bruise on his face. Ring a bell, *Dooley*?"

Oh.

"He wouldn't say what happened," she said. "My mother wanted him to call the cops, but he wouldn't do it. He said he was afraid what would happen if he got the cops involved. He said, you know how it is with bullies, you tell on them and all you get is bullied more." Yeah, Dooley knew all about that. "He wouldn't even say who did it. But now I know it was you, and you have the nerve to come up here and tell me you're sorry about him?"

"Who told you?" he said. He didn't even bother trying to sound indignant.

He read contempt in her eyes. "Now you're playing dumb. Friday night you looked ready to rip his head off, and now you don't remember?"

It must have been either Gillette or Landers.

"What else did they say about me?"

She held herself tall, reminding him of a little bird puffing out its feathers to make it look bigger than it really was. But he knew from the tremble in her lower lip and the way her eyes jumped from him to around him and behind him—probably hoping to see someone else, anyone else, nearby—that she was afraid to be up here alone with him.

"Everything," she said.

If she knew everything, then it had to have been Gillette. To hell with Dr. Calvin. He wanted Gillette.

"Were you up on this bridge the night my brother died?"

"*What?*" Dooley said. "No!"

"You said you didn't know my brother, but you did. You beat him up."

"I didn't beat him up. He was hassling a kid. I tried to get him to stop. He shoved me. I tried to get him to back off. That's all."

"Peter was there, too. He told me what happened."

So it had been Gillette *and* Landers.

"Then he lied to you," Dooley said. "So did your brother."

"Mark would never lie to me."

Oh boy.

"Maybe you didn't know your brother as well as you thought you did."

She didn't like that.

"Look," he said, "I'm sorry he died. But I didn't have anything to do with it. I just saw him fall."

She looked at him a moment like he was Satan, complete with horns and a tail. Then she turned and walked off the bridge.

■ ■ ■

Dooley went to every single place he could remember having been with Gillette. He ran into people he used to know, most of whom were surprised to see him out, some of whom probably wished he wasn't, a couple of whom offered him some refreshment, all of whom were amused when he said, no, he didn't do that anymore. None of them had seen Gillette. None of them knew where he was living now. ■

Seventeen

If Gillette was at school on Monday, he was keeping a low profile because Dooley didn't see him. Same thing on Tuesday.

On Wednesday when Dooley was leaving school, he ran into Rhodes. Bracey was with him. So was Landers. Landers scowled at him. Dooley wished he could at least remember Megan coming onto him. It would make that scowl worthwhile. But he couldn't.

"Have you seen Gillette?" Dooley said.

"No," Rhodes said. He seemed surprised. "I was going to ask you the same question."

"Me? Why?"

"He's missing."

"Missing? You mean, he's skipping class?"

Rhodes shook his head. "His mother called me."

"You know his mother?"

"Sure," Rhodes said, surprised again, as if he was wondering if there was some reason he shouldn't know her. "She's nice. She works hard, you know, with four kids and she's all on her own. You don't know her?"

Dooley shook his head.

"Well, she said she hasn't seen Eddy since he left home to come to my party. She sounded really worried. You don't know where he is?" Rhodes said.

"Why would I know that?"

Rhodes blinked behind the lenses of his glasses. "Eddy said you and he used to be tight," he said. "He said you'd had some kind of falling out. You two really got into it at the party." Rhodes had mentioned that once before. The first time he'd said it, Dooley couldn't remember what had happened. He still couldn't. "I saw you talking to him after that. I thought maybe you had buried your differences."

"I haven't seen him," Dooley said.

■ ■ ■

Dooley stopped short at lunchtime on Thursday when he saw his uncle's car was parked in front of the school. His uncle got out and waited for Dooley to approach.

"What's wrong?" Dooley said. It had to be something. Why else would his uncle be there?

"The police want to see you."

"What about? The smash-and-grab? Did they get any prints?"

"No," his uncle said. "All they have is that your wallet was at the scene. It's not enough to charge you. The shape you were in, you could easily have dropped it. But I don't think that's what they want to talk to you about. It was a different guy who called." Dooley's uncle was an in-charge, on-top-of-everything kind of guy, but he looked worried. That shook Dooley.

"Did you ask him what it was about?"

"I did."

"And? What did he say?"

"He said it was about a police matter," his uncle said. "Do you have any idea how many times I said that when I was a police officer?" He shook his head. "I gotta tell you, it has a whole different effect when someone says it to you instead of the other way around."

The cop who wanted to see Dooley, a detective named Joyeaux, thanked Dooley for coming in. He said that he wanted to ask Dooley a few questions and that Dooley wasn't a suspect, they were just contacting people they thought might be able to help them out.

"Help you out with what?" Dooley's uncle said, clearly impatient that the detective wasn't getting right to the point.

"When was the last time you saw Edward Gillette?" Joyeaux asked Dooley.

"Who the hell is Edward Gillette?" Dooley's uncle said.

"A guy I know," Dooley told his uncle. To the detective he said, "I saw him at a party on Friday night. I heard he was missing. Did something happen to him?"

"Is that what this is about?" Dooley's uncle said. "Some kid who's missing?"

"Edward Gillette hasn't been seen since last Friday night," Joyeaux said. "Did you talk to him at the party, Ryan?"

Dooley was willing to bet that the detective already knew

the answer to that. Gillette's mother must have reported him missing. She'd also called Rhodes's house, so unless the cops were brain-dead, they had already talked to Rhodes and had got a rundown of who was at the party and who had talked to Gillette.

"I remember seeing him," Dooley said. "But I don't remember talking to him." He glanced at his uncle. His uncle didn't say anything. "I was high," Dooley said, looking at Joyeaux, avoiding his uncle now. "I had a few drinks. Some other stuff too."

"What other stuff?" Joyeaux said.

"Rohypnol," his uncle said, his tone dry. "Ryan ingested some Rohypnol that night. He thinks someone slipped it into his drink."

Joyeaux looked surprised and suspicious both at the same time. He hadn't known about the roofies, which made sense to Dooley. Whoever had spiked his drink sure wasn't going to tell the cops about it, assuming the cops had talked to that person. Dooley couldn't tell if Joyeaux believed him or not.

"What if I told you there were people at the party who saw you talking to Edward Gillette?" Joyeaux said.

There wasn't much Dooley could say. "If that's what people saw, then I guess that's what must have happened." He wished things had happened differently, but apparently they hadn't.

"What if I said there were people who saw you and Edward Gillette in what appeared to be some kind of altercation?"

Dooley shrugged. He already knew what had happened;

Rhodes had told him. He'd probably told the police, too. Probably so had anyone else who had been at the party, had seen Dooley and Gillette, and had been questioned by the police.

"Where are you going with this?" Dooley's uncle said. "Are you trying to suggest that Ryan did something to this kid?" He sounded annoyed, but when he glanced at Dooley, Dooley saw that he looked worried.

"Edward Gillette left home late Friday afternoon. He was last seen at a party on Friday night. Ryan was at that party."

"So were a lot of other kids," Dooley's uncle said.

Joyeaux nodded. His tone was conciliatory when he said, "We're just trying to get a picture of who Edward talked to, what went on at the party, who he left with, and where he might have gone. His mother is worried about him. She says this isn't normal behavior for Edward."

Dooley had a hard time believing that. It was possible Gillette had changed. It was possible that he was trying, just like Dooley was. But Dooley had a hard time believing that, too. He glanced at his uncle. He bet his uncle was thinking what he would do if Dooley had left home on a Friday and still hadn't showed up by the following Wednesday.

Joyeaux turned to Dooley. "When did you leave the party, Ryan?"

"I don't know."

"Did you talk to anyone before you left the party? Did you say goodnight to anyone or maybe arrange to meet anyone—" Dooley knew he meant Gillette. "—somewhere after the party?"

"I don't remember."

"The police questioned you that night, didn't they, Ryan?"

"They questioned him the next day," Dooley's uncle said.

"In conjunction with a smash-and-grab at an electronics store," Joyeaux said, not taking his eyes off Dooley.

"He wasn't charged," Dooley's uncle said. Dooley could tell he was annoyed.

Joyeaux turned to him. "It would be a lot better if you let Ryan answer the questions," Joyeaux said.

Dooley's uncle scowled at Joyeaux but didn't say anything.

Joyeaux turned back to Dooley.

"The police questioned you in conjunction with a smash-and-grab, is that right, Ryan?"

"Yes," Dooley said.

"Did you and Edward do that together?"

"You said you wanted to talk to him about this kid's whereabouts," Dooley's uncle said. "You didn't say you wanted to talk to him about the electronics store."

"I'm just trying to get a picture of what happened the night Edward was last seen," Joyeaux said. "It might give us some idea of what happened to him." He was smooth-talking Dooley's uncle, but Dooley's uncle wasn't buying it. Joyeaux turned to Dooley.

"Do you know where Edward Gillette is?" he said.

"No," Dooley said.

"Did you do anything to Edward Gillette?"

"No!"

"That's it," Dooley's uncle said. He stood up abruptly, glowering at Joyeaux before turning to Dooley. "Let's go."

■ ■ ■

On the way home in the car, Dooley's uncle said, "This Edward Gillette—who is he, exactly?"

"Someone I used to know."

His uncle gave him a sharp look. "You mean, someone you *know*."

"I mean, someone I knew from before," Dooley said. "We used to hang out together."

"Define hang out."

"You know what I mean."

"I'm *afraid* I know what you mean," his uncle said. "You want to put my mind at ease?"

"I can't," Dooley said. "You're right."

"And now you're hanging out with him again? What the hell's the matter with you, Ryan?"

"I'm not hanging out with him. It turns out he goes to my school." It was kind of funny if you looked at it in the right light: two guys who had made a career out of avoiding school as much as they could get away with, and here they were, both in the same school, both, as far as Dooley could figure, attending *or else*.

"It didn't occur to you to mention that to me?" Dooley's uncle said.

"I didn't think it was important. He's not in my life anymore."

"He was in it Friday night."

"Turns out he was a friend of the dead kid, Mark Everley. The party was a sort of memorial for Everley—his sister wants to start a scholarship in his name. I guess that's why Gillette was there."

"Tell me again why you didn't ask me if you could go to the party."

"Come on," Dooley said.

"Tell me, Ryan."

Jesus. He was serious. Fine.

"Because I didn't think you'd let me go."

"Now you see why?"

Yeah, now Dooley saw why.

■ ■ ■

Jeannie was in the kitchen in silver slippers that looked like sandals and that had skinny little straps on them and a red silk robe with a big dragon on the back. She was humming while she made Sunday morning breakfast—sausages and French toast. Dooley's uncle was at the kitchen table in relax-fit jeans and a gray T-shirt. He was drinking coffee. Every so often he glanced over at Jeannie. Dooley was at the table, too, flipping through the newspaper from the day before and smelling the sausages. He was working on a second cup of coffee and thinking about French toast swimming in maple syrup—the real stuff that his uncle insisted on, he had a friend in Quebec who shipped him up a dozen cans every year—when the doorbell rang.

"Get that, will you, Ryan?" his uncle said.

Dooley got it.

It was the homicide detective from the ravine, Detective Graff.

"Hello, Ryan," Graff said. "You home alone?"

"My uncle's here."

"Let's go talk to him," Graff said, stepping into the front hall and forcing Dooley to back up. Graff was a little shorter than Dooley, but he had a swagger that made him seem taller. Dooley believed it was their guns that gave cops that confidence. That and the fact that everyone knew how much grief you could earn by messing with a cop. Graff followed Dooley through to the kitchen.

Dooley's uncle looked up, surprised.

"He's a cop," Dooley said.

"I know," Dooley's uncle said, standing up. "Graff, right?"

"That's right," Graff said.

"What's this about?" Dooley's uncle said.

"I'd like Ryan to come in," Graff said. "I'd like to talk to him."

"About?"

"About Edward Gillette."

"He already talked to someone about that."

"There's been a new development."

Dooley and his uncle waited. Dooley didn't know about his uncle, but he had a bad feeling. After all, Graff was a homicide cop.

"They found Edward Gillette," Graff said. "He's dead."

"Dead how?" Dooley's uncle said.

"Massive trauma to the head," Graff said. "A guy out walking his dog found him in a ravine a ten-minute walk from this house. He was in a ditch, covered with scrub and leaves." ■

Eighteen

In the interview room, Graff told Dooley—again—that he was not a suspect. He said he just wanted to ask Dooley some questions. He told Dooley he didn't have to answer if he didn't want to. But he warned him that if he did answer, anything he said could be used in a subsequent criminal proceeding. He told Dooley he had the right to have a parent or guardian present.

"He knows the drill," Dooley's uncle said. "And I'm here. Let's get on with it.

Graff asked him how he knew Edward Gillette.

Dooley said, "We used to hang around together."

"You used to do more than that, didn't you, Ryan?"

Dooley felt his uncle's eyes sharp on him.

"Yeah," Dooley said.

"You did some purse snatchings together, didn't you, Ryan?"

Dooley felt his uncle tense up.

"You were pretty tight, weren't you, Ryan?"

"For a while," Dooley said.

"And then what?" Graff said.

Dooley shrugged.

"The woman, right?" Graff said.

Dooley stared down at the tabletop.

"What's that got to do with anything?" Dooley's uncle said. "He did his time. He's been keeping his nose clean since he's living with me."

"Except for last Friday," Graff said. "Tell me about the party, Ryan."

"I don't remember," Dooley said.

"I heard you partied a little too hearty."

"Someone slipped him something," Dooley's uncle said.

Graff looked pleasantly at him. "Oh," he said. "You were there?"

Dooley's uncle didn't like that.

"He's my nephew. I trust him."

Graff opened a file folder and thumbed through the pages inside. He slid the folder over to Dooley's uncle. Dooley's uncle read the top page. He looked at Dooley.

"Come on, Ryan," Graff said. "You and I both know you were an early bloomer when it comes to club drugs. Edward Gillette, too."

"You said he wasn't a suspect," Dooley's uncle said.

"He isn't," Graff said. "I'm just trying to get some facts straight. Like, for instance, this altercation you and Edward had at that party last Friday night."

"I don't remember," Dooley said.

"It came to blows," Graff said. "A couple of the kids who were there had to break it up."

Dooley looked at him. This was the first he'd heard of that.

"I don't remember," he said.

"What were you doing between the time you left the party and the time you were arrested on that smash-and-grab?"

"I don't remember."

"Was Gillette with you?"

"I don't remember."

"Did you kill Edward Gillette, Ryan?"

Dooley's uncle stood up before Dooley could say anything. He grabbed Dooley's arm and Dooley got the message that he should stand up, too.

"Not a suspect, my ass," Dooley's uncle said.

"What about Mark Everley?" Graff said. "Did you push him off that bridge, Ryan?"

That stopped Dooley's uncle short. "What are you talking about?" he said. "I thought the Everley kid fell because he'd been drinking and fooling around up there."

Graff just looked at him, maybe wondering how Dooley's uncle knew that and probably coming up with an answer good and fast. He didn't say anything.

■ ■ ■

By the time Dooley and his uncle got home, Jeannie was gone. She'd left the French toast and the sausages and a note on how to warm them up, but neither Dooley nor his uncle was hungry. His uncle spooned coffee and poured water into the coffeemaker and stood at the counter while the coffee brewed. He said, "Is there anything about Edward Gillette I should know, other than what Graff told me and you didn't?"

"No," Dooley said.

"You had some kind of fight with him at that party. What was it about?"

"I don't remember."

"If I was Graff, I'd think you were rehearsing your defence," his uncle said irritably.

Had it really come to that? Was his uncle really wondering whether or not he should believe Dooley?

"Maybe it was because Gillette told Beth about me."

"Beth?" his uncle said.

"The girl I told you about."

"The girl who was the reason you went to the party?"

"Yeah."

"What did he tell her?"

Here it came—crunch time.

"There was this thing that happened with Mark Everley," Dooley said.

Dooley's uncle was quiet for a moment. Dooley imagined him thinking, *What now*? "Does it have anything with why Graff asked you that last question?" he said.

"Maybe," Dooley said. "Probably."

His uncle waited. Dooley wondered how he would take the story.

"Well?" his uncle said when Dooley didn't continue.

"It's complicated," Dooley said.

"It's Sunday," his uncle said. "I've got nothing but time."

Dooley took a deep breath. Where to start?

"Mark Everley came into the store a couple of months ago, just after I started working there. I didn't even know who he was. He was with another guy I didn't know either." Turned out it was Landers.

His uncle was still standing beside the coffeemaker. He had a clean mug in his hand. His uncle was a coffee addict, but he wasn't reaching for the pot. He was watching Dooley.

"There was this girl in the store. She was . . . different. Someone said she had Down's." His uncle nodded, but just barely. "Everley started making fun of her behind her back, the way she looked, the way she walked, the way she talked. He was trying to get laughs from the guy he was with." He could see it as he described it. He still couldn't understand what kind of person would do something like that. They seemed to know who she was. It was Landers who had pointed her out. He had also looked around the store, like he was checking to see if someone else was there with her. "The girl caught on. She knew what he was doing. You should have seen the look on her face." Poor kid. She'd been crushed. Something else, too. Something that told Dooley this wasn't the first time some jerk had made fun of her like that. Something that also told Dooley that she was way smarter than Everley gave her credit for.

"Anyway, she came up to the cash and I rang up her rental." *The Little Mermaid*. "She left. And I said to Everley, why don't you leave her alone?" Boy, Everley had perked up at that. Dooley didn't get it at first. "He laughed. He said, You gonna make me?"

Dooley's uncle shook his head. Dooley bet he had a pretty good idea where this story was going.

"Anyway," Dooley said, "then Everley and the other guy went out of the store. The girl was out there. I think she was waiting for someone." He wasn't sure about that, though, because no one ever turned up to get her. "And he started in again." He knew Dooley was watching him. He looked right at him. "So I went outside," Dooley said.

His uncle shook his head again, but he didn't say anything.

"He was being loud, you know?" Dooley said. "And he didn't care that people were walking by looking at him." Boy, all those people, and what had *they* done? Absolutely nothing besides stare and then just move it along. "The girl was really upset. She was covering her ears. So I stopped him."

"Stopped him?" Dooley's uncle said. He still hadn't moved to fill his mug.

"I told him to knock it off. He just kept running his mouth." Only now he was making fun of Dooley: look at the video store clerk, offering excellent customer service out there on the sidewalk, did he really think he could tell *anybody* what to do? "He wouldn't stop. So I grabbed his arm and pulled him away from the girl. He didn't like that." Well, that wasn't entirely true. Everley had got this crazy look in his eyes, like, yeah, here we go, bring it on. "He threw a punch at me." Dooley could tell right away that Mark Everley had thrown a lot of punches. He was like some guys Dooley had crossed paths with, guys who thought they were tougher than anyone else and who really got off on proving it. Guys who liked to get things started just so that they could finish them off. "I connected first."

"You hit him?" his uncle said.

"You would have, too, if you'd been there," Dooley said. "He was asking for it."

His uncle stared at him.

"Okay, so maybe you wouldn't have. But he threw the first punch, and he was giving that girl a hard time. It wasn't right."

"And the guy he was with, that was Edward Gillette?"

Dooley shook his head. "That was another guy. But Gillette was hanging around, too. He saw it happen. He told Beth."

He could see his uncle didn't get it.

"Beth is Everley's sister," Dooley said. "The way Gillette told her the story, I beat up Everley."

"Did you?"

Yeah, it had come to that. His uncle didn't know what to think anymore, but he was leaning toward the worst.

"No."

"How many times did you hit him?"

"I think maybe two or three times—and only because he was hitting me. The guy was crazy." That didn't even begin to describe it. It seemed to Dooley that Everley was having the time of his life. The guy loved to fight. He liked to inflict pain. Maybe he even got off on getting some back. "Then the guy who was with him stepped in and told him he should forget it, he should walk away." Dooley believed Landers had done that only because, unlike the teasing, the fight had drawn a crowd, and a few people were muttering about calling the cops. He also believed that if there had been no one else around, Landers probably would have jumped in and started swinging at Dooley alongside Everley. Landers seemed like the kind of guy who had no trouble with two against one so long as he wasn't the one.

"Did you break anything?" Dooley's uncle said.

Dooley shook his head. "He ended up with a swollen eye and some bruises. But all I did was stop him. I didn't beat him up. Believe me, I know the difference."

"Why would Gillette tell this girl you beat up her brother if you didn't?"

Dooley hesitated.

"I think he's afraid of me," he said at last.

His uncle looked at him for a moment before finally pouring himself a cup of coffee. He stirred some of Jeannie's Sweet 'n' Low into it and sat down at the table. Dooley sat opposite him.

"And he's afraid of you because . . .?" his uncle said, slowly, drawing out the question as if to put off having to hear the answer.

And what a question. It was the big one—the biggest one—and the answer was the thing Dooley had never told another living soul, the thing he'd been carrying around with him for nearly two years now.

"Ryan?" His uncle was leaning across the table now, eyes hard on Dooley. "You've been doing pretty well since you moved in here. Going to that party, that's turning out to be a big mistake. If you're going to straighten it out, you're going to have to *be* straight—with me, anyway."

It was easy to say, but harder to do. The thing was, nobody knew—unless Gillette had told someone. But why would he do that? You told most people something like that, and they'd go straight to the cops. The first time Dooley had run into Gillette after he moved in with his uncle, he'd caught the panic in Gillette's eyes and had realized that Gillette was afraid of him, afraid of what Dooley might do to him. But if Dooley told his uncle that . . . or if Gillette had said anything to anyone . . .

His uncle was still looking at him, still waiting, his last words visible in his eyes: *You're going to have to be straight.*

"That last time I got busted," Dooley said, "you know, the thing with that woman?"

His uncle nodded, but Dooley could see he didn't want to think about that.

"Gillette was with me," Dooley said.

His uncle slumped back in his chair. "Go on."

"That's it," Dooley said. "He was there. He's the one who set it up." Before his uncle could say anything, Dooley added, "I'm not saying it's his fault. I went in there, same as him, I was the one who hit that woman. But Gillette was in on it. I got caught. He didn't."

"You didn't tell the police there was anyone there with you," his uncle said—a statement, not a question, because, of course, his uncle had read his file.

Dooley just gave him a look. His uncle shook his head.

"I didn't hear from Gillette the whole time I was in lockup.

Then, after I got out, I bumped into him on the street. He looked kind of scared. Of me. You know?"

"Scared?" his uncle said. "He should have been grateful." He peered at Dooley. "There's more," he said wearily.

"It was the wrong house," Dooley said. "A guy I met inside told me. He heard it from someone who knew Gillette. The house we were *supposed* to be in—that one was empty. The people were out of town on vacation. Gillette knew which one it was. But he screwed up. We were in the wrong house. That's why that woman showed up the way she did. I kept my mouth shut about Gillette. I figured if it had been the other way around and he had got caught, he'd do the same thing. Then I find out he screwed up and he didn't even have the guts to tell me."

"Did he know you knew?" Dooley's uncle said.

Dooley nodded. "I told him."

"When?"

"Last week."

His uncle finally took a sip of his coffee. He was quiet for a few moments after that.

"Who else knows about this?" he said finally.

"The guy who told me," Dooley said. "And the guy who told him, I don't know who else. Nobody who would tell the cops, if that's what you mean." His uncle didn't say anything, but Dooley had the feeling that was exactly what he meant. His uncle stared so hard at Dooley that Dooley couldn't help it; he squirmed. Geeze, he wished things were different.

"Ryan," his uncle said. "Is there any chance you did

anything to Gillette the night of the party?"

"I don't think so."

"Look at me, Ryan,"

Dooley met his uncle's eyes.

"Did you do anything to Edward Gillette?"

"I don't think so," Dooley said again.

His uncle watched him closely. Finally he said, "Do yourself a favor. You didn't give the guy up two years ago. Don't do it now. Don't bring him into it. Okay?"

Dooley nodded.

"I mean it, Ryan."

So did Dooley. He could imagine what Graff would think if he knew about Dooley and Gillette: Dooley does time without giving up Gillette. Then Dooley finds out Gillette is the whole reason things went bad, the whole reason Dooley did what he did, the reason, when you got right down to it, that Dooley ended up doing time. So when Dooley gets out, he's already got a reason to want to get even with Gillette. Then Dooley gets interested in a girl and Gillette is stupid enough to poison the girl against him. Yeah, Graff might think Dooley had more than enough reason to want Gillette dead.

"The thing Graff asked me about Everley," Dooley said slowly. "You know, did I push him—why would he ask me that? I thought you said they decided it was an accident."

His uncle sipped his coffee. "Maybe he was just trying to shake you up," he said. "You know, try to scare you so you'll give it up on that Gillette kid. Or maybe something else came up and they took another look at Everley. I guess we'll find out when they're ready to tell us."

"What do we do until then?" Dooley said.

"We wait, Ryan. There's nothing else we can do." ■

Nineteen

That night, lights out, Dooley was in the bed in the room that he guessed at one time was his uncle's guest room, staring at the ceiling and thinking about Gillette. He'd met him back in junior high. They hadn't gone to the same school, but they hung out with some of the same people, and for a while there Dooley and Gillette had really hit it off. They fooled around together. They shoplifted stuff together—CDs and DVDs mostly—that they could sell for cash. They grabbed a few purses, but that was a pain in the ass. Too many of the women they went for, older ones who looked like they didn't have much fight in them, turned out not only to be loud and aggressive, but strong, too, like they worked out or something. It turned out that some of them did. Dooley found that out when he got arrested on a purse-snatch and went to court and the woman, who had gray hair for Christ's sake, looked all smug when she told the judge that she went to the gym almost every day, where she did a weights class and a pilates class. She sounded so proud of herself that Dooley was surprised she didn't peel off her jacket and show them all her biceps. After that time, once Dooley was in the clear again, Gillette came up with the idea of breaking into people's places when the people weren't there. He said it would be easier. They could take their time. They could walk away with more stuff than they could ever get in a purse, only now with no witnesses and no more pissed-off, middle-aged women with wrinkled faces and buff biceps whose attitude was: Bring it on, punk.

The thing with going into people's houses: you had to figure out when the people would be gone and roughly when they were likely to come back. You had to be careful, though, because the last thing you wanted was some nosy neighbor seeing you hanging around and getting suspicious and giving your description to the cops who eventually came to investigate the break-in. Gillette decided he was the expert when it came to that. He enjoyed scouting out places for them. He liked houses that backed onto ravines—nobody to see what was going on at the back of house like that—or that were located opposite parks or school yards, places where a couple of guys could hang out and fool around, you know, boys will be boys, without arousing too much suspicion and where they could keep an eye on who came and who went and when they came and went.

Dooley liked the rush he always got when he and Gillette were actually jimmying open a back door or a window. He liked sliding into a house he'd never been in before, keeping silent and praying there wasn't a person or a dog in there somewhere that they hadn't counted on. He liked moving fast through the rooms, looking for stuff they could take that would give them a decent return on the risk. He liked the adrenaline high he always got from wondering if, this very second, while he was scoring an iPod or some jewelry, the man or woman of the house was about to insert a key into the front door or back door and enter the house and hear something or see something and . . . Jesus, it was scary, but it was great, especially if, like Dooley, you were on something.

More than anything else, though, he liked the way each house was like a giant surprise package. Until you actually got inside, you never knew what you were going to find. You could tell from the outside if a place was freshly painted or if it needed a paint job. But you couldn't tell if the furniture was going to be sparse and ultra-modern or if the rooms were going to be crammed full of old-fashioned, overstuffed sofas and armchairs. You couldn't tell whether the kids' rooms were going to be overflowing with toys and electronics or whether you'd find porn videos and magazines on the top shelf of a closet in some teenager's room or, you never know, in the parents' room. Some places were really nice—fresh and new, warm and cosy, the kind of place Dooley wished he lived in but couldn't quite imagine himself fitting into. He liked to lie down on the beds that looked comfortable and was always pleased when they turned out to feel as cushiony as he'd hoped. He liked to check out the clothes in the closets and always wished he could take some of the stuff that was especially nice, but clothes were bulky and you couldn't get much for them and you sure couldn't walk around wearing them because what if the person whose house you had robbed saw you on the street, just by chance? It wasn't worth the risk.

Every place he had ever broken into, he had broken into with Gillette—including the last place, the place where the woman lived. He hadn't admitted it to anyone—not his uncle, not even Dr. Calvin—but that woman had kept him up more nights than Lorraine ever had. Gillette had picked the house. He said the location was perfect. There were a lot of old people who lived on the street, and they all went to bed early. By ten o'clock, he said, the street looked like it was blacked out. And the people who lived in the house he'd picked out were out of town. Gillette had watched them put a bunch of suitcases in the back of the car and drive away. He said with that many suitcases, they'd probably be gone for a couple of weeks, which was good. He said that if they went into the place sooner rather than later, it would be weeks before any even noticed that stuff was missing. They'd have it sold, he said, before the woman and her husband even got to where they were going. Gillette even slipped around back after they were gone. He pretended to be looking for his dog, in case anyway saw him. But he said he was pretty sure no one did. He checked the place out. He said they could get in a back window, easy.

They decided to go in the next night. Dooley killed the day by getting stoned. He didn't say anything to Gillette, but the truth was, he was pretty wasted by the time they got to the place. Gillette was right about the street being quiet. There were no lights on anywhere. Gillette seemed to hesitate when they were standing out on the sidewalk.

"Come on," Dooley urged him. He'd brought his baseball bat with him. He took it whenever he and Gillette went out together. His working theory at the time: he could always tell whoever wanted to know—like the cops—that he was on his way home from a pickup game in the park.

Gillette still didn't move. Dooley glanced around. True, there were no lights on anywhere. But you never knew when some old lady was going to get up to use the bathroom and then look out the window on her way back to bed. Old people like that, they know who belongs in the neighborhood and who doesn't. Gillette was looking around and frowning.

"What's the matter?" Dooley said.

"Nothing," Gillette said. He nodded down the street. "Come on."

He led Dooley around the side of the house. They pried open a window, no sweat. And then they got to work. Dooley was in the dining room, checking the credenza, when he heard Gillette mutter a single word: "Shit." Then Gillette yelled, "Look out!" which is when Dooley grabbed his baseball bat, which was propped up against the credenza. He saw a shadow coming at him, and he swung at it.

His lawyer asked him later, "What were you thinking?" Dooley didn't answer. What could he say? He saw that shadow and everything in his head just went red, then it went black, and he swung.

The shadow turned out to be a woman who, if you asked Dooley, would have made a good stealth burglar. She was fifty-four years old and she walked like a cat, even in high heels.

The bat connected with her head—no, that wasn't right. Jesus, after all that therapy, after all those groups, he could at least say it right to himself when he was lying alone in his room in the dark, couldn't he? He swung his baseball bat and he cracked her a good one on the head. He could still hear the sound the wood and the bone had made when they came into contact with each other. When he heard it that night, something lurched in his stomach, and he dropped the bat. He looked at the woman lying there on the floor. Even as out of it as he was, he couldn't believe what he had done. Then he ran. Gillette was already gone. It wasn't until Dooley was maybe ten blocks away that he realized he'd left the bat on the floor next to the woman.

The cops got prints off the bat and matched them to prints of his that they had taken when he'd been arrested a couple of months earlier for that stupid purse-snatching, that middle-aged lady body-builder. They arrested Dooley.

It turned out that the woman had suffered permanent brain damage and permanent motor damage. Her husband had sat in the front row during Dooley's trial. Before sentencing, he told everyone that his wife was probably never going to walk again, might not talk either. He stared at Dooley when he said it.

At first Dooley had felt bad, about being caught, not about the woman. Now he felt bad about everything.

■ ■ ■

How do rumors get started? Who's rumormonger zero, the one who sees something or hears something and decides he (or she) is going to take responsibility for putting it out there? Dooley wondered about that on Monday, when his uncle insisted that he go to school even though school was the last thing Dooley wanted to think about.

"You've got to hold it together," his uncle said. "You're not charged with anything. And you're still on a supervision order. One of the conditions is you have to attend school regularly."

"Even if I can't concentrate?"

"Force yourself, Ryan. As long as they haven't made an arrest, they're still investigating."

"What if they've already made up their minds? What if all they're doing is investigating ways to make it stick to me?"

"Well, then you're screwed," his uncle said. Dooley couldn't tell if he was kidding.

As soon as Dooley got to school, he noticed that people were looking at him a certain way, even his teachers. Also, people whispered behind their hands to each other, even his teachers. The only person who came up to him and said anything was Rhodes. He said, "They talked to me about Eddy. They talked to Bracey and Landers. They probably talked to everyone who was at the party."

Dooley had the impression that Rhodes was trying to make him feel better. If he was, he wasn't succeeding. Dooley was willing to bet that no one else had had a beef with

Gillette that night, that no one else had history with Gillette, and that no one else had a record like Dooley's.

"So what did they say to you?" Rhodes said.

"The usual," Dooley said. "When did I see him last, did I have any problems with him, that kind of stuff."

"And?" Rhodes said.

Dooley didn't want to talk about it. Then he didn't have to—the bell rang.

■ ■ ■

At lunchtime, Dooley walked down the street to the Chinese restaurant that he always went to. He ordered cashew chicken, steamed rice, and green tea. This time he didn't read while he ate. Instead, he wondered what his chances were.

The first thing he thought about (and, boy, there were countless people who would have loved this one, from Calvin to Kingston to his uncle) was that he was in this mess because he had screwed up. If he'd stuck to ginger ale, none of it would have happened.

Maybe.

You could stick to ginger ale and someone could still slip something into your drink. But if he hadn't been drinking, he would have noticed that, right? If he'd been behaving the way he was supposed to and someone had slipped something into his drink and he'd started feeling all loopy and weird, he would have known something wasn't right (although he may not have been able to do much about it). But after a couple of glasses of champagne and (if he was being honest with himself) who knew how many other drinks, it was hard to tell what was what. So it was his own damned fault. No one had twisted his arm; no one had forced him to swallow any of those drinks. He had to accept responsibility for that.

The second thing: he wondered if they were going to arrest him, even if it was only on the smash-and-grab, and, if they did, what his chances were of staying out of custody. Probably not good, given that he was out on supervision now, the idea being he could stay out (and supervised) if he kept his nose clean, and he could expect to go back for the remainder of his disposition if he got into any trouble. The number one most important thing right now: pray he didn't get arrested and, for fuck's sake, don't do anything else that would attract the attention of the cops.

He'd met a guy one time who had told him that being outside was always better than being inside, even if you were only out on bail. Dooley had been quick to agree. If you were out, you weren't locked up. People couldn't tell you what to do (although they could lay some conditions on you, tell you what *not* to do). They couldn't tell you when to do it. They couldn't stop you from having at least some fun. But, no, this guy meant something different. This guy said, first, if you hadn't done whatever you'd been arrested for—which, frankly, had never been the case with Dooley—and you were outside instead of inside, it was good because, first, when you finally went to court, you didn't come in as a prisoner, you came in as a free person, which influenced how other people looked at you and how you felt about yourself and how you acted. Second, it was good because if the cops had arrested you, that meant that they were committed to you being the one who had done whatever it was. But—always assuming you really hadn't done it—if you were outside, you could at least try to do something to get yourself off the hook. You could do things you'd never have a chance to do if they decided to remand you until your court date.

Take Dooley's situation—Dooley chewed on his cashew chicken at the same time he was chewing on this—assume it came down to the cops (read: Graff) thinking that Dooley had had something to do with what had happened to Gillette. In that case, Graff would be working that side of it. Dooley, on the other hand, was pretty sure that he'd had nothing to do with it—he wished he could be certain, but he wasn't. And there weren't too many people who were going to be working Dooley's side of it. So it was up to Dooley. If they arrested him, or if, for whatever reason (and there were plenty to choose from) Al Szabo decided to send him back, there would be nothing he could do to try to prove he hadn't been involved (still assuming he hadn't). But that hadn't happened yet. He was still out, which meant he could do *something*. What, he wasn't sure. But something.

He chewed some chicken.

He didn't remember much about what had happened at the party after he'd had that second Coke and whatever-the-hell it was. But there had been plenty of people at the party—people who *had* seen things, people who had talked to the cops, people who might be willing to answer a few questions if Dooley asked them.

Who to ask? Who had been there? Who did he remember?

He started with the girl who had been with Rhodes that night, for the simple reason that she was the first person he ran into, almost literally. He was striding down the hall, running down the list of people whose names he remembered and trying to think of others whose faces he remembered, when she stepped right in front of him. It turned out she was coming out of the girls' bathroom. She looked annoyed at first, like how dare someone be standing in the exact place she wanted to be, but as soon as she registered who he was, she lightened up. He saw for the first time that she had green eyes and a cute little nose. She was waiting for him to say something. So he said, "Hi."

"Hi, yourself," she said, offering him a little smile.

"Jen, right?" he said.

"Right." She sounded amused by his uncertainty.

"Look, Jen, this is a little embarrassing—"

Her smile got wider. She had great teeth—straight as soldiers on parade, white as newly scrubbed porcelain.

"—but I was wondering, last weekend, at that party . . ." Geeze, he wished he'd never taken that glass of champagne from Bracey. "What do you remember?"

"What do *I* remember?" She laughed. "I remember everything. What do *you* remember?"

He met her sassy green eyes. Well, he told himself, it was hardly the first time someone had asked him that question. He told her more or less what he recalled (he left out the part about calling his uncle—how lame was that?—and the part about Landers and the maid—he didn't know what she thought of Landers, so why complicate things?). He ended with shooting pool with Bracey after Landers had made his toast.

"After that," he said, "it gets a little hazy."

"You're one of those guys, when they drink, they get aggressive, right?" she said.

Dooley waited.

"I saw you shoving Eddy around," she said. He wondered if the cops had talked to her yet. He wondered how many other people had told Graff what she was telling him now. "Before that, you went after Peter."

"Do you know what that was about?"

"Yeah," she said. "First, he was pissed off because he thought you were hitting on Megan."

"First?" Dooley said.

"Yeah. Then he started telling everybody you beat up Mark one time. That sure was news to Beth." She shook her head. "She's all broken up about him being dead. She's doing that whole scholarship thing. But I get the impression she and Mark didn't communicate much. Anyway, when she heard what Peter was saying, she freaked out. Win calmed her down, but she left pretty soon after that. That's when you went after Peter. Win and Marcus had to break it up."

Jesus. Rhodes hadn't told him *that*. Dooley hoped that she was exaggerating. Hoped? Hell, he prayed.

"And after that?"

Jen shrugged. "After that I saw you shoving Eddy around."

"Do you know what *that* was about?"

She shook her head. "I didn't stick around to find out, either. It was getting boring, you know?" She looked hard at him, like she was trying to decide whether to tell him something. In the end she just said, “I gotta run.”

■ ■ ■

Dooley circled the schoolyard after school, approaching girls mostly. Some of them backed up a pace when he stopped to talk to them. Some of them looked surprised and a little interested when he went up to them. One of them finally told him where he could find Megan. It turned out she lived only a few streets away from Dooley’s uncle. She grinned at him when she answered the door and came out on the porch to talk to him.

“I don’t remember everything,” she said. “I was having fun, you know?”

He had an idea, but just so he was clear: “Drinking?”

“Yeah, that. And other stuff.”

“Drugs?”

“A little smoke,” she said. “I’m not into anything else.”

“Did I hit on you?”

She laughed. “I wish,” she said.

“But Landers . . . Peter thought I did,” Dooley said.

“Peter gets jealous,” she said. “Over nothing.” She stepped in close to him. “You have a girlfriend, Dooley?”

He stepped back. “Did you notice what time I left?”

She shook her head. “After that thing with Peter, I had to stick pretty close to him. I didn’t want him to hurt you. Or vice versa. Especially vice versa.” She winked at him, which made him wonder how much she had heard about him. “I lost track of you.”

“What about you? When did you leave?”

"Around two."

"With Landers?"

"With Peter, yeah. Also with Marcus and Eddy."

That was news. "Gillette left with you?"

She nodded.

"Did he go home?"

"I have no idea," she said. "We got into a cab . . ."

"You and Landers and Bracey and Gillette?"

"Yeah," she said. "Well, me and Peter anyway. I had a lot to drink and Peter was all over me. I think the cab driver threatened to throw us out." She thought for a moment. "Or maybe Peter just said that, you know, kidding around. I think the cab stopped a couple of times. Maybe the other two got out along the way. You should ask Peter. I think he was in better shape than me. All I remember is he walked me to the door and then he took off. He's afraid of my dad. My dad always blames Peter if I come home drunk or whatever."

"Where did Peter go when he left you? Home?"

"I guess so," Megan said.

"And you don't know where Gillette got out of the cab?" It sounded like she didn't even know if he'd got into the cab in the first place.

"Sorry," she said, smiling up at him. If anyone else looked at him the way she was looking at him now, he'd have thought it meant something. But he was getting the idea that Megan just liked to put it out there for fun. She liked to play.

Before he left, she told him where Bracey lived. When Dooley turned to leave the porch, he saw Landers standing down on the front walk, his lip curled up like he was trying to avoid a bad smell. Dooley went down the porch steps. Landers blocked his way. He was as tall as Dooley and looked like he was in pretty good shape. Looked like a scrapper, too. Dooley thought about asking him the same questions he'd asked Megan, but decided against it. He was pretty sure Landers wouldn't answer anyway. He was getting more and more sure about a lot of things to do with Landers. So instead of saying anything, Dooley met Landers' eyes and let him see in them everything he had probably heard about Dooley. Then, holding that look, he stepped around Landers.

He went to Bracey's house next, but Bracey wasn't home. No one was. He checked his watch. Time for work. ■

Twenty

He ran into Bracey on the way to the video store. Bracey was standing outside a pizza place, chewing on a slice that he had rolled up so that he could jam it into his mouth more easily. His face changed when he spotted Dooley. Bracey wasn't like Everley or Landers. He was more like Rhodes, quieter, not a scrapper. He tossed what was left of his pizza and turned away from Dooley, trying to be casual about it but, Dooley guessed, eager to be on his way. When Dooley caught up with him and dropped a hand on his shoulder, Bracey stiffened, making Dooley feel like The Ice Man, a superhero who could freeze people solid just by touching them. Used to be Dooley would get off on a power like that. Now he just thought: shit.

"Hey, Marcus, I need to ask you something," he said, pushing some jolly into his voice so Bracey wouldn't wet himself. He circled around Bracey so that he could look him in the eye.

Bracey was as twitchy as a rabbit. "I heard they found

Eddy," he said.

"I heard he left the party with you," Dooley said.

Bracey's eyes widened. "What are you saying? Are you saying you think *I* had something to do with what happened to him?"

"You all went home in a cab together, you and Landers and Gillette and Megan, right? Where did you let Gillette off?" Dooley said.

"Eddy didn't come with us," Bracey said.

"But Megan said—"

"Megan was wasted. We walked down to St. Clair together. Peter, Megan, and I got in a cab—we all live in the same direction. Eddy said he was going to take the bus."

"What about me?"

"What about you?" Bracey said, surprised.

"When did I leave?"

"How would I know?"

"So you didn't see me leave?"

"I saw you take a few swings at Eddy. And at Peter."

"That's it?"

Bracey nodded.

"But you saw Gillette get on the bus?"

"Sure," Bracey said. He thought about it for a moment and then frowned. "A bus was coming just as we got into the cab. So, yeah, he must have got on."

Must have.

"You didn't see him get on?"

Bracey looked at him.

"He said he was going home," he said. "So he must have

got on." But Dooley could tell that he was wondering now. And that made Dooley wonder, too.

■ ■ ■

Mostly work was stupid and boring, especially on Monday nights. On Monday nights, the biggest challenge was to find some way to look busy (if you were on shift with Kevin, which Dooley was) so that Kevin didn't drive you crazy with his *Have you done this? Have you done that*? and you didn't, as a result, want to kill him. Dooley was walking the aisles, checking to make sure that the new titles were displayed face out and that everything was in the right section and, within each section, that everything was shelved so that the customers could find things right away, assuming they knew the title they were looking for (they didn't always) and assuming they could spell (they couldn't always). That meant a lot of re-shelving, some of it on account of customers picking things up and then changing their minds and putting things back down wherever they felt like instead of in the right place, and some of it on account of Linelle, who had her own system of shelving, based, Dooley believed, on her contempt for the alphabet, the film industry, and the customer—not necessarily in that order. Linelle put stuff where people would be least likely to look for it, like *Pretty Woman* in the Fantasy section or *Natural Born Killers* under Education/Self-Help.

He heard the electronic *bong* that sounded every time someone came through the door, but he didn't turn to see who it was. Kevin was up front at the cash. Let him keep an eye out for potential shoplifters. Dooley continued with his alphabetizing. He didn't stop until he heard a sound like a whoop, someone either thrilled about something or mad about something. He started to turn toward the sound when someone clamped his arms to his sides. What the—?

Oh.

It was her.

She hugged him tightly and beamed at him.

"Hey, Alicia," Dooley said. "How's it going?"

He glanced around, looking for the woman who had started coming in with her after the incident with Everley and Landers. Who he saw instead was the geek from school, Warren, standing halfway up the aisle gaping at him. Dooley gently pried Alicia's arms loose. He looked at Warren, who came down the aisle now and took one of Alicia's hands and pulled her away from him. He said something to her in a quiet voice and she said something back. Dooley walked up to the cash so that they could have some privacy.

"You finished straightening all the titles?" Kevin said, without looking up from what he was doing, which was reading some new inserts to the employee manual.

Before Dooley could answer, a voice behind him said, "It was you?"

Dooley turned to look at Warren. Alicia wasn't with him. She was over in the documentary section, probably looking for the penguin movie that she had already rented half a dozen times.

"It *was* you, wasn't it?" Warren said. He sounded stunned.

Out of the corner of his eye, Dooley saw Kevin straighten up, his radar telling him that something was going on in *his* store.

Alicia came toward the cash with a DVD case. She held it out to Dooley, even though he was standing in front of the counter and Kevin was behind it at the cash register. Dooley ducked through the opening, nudged Kevin aside, and took the DVD case from her. He was right; it was the penguin movie again. He smiled at her as he scanned the case and told her how much it was. He waited patiently while she hunted in her pocket for the money. She had the exact change. She always did. Dooley put the DVD in a bag and passed it across the counter to her. Warren was still staring at him.

"Wait for me over there," he said to her, pointing to the new releases. "I won't be long, I promise." She did what he told her.

"She usually comes in with someone else," Dooley said.

"My cousin," Warren said. "You're really the one?"

"He's the one what?" Kevin said. It was driving him crazy that he didn't know what was going on.

Dooley slipped out from behind the counter and headed back to where he had been re-shelving in the Action/Adventure aisle, putting back the Bruce Willis, Sylvester Stallone, and Steven Sagal movies that Linelle had shelved in the Comedy section. Warren trailed after him.

"Look," Dooley said, "it's no big deal."

"Yeah, but of all the people—" He shut up when Dooley gave him a look. "What I meant was—"

"Forget it, okay?" Dooley said. Jesus, he'd done what any decent person would have done and this guy couldn't get over it. What did that say about Dooley? "You should just buy her that movie," he said.

"What?"

"The penguin movie. The number of times she's rented that one, she could have bought it already, plus another one."

"If she owned it," Warren said, "she wouldn't have to come here and rent it every week."

"My point," Dooley said.

Warren shook his head. "She *likes* coming here. She likes to come and see Ryan. That's you, right?" Like he still couldn't believe it. "One of the reasons they were giving her a hard time," he said, "is because of me. They told her, no wonder she's the way she is, she has me for a brother."

■ ■ ■

Two days later, Dooley felt like a guy who had been holding his breath forever. He hadn't heard any more from the cops. He got up every morning, as usual. He went to school every day, as usual. He did his assignments. He occasionally stuck up his hand in class but wasn't ever called on, which was fine with him. He went home every day to change for work, he spent his breaks doing homework, and he reached for the phone maybe a hundred times to call Beth. But that's all he did—reached out, maybe picked up the receiver, maybe looked at it, and then put it back down again.

He was up at the cash Wednesday night, telling a kid, sorry, no way, unless you can prove to me you're eighteen, you are not renting that game, when he heard "Jesus H. Murphy!" and saw Kevin charge out of the store. Dooley turned to look through the window. Kevin was out on the sidewalk flapping his arms at a scruffy guy who had his hands on the glass and his nose pressed against it, peering into the store. The guy paid no attention to Kevin, whose mouth was flapping. Dooley made out a few words: loitering, vagrant, police. Whatever. Dooley snatched the game from the kid's hand. "Come back when you're eighteen," he said, and seriously wondered what kind of boring excuse for a life you'd have to have at eighteen to want to rent that piece-of-crap game. Another customer approached the counter with a couple of DVDs. Dooley was reaching for them when someone thumped on the glass. Dooley turned to look. It was the scruffy guy. He thumped again, harder this time, when Dooley made eye contact with him. The glass in the window shook.

"If you don't stop that, I'll call the police," Kevin said, his voice loud and clear even through the window.

It all came together in a nanosecond. The scruffy guy went from being just another drugged-up or cheap-liquored-up or maybe just plain fucked-up nuisance of a bum to being a drugged-up or cheap-liquored-up or maybe just plain fucked-up nuisance of a bum with a backpack slung over one shoulder—a red backpack with black trim and net pockets. Dooley scooted around the counter and headed for the door.

"Hey!" the customer said.

"Back in a minute," Dooley said. He went outside where the first thing Kevin said to him was, "It's not time for your break yet. Get back inside and watch the store."

The homeless guy swung away from the glass so that he was face to face with Kevin, who wrinkled his nose and scuttled back a pace.

"Why don't you let me handle this?" Dooley said.

Kevin looked from Dooley to the homeless guy and said, "You've got three minutes to get rid of him before I call the cops."

Prick, Dooley thought. He waited until Kevin went back inside the store before he said to the homeless guy, "Are you looking for me?"

"I heard someone was looking for this," he said. He untangled himself from the backpack and held it out to Dooley. "I heard there was a reward." He talked in a slurry mumble. Dooley had to listen closely to get what he was saying.

Dooley told the guy that he was the one who was looking for the backpack. He told him that all he had on him was fifteen dollars and change. He said the nearest ATM was a few blocks away and his break wasn't for another hour. He gave the guy what he had on him and asked him if he could stick around until he got off. The guy just shrugged and handed Dooley the backpack. Dooley wondered if he was simple-minded or fogged; he'd handed over the pack without being paid in full.

"Where did you find it?" Dooley said. The guy gave him

a blank look. "The backpack," Dooley said. "Where did you find it?"

"On a kid," the guy said. "He was dead."

On a kid. Geeze.

"Did you see him go over?" Dooley said.

The guy shook his head.

"Did you see anything?" Dooley said.

The guy looked at him. "I saw you."

Dooley wondered if he was the person he had seen going around the corner back there in the ravine that night. He said, "Wait here, okay? I'll be back out on my break. One hour."

Dooley went back inside the store. By then, Kevin was in the games section, harassing some kids. At least, that's what it looked like. Dooley stashed the backpack in one of the cupboards under the counter. He looked out the window a couple of times and saw that the guy was still out there, standing patiently next to a utility pole, reading an advertisement that promised you could make *Big $$$$ In Your Own Home!!!* Then things got busy. Dooley rang up more rentals than he would have thought possible for a Wednesday night until, finally, it was time for his break. He looked outside again. The homeless guy was gone. Dooley went outside to look for him—he spent his whole break checking the neighborhood. The guy was definitely gone.

■ ■ ■

When Dooley went off shift, he took the backpack with him. His uncle called to him from the back of the house when he came through the front door. Dooley tossed the backpack into the hall closet. His uncle was sharp enough that he would notice it and, if Dooley lived up to his promise to be straight, probably tell him what an idiot he was for monkeying with it. He went through to the kitchen.

"I want you to come home right after school tomorrow," his uncle said. "We have an appointment."

"Appointment?"

"With a lawyer. Just in case this thing goes somewhere."

What did that mean—*goes somewhere*?

His uncle looked at him for a few moments.

"You okay, Ryan?"

Other than needing a lawyer just in case the cops decided to charge him with a murder, never mind that smash-and-grab he couldn't believe he had done, no matter how out of it he was, "Yeah, sure. I'm going upstairs, okay?"

He snagged the backpack from the hall closet on his way. ■

Twenty-One

Dooley dropped the backpack onto his bed. The smartest thing to do, he knew, would be to go right back downstairs, show his uncle the backpack, tell him exactly how it had come into his possession, and get his uncle to take it to the cops. Graff would probably be suspicious. He'd probably have his own ideas about how Dooley all of a sudden happened to have Mark Everley's backpack and was surrendering it. But Dooley could describe the guy who'd given it to him and Kevin could back him up that the guy had showed up at the store. Yeah, let the cops handle it. That was the probably the smart thing to do.

But he didn't do it. He couldn't. Not with all the stuff that was swirling around in his head.

Gillette was dead.

Dooley had a past with Gillette.

People had seen Dooley and Gillette in some kind of fight together the night Gillette disappeared.

The cops wanted to know, Ryan, did you kill Edward

Gillette? (What if Graff found out that Gillette had been with him that night in the house? Maybe it had been a mistake to tell his uncle. Jesus, what had he been thinking? His uncle used to be a cop. Once a cop, always a cop. What if his uncle had second thoughts? What if he felt obliged to tell Graff everything he knew? Or what if Graff decided to question his uncle formally? There was no way his uncle would sit there and lie to a fellow cop. For sure there was no way he'd lie in court, if it came to that.)

There was more.

Gillette had come up to him that time and asked him if he thought someone had pushed Everley off that bridge. Why would he ask that? Boy, there was a question Dooley wished he had asked, but it was too late now.

And now the cops were saying: Hey, Ryan, did *you* push Mark Everley?

That was something else. Everley was dead. Gillette was dead.

Everley and Gillette hung around together.

What were the chances that two guys who hung around together would die within a couple of weeks of each other, one maybe an accident, maybe not, the other definitely not?

What was going on?

Whatever it was, Dooley didn't want to be involved in it. He didn't want to go down for it, either. Which meant that he should at least take a look at Everley's backpack, be on top of the situation for a change, be the one finding things out instead of the one the cops sprang stuff on. Besides, he'd been the one to find the backpack.

He sat down on his bed and opened the pack. Beth had said her brother always had it with him. He had his camera in it. He had notebooks that he wrote in. Who knew what else was in there?

Sure enough, there were four notebooks, the hard-covered kind, held together with a big rubber band. But there was no camera. He wondered if that was why the homeless guy had taken off without waiting for more money. Maybe he'd already taken the camera. Maybe he'd sold it.

Besides the notebook, Dooley found a lighter, half a pack of cigarettes, a couple of pens, a mechanical pencil, a strip of rubbers, a copy of *Hamlet* with a school stamp in it, and, in a small pocket, some loose change, and a key ring with three keys on it.

He pulled the rubber band off the notebooks and flipped through them one by one. They were filled with writing and sketches. Stories, Beth had said. She'd said some of them were good. Dooley scanned some pages and read others. He wondered if Beth had actually read any of her brother's stories. If she had, he wondered what she liked about them. They were all about gangs and violence, guns and knives, grudges and revenge—and they all read like the storylines of direct-to-DVD movies, the kind that no-talent guys like Jean-Claude Van Damme made and that only left the Action/Adventure shelf to go to the sale bin, five-ninety-five, they were that bad.

Some stuff fell out of one of the notebooks—a business card and some scraps of paper. The card was for someone named Bryce Weathers. It had the name, address, and phone number of an immigrant and refugee organization on it and someone—Everley?—had scrawled another name on it: Sara. Dooley flipped it into his wastepaper basket. Ditto the scraps of paper—they looked like something Everley or someone else had photocopied from the newspaper and then ripped up.

He jammed the notebooks back into the backpack and started to re-zip all the zippered pockets s when he felt something else. Something small and hard. He looked into the pocket, but didn't see anything. He saw then that there was a hole in one of the seams. He pushed his finger through it and poked around. There was something in there all right, something that had slipped into the lining. He pulled it out. It was a small rectangular object, maybe half an inch wide, three inches long, and a quarter of an inch thick. The lettering on it said USB Storage, 512 MB. A data storage device. Dooley wondered what was on it. A guy who wrote stories might write other stuff. It was possible.

He took the device into the middle bedroom, which his uncle had turned into an office and study. The place was lined with bookshelves. It also had a big oak desk and, beside that, a computer table with a gigantic, ancient desktop computer on it. Dooley checked it out, but there was no place to plug in the storage device. They probably hadn't been invented when Dooley's uncle had bought the computer, which was probably back when Dooley was in elementary school. Okay, so that wasn't going to work. He needed a more up-to-date computer. And he knew just where to find a whole roomful of them.

He went back into his room, closed the door, tossed the USB data device onto his dresser, and dropped the backpack into his closet. He would take the device to school tomorrow and check it out. After that, he would do the smart thing. He would tell his uncle about the backpack after he'd checked out the device and let his uncle stickhandle its surrender to the cops. He wondered if the cops would return it to Beth right away or if they'd hang onto it for a while, and supposed that depended on how they were looking at Everley's death, whether they really thought someone had pushed him or whether Graff had been trying to bluff him.

He got ready for bed and then lay there, thinking about Beth. She was why he'd gone looking for the backpack in the first place. He wanted to make her happy—well, less sad—by offering her something to make up for refusing to be hypnotized. The way it looked now, he'd have to get hit by a car or pushed over a cliff to accomplish that goal. She seemed to hate him as much as she'd loved her brother. And that was something, too, the fact that she was so fierce in her love for Everley. Either the guy must have had some good qualities or Beth was one hundred percent blind to his shortcomings. Dooley thought maybe it was a combination of both.

■ ■ ■

Dooley grabbed the USB device off his dresser the next morning and dropped it into the pocket of his jean jacket. During his spare, which was just before lunch, he went into the computer room. There was a teacher in there, watching over the equipment while she graded test papers. Her name, Dooley knew, was Ms Hurley, and she was new to teaching. The expression on her face when Dooley appeared and asked if he could use a computer was both startled and nervous. She started to say something—it seemed to Dooley that she was getting ready to say no, maybe to make up some lame excuse why he couldn't—when two girls appeared with the same question. Ms Hurley assigned the girls a machine right up front, making them a buffer, Dooley realized, between herself and him. She waved Dooley to a machine at the back of the room, which was fine with him.

He had no trouble finding a place to plug in the device. He had no trouble looking at the directory—there were a lot of files on the device, and, from what he could see, most of them were big. Geeze, did Everley have entire novels on there or what? He clicked on a couple of the files names, but all that came up on the screen was page after page of gibberish. Some files he couldn't open at all.

"Problem?" said a quiet voice beside him.

Dooley turned cautiously and saw Warren, two computer stations away—when had he come in?—craning his neck to look at the screen in front of Dooley.

"Looks like you're using the wrong program," he said. He didn't come any closer, either respecting Dooley's privacy or afraid to approach him.

"How do I know what's the right program?" Dooley said. He'd never taken much interest in computers. He hadn't had much access except at school and then there had always been so many restrictions on what you could and couldn't do that what was the point?

"Well, what kind of files are they?" Warren said.

Dooley was lost and felt stupid because of it.

"You want me to take a look?" Warren said.

Dooley hesitated. Then, what the hell, he was getting nowhere on his own. "Yeah, okay," he said.

Warren got up, came over to where Dooley was, hooking a chair on the way, and sat down next to Dooley. Dooley moved his own chair over so that Warren could get a good look at the screen. The chair legs scraped against the surface of the floor. Ms Hurley looked up from what she was doing. As soon as Dooley made eye contact with her, she looked down again, her cheeks pink. Warren glanced at her, then at Dooley. He kept his voice quiet when he said, "Well, there's your problem right there."

"What?" Dooley said.

"They're not data files."

Dooley looked blankly at him.

"They're images, right?" Warren said.

"Images?"

"Photographs," Warren said, sounding surprised to be telling Dooley what was on the device instead of the other way around. He clicked the mouse, pulling up one screen after another, clicking in and out of them so fast that Dooley didn't have a chance to even understand what he was looking at. "I didn't think so," Warren said at last.

"Didn't think what?" Dooley said.

"They don't have the right program here. You can't access these files."

"Oh." Dooley looked at the computer screen. "What kind of program do I need?"

When Warren told him, Dooley didn't know what to do with the information.

"If you want me to," Warren said, "you could come over to my place after school. You can take a look at them there."

"I can't," Dooley said.

Warren's face changed. "Okay, well, whatever," he said.

"I don't mean I don't want to," Dooley said, because he knew that's what Warren was thinking. "I mean I can't. I have an appointment."

"Okay, so what about now?" Warren said. "I live about a block from here."

"Okay," Dooley said.

"Yeah?" Warren said, his mood buoyed.

"Sure," Dooley said. He reached to pull the USB out of the port at the back of the computer. "Whoa!" Warren said. "You have to eject that first." He showed Dooley how.

■ ■ ■

They went out the back way—Warren's idea, not Dooley's—and at first Dooley was glad. After all, who wanted to be seen with a geek like Warren? He looked at Warren as they walked quickly across the school yard and saw that Warren was scanning the area, checking, Dooley realized, to see if anyone noticed that he was with Dooley and pleased (it seemed to Dooley) that a few of the people who were outside glanced in their direction. Dooley thought then that maybe Beth was right. Maybe, despite everything that he had done and all the regrets he had, some people did think he was kind of cool. Warren was sure acting as if he did.

It turned out that Warren lived on the next street over from the school. You could see the football field from his bedroom window. The house was small, but neat, and it smelled like a bakery.

"My mom makes extra money baking and decorating cakes," Warren said when Dooley sniffed the air appreciatively. He didn't say why she needed the extra money, and Dooley didn't ask.

Warren's room was smaller than some bathrooms that Dooley had been in. It contained one single bed; one desk, the kind with the writing surface that you folded down when you needed to work and folded back up again out of the way when you were done; one triangle-shaped computer table that was wedged into a corner, and a set of bookshelves that ran all the way up to the ceiling and that was jammed with books and stacks of computer magazines. Dooley figured he had come to the right place.

Warren sat down at the triangle-shaped computer table and within minutes started displaying photographs on his computer screen. There were dozens of them—landscapes and portraits, shots of people Dooley had seen around school and shots of complete strangers. Shots of Rhodes and Bracey and Landers and of their girlfriends. Shots of Beth that took Dooley's breath away.

"These are pretty good," Warren said.

Dooley looked at him. "Why do you say that?"

"The composition is interesting," Warren said. "And the framing. There are no lampshades growing out of people's heads, you know, stuff like that that amateurs do. They look into the camera and they just snap away. They don't think about what's really there. Plus, the portraits are nice. Tight, you know. Focused right in there on the subject. They give you a sense of what the person is like, you know." He showed Dooley four different pictures—one of Rhodes, one of Landers and Bracey together, one of a Rhodes and Bracey, and one of Beth. Dooley stared at the one of Beth—she looked like an angel, sweet and kind and soft, which, in a way, she was. But that wasn't all she was.

"How can you know from a picture what someone is really like?" Dooley said, because he'd seen a different side of Beth, one that was angry and stubborn.

"Well, the ones I know, these pictures pretty much confirm how I feel about them," Warren said. He clicked the mouse, his finger twitching so fast that the screen went from pictures to disk indexes and folders, to more pictures. Then he said, "Stalled" and looked expectantly at Dooley.

"What?" Dooley said.

Warren nodded at the screen. A little box had popped up, asking for a password. Dooley shook his head.

"These aren't yours, are they?" Warren said, his tone telling Dooley that he had probably known it right from the start.

"No," Dooley said. There didn't seem to be any point in lying. He waited to see what Warren would say next.

Warren looked at Dooley and shook his head. Then he

turned back to the screen. "Some of these files are password protected," he said. "I can't get into them unless you give me the password."

"I don't have it," Dooley said.

Warren leaned back in his chair.

Dooley looked at the stacks of computer magazines on Warren's shelves. Warren must know a lot about computers if he had all those magazines.

"There must be some way to see what's in them," Dooley said.

Warren shook his head. "You put a password on these files and it's like locking them up in a safe. If these were my files and I put a password on them and then I forgot the password, it would be like I forgot the combination to the safe. There'd be no way I could get into them."

Dooley wondered why Everley had files that were as good as in a safe. He said, "There's always someone who can get into a safe."

Warren sat quietly for a few moments, staring at the computer screen.

"Whose flash drive is this?" he said finally.

"What difference does it make?"

"Most people, when they make up a password, they either make up something complicated that they have to write down or they use something that they know they're going to remember. If you know the person, you can at least come up with some possibilities—that is, if the password is something that means something to them. If it's something complicated that they wrote down and hid somewhere, that's another story."

"So either the password is written down somewhere," Dooley said. He thought about all that scribbling in all those hard-covered notebooks in Everley's backpack, which right now was in Dooley's closet. "Or it's something that someone might be able to figure out."

"Well," Warren said, "you've got the flash drive, so you know who it belongs to, right?"

Dooley didn't say anything.

Warren stared at the computer screen for a few moments. Then, without looking at Dooley, he said, "It belongs to Mark Everley, doesn't it? The people pictures—they're all people he hung around with. And that's his sister."

Dooley reached for the flash drive. Warren put out a hand to stop him.

"I have to eject it first," he reminded Dooley. Then he said, "I'll take a shot at it if you want me to."

"You mean, you can figure out how to open those files?"

"I can't guarantee anything," Warren said. "But I can try."

Dooley looked into Warren's small gray eyes, set in his too-round face with its not-too-great complexion, surrounded by his wispy blond hair.

"Leave it with me overnight," Warren said. "If I can't crack it, I'll give it back to you, no harm done." When Dooley still hesitated, he said, "Let me try, you know, for my sister. Okay?"

"Okay," Dooley said.

■ ■ ■

Dooley went straight home after school so that he could go with his uncle to meet the lawyer his uncle had hired. It turned out the lawyer, a woman in her forties wearing a sharp-looking suit, had come to the house. It turned out she was there because Dooley's uncle had called her as soon as he opened the door to the police, who had a warrant to search the house—again. By the time Dooley got there, they had torn apart Dooley's bedroom, his uncle's bedroom, both bathrooms, the living room, the dining room, Dooley's uncle's home office, and the laundry room and storage area in the basement, and were working on the kitchen. But as far as Dooley could see, they had found all they were going to find and that amounted to exactly one item, which Dooley saw sitting on the coffee table the minute he walked into the house. Dooley's uncle was sitting on the couch, staring at it. The lawyer in her sharp-looking suit was standing on one side of the table talking to Detective Graff. All three of them turned their heads when Dooley entered the room. Dooley noticed right away that his uncle looked completely different from any other time Dooley could remember. Sometimes Dooley's uncle looked annoyed. Sometimes he looked downright pissed-off. Occasionally he looked amused. But right now? Right now he looked mostly tired and when he turned his head to Dooley, Dooley was surprised to see a dull flatness in his eyes, like he didn't care about anything any more.

"Ryan," Detective Graff said, his voice nice and loud and, Dooley noticed, very upbeat. "Look what we found."

He nodded at the backpack that was sitting on the coffee table. It was red with black trim and net pockets.

The lawyer was all of a sudden telling Dooley what Dooley already knew—that he didn't have to say anything, he didn't have to answer any questions, that he had a right to talk to his lawyer in private. Dooley glanced at his uncle, who didn't even look up at Dooley now. Nor did he go with Dooley and his lawyer, whose name was Annette Girondin, when they went with Graff so that Graff could ask Dooley some questions, which made Dooley think he was more or less fucked this time.

■ ■ ■

Annette Girondin and Detective Graff argued about the backpack. Apparently the search warrant was related to Edward Gillette and was focused on either the murder weapon or on clothes that Dooley had been wearing that might have blood on them that could tie him to Gillette's death or any other biological evidence like, say, soil or anything else from the park where Gillette's body had been found. But now Graff was saying that he had some questions about the death of Mark Everley in addition to questions about the death of Edward Gillette. When Annette Girondin said that she thought that death had been accidental—which Dooley believed his uncle must have told her—Graff said at the very least Dooley had to account for how he came to be in possession of a deceased person's personal property, which property the decedent's family had claimed the decedent had

had with him at the time of his death. He turned to Dooley for an answer to this question.

"You don't have to answer," Annette Girondin told Dooley.

"His sister told me it was missing," Dooley said to Graff. "She was really upset about that. She wanted it back. So I put out some feelers, you know?"

"No, I don't know," Graff said. "Why don't you tell me?"

"He went off the bridge down there in the ravine," Dooley said. He was pretty sure he wasn't imagining Graff's reaction to how he put it—*went off the bridge*. "There are lots of people down there. Homeless people. So I asked around. I said if anyone found it, there'd be a reward. Some homeless guy turned up at my workplace and gave it to me."

"At your workplace," Graff said. "You mean the video store?"

"Yes," Dooley said.

"This homeless guy, does he have a name?"

"I didn't ask," Dooley said. "But I can describe him." As he told Graff everything he could remember, he realized that he could have been describing any one of dozens, maybe hundreds, of down-and-outers in the city. He wished he'd paid closer attention to the guy.

"And you gave this person a reward," Graff said.

"Yes." Dooley could tell Graff didn't believe him.

"How much?"

"Everything I had on me—fifteen dollars." He thought about telling Graff that he'd offered to take the man to the bank machine to get him more money, but decided that would make it worse. First, he'd have to say that the homeless guy had disappeared before he got his break and could take him to the bank machine. Then he'd have to look at the expression on Graff's face while Graff wondered what kind of homeless person would turn down an offer of more money, except maybe one that was a figment of Dooley's imagination.

"I don't suppose anyone else saw you with this homeless person?" Graff said.

"Kevin," Dooley said. "My shift manager. He can tell you call about it." Well, he could tell Graff that a homeless guy who fit Dooley's description had turned up at the store and that Dooley had gone out and talked to him. But had Kevin seen the guy give Dooley the backpack? Dooley wasn't sure. Kevin was a nosy guy. Maybe he'd watched it out the window. "Yeah," he said to Graff, "talk to Kevin. See if he remembers anything."

Graff said that he would do that. Then he said, "Tell me again about the night that Mark Everley died."

"You said you wanted to talk to him about the murder of Edward Gillette," Annette Girondin said.

"You were the one who found Mark Everley, that's what you told me that night, correct?" Graff said.

Dooley said, "Yes."

"At the time, you told me that you *thought* Mark Everley went to your school, but you weren't sure. You remember that, Ryan?"

Dooley said, "Yes" again, knowing where Graff was going this time.

"You didn't tell me that you had been in a street fight with Mark Everley two months ago, Ryan—a street fight that Edward Gillette witnessed."

Who had told Graff that? Dooley bet anything it was Beth.

"It wasn't a street fight," Dooley said. Jesus, trust a cop to put that kind of spin on it.

"But it was a fight."

"He was hassling a girl. I told him to back off. That's all."

"You made that point with your fists, isn't that right, Ryan?"

"I told him to leave the girl alone. He came at me. All I did was defend myself."

"Like you defended yourself against that woman, right, Ryan? You've got a real temper, don't you? Is that what happened that night in the ravine, Ryan?" Dooley hated the way Graff kept saying his name. He sounded like a salesman. "Did Mark Everley give you a hard time? Did he come at you again? Did you have to defend yourself, Ryan? Because if that's what happened, you should say so. Self-defence, you know, it happens, right?"

"Don't answer that, Ryan," Annette Girondin said.

"Come on, Ryan. We know you knew Mark Everley. We know you had at least one fight with him. Maybe there were more. Were there, Ryan?"

"No."

"We know that Edward Gillette was a witness to that fight. What happened, Ryan? Was Edward in the ravine that night, too? Did he see something? Was he holding it over you? Is that what the fight was about at Winston Rhodes's party? Did Edward Gillette threaten you? Did he say he was going to the police? Is that why you killed him?"

"I didn't kill him," Dooley said.

"Oh," Graff said, sounding surprised now. "You're sure about that? Because the last time we talked, you weren't sure about anything. You said you didn't remember what happened that night. But now you're sure you didn't kill Edward Gillette. Is that what you're telling me, Ryan?"

Dooley just looked at him. He didn't need Annette Girondin to tell him that he didn't have to answer.

Detective Graff stared at him for a few moments. Then he smiled, like, hey, he'd only been kidding, and said, "What were you looking for in the ravine the day after Mark Everley died?"

"What?"

"The day after Mark Everley died," Graff said, his voice friendly now, like a guy reminding his buddy of some pleasant event they'd shared and he now wanted to reminisce about. "I saw you down in the ravine, remember? It looked to me like you were looking for something. What was it? Did you leave something or maybe drop something at the scene?"

"I was just taking a run."

"Why did you get your uncle to ask around and see if the police had any idea where Mark Everley was before he died?" Boom, boom, boom. The guy was like a one-man assault squad the way he kept lobbing questions at Dooley from different directions. "Were you afraid someone saw you with Everley that night, Ryan? Were you checking to see if you were in the clear?"

Dooley didn't answer. What was the point? Graff would never believe him.

"The night Mark Everley died, you told me you left the video store at nine o'clock, correct?"

Dooley nodded.

"Tell me again exactly what you were doing between the time you left the video store and the time that kid on the bike came by and saw you standing over Mark Everley's dead body."

Annette Girondin shook her head impatiently. "Don't answer that, Ryan." She looked at Graff. "Ryan has explained how he got the backpack. Why don't you check out what he told you? And since Mark Everley's death was accidental, I suggest you move on. If you have any more questions about Edward Gillette, ask them. Otherwise . . ."

"Where were you the night Mark Everley died, Ryan? Were you two drinking together?"

"Don't answer that. Ryan."

"I don't drink," Dooley said.

"I bet you don't do drugs, either," Graff said.

Dooley looked right into the detective's eyes. The man was aching to nail him.

"I didn't kill Gillette," he said. "And I had nothing to do with whatever happened to Everley."

"Don't say another word, Ryan," Annette Girondin said. "In fact, unless Detective Graff is charging you—"

"I didn't see Mark Everley that night until he took a header off that bridge," Dooley said.

"You just stole his backpack off him after he landed, is that it?" Detective Graff said. "What did you do with his camera? Did you sell it? Oh, no, that's right, you said some homeless guy had the backpack."

"Check with my manager," Dooley said. "Check with Kevin. He'll remember the homeless guy."

"Come on, Ryan," Annette Girondin said, standing up. "We're leaving."

"Where were you between the time you left the video store and the time Mark Everley went off that bridge?" Detective Graff said.

Dooley said nothing.

"Why did you kill Edward Gillette?" Graff said.

Jesus. ■

Twenty-Two

"You okay?" Dooley's uncle said after Annette Girondin left the house.

"Other than I have a homicide cop accusing me of killing two guys, I'm fine," Dooley said.

His uncle shook his head. "You should take up running, maybe martial arts, boxing, something. You're wrapped too tight, Ryan. You work at keeping it in, but if you don't find an outlet, one of these days you're going to explode."

"Graff thinks I already did. Twice."

"Well, that's your past catching up with you—at the ripe old age of seventeen." He'd been standing in the front hall, watching for him, Dooley realized, when Dooley and Annette returned to the house. He had tidied the place up—well, the first floor at least—and now that Annette was gone, he was sitting on the couch working on a bottle of beer. He'd offered one to Annette Girondin, but she had declined. He hadn't offered one to Dooley. He took a long swallow of it now and looked at Dooley. "Is there anything you want to tell me?"

"Besides I didn't do it?" Dooley said.

His uncle took another swig of beer. "Yeah," he said. "Way too tight."

"You used to be a cop," Dooley said. "What do you think are the chances Graff can nail me for something I didn't do?"

His uncle's expression soured. "You mean, do I think the prisons are full of innocent people?"

"David Milgaard," Dooley said. "Donald Marshall, Rubin Carter, Clayton Johnson, Thomas Sophonow, Steven Truscott, Robert Baltovich—"

His uncle waved a hand to silence him.

"You know," he said, "this wouldn't even be an issue if you had come straight home from work the night that kid went off the bridge—like you were supposed to—and if you had gone to work the night that other fellow disappeared—*like you were supposed to.*" He set down the beer bottle. "You've been straight with me, right, Ryan?"

"Yeah," Dooley said. He looked at his uncle, who wasn't a big guy, but who you could tell was tough, you could tell he'd never back down and he didn't scare easy, but who looked worried now. "I screwed up a couple of times, I admit it. But I never killed anyone."

"Annette's good," his uncle said.

Which, Dooley knew, meant that she was expensive.

"I have some money saved," Dooley said. "You know, from work."

"Yeah, well, let's see where this goes," his uncle said. He got up off the couch. "I'm going to start supper. Jeannie's coming over. Go clean up your room. They really did a number on it."

His uncle wasn't kidding. The cops had tossed his bed. They'd pulled everything out of his closet. They'd emptied his drawers. They'd even gone through the small collection of books on the shelf above his bed. It wasn't until nearly two hours later that everything was finally off the floor and he was up-righting his wastepaper basket, which, thank God, contained nothing but paper, including the business card he had found in Everley's backpack.

■ ■ ■

Dooley's uncle was at the kitchen table when Dooley got up the next morning. He had a mug of coffee in front of him, which was normal. He didn't have the newspaper open in front of him, which was not normal. When he turned to look at Dooley, Dooley got a sick feeling.

"What's the matter?" he said.

"I called this guy I know," his uncle said.

Dooley glanced at the clock on the stove. It was eight o'clock in the morning.

"Joe DeLucci," his uncle said.

Dooley recognized the name. He was the cop his uncle had asked whether anyone knew where Mark Everley was the night he went off the bridge.

"Sit down, Ryan," his uncle said.

Dooley sat and looked across the table at his uncle with his gray-and-black spiky hair, his barrel chest, his piercing eyes, and, more prominent today, the worry lines over the bridge of his nose.

"They're saying now it could be that Mark Everley was pushed off that bridge."

"*What?*"

"Scuff marks, marks on his clothes, the way he fell, all that kind of stuff."

"You said they thought it was an accident."

"Yeah, well, now they're not so sure. Or maybe Graff is just being pig-headed." His uncle had his hands wrapped around his coffee cup, but so far as Dooley could tell he hadn't yet taken a sip. Dooley couldn't even tell whether the coffee in the cup was still hot. "You had nothing to do with that, right, Ryan?"

"What? No!"

"You just happened to see him go over. It's a coincidence you were in the ravine at the time, that's what you're saying?"

"You think I *kill* people?" Jesus.

His uncle stared at Dooley for far too long before he finally shook his head. He looked more defeated than convinced.

"I'll tell you what," Dooley said. "If I was going to kill someone, it would be over something important. It sure wouldn't be over some asshole like Mark Everley making some girl cry."

"Tell me why I'm not taking comfort in that," Dooley's uncle said.

"I didn't kill Eddy Gillette. And I didn't kill Mark

Everley. I don't kill people." Jesus, like he had to say that.

"Tell me again exactly what you were doing that night."

Dooley hesitated. Big mistake.

His uncle's fist came down like a sledgehammer on the table, making it and Dooley jump and the coffee in his mug slop over onto the tablecloth.

So Dooley told him.

"What the hell's the matter with you?" his uncle said when he had finished. "Why do you want to go and upset those people?"

"I just wanted to take a look," Dooley said. "You know, see if I could see how she was?"

"Didn't I tell you to leave it alone?" his uncle said. "I bet you were one of those kids, Lorraine would tell you not to do something and you'd be right there doing it and probably thumbing your nose at her at the same time, right?"

Boy, he was mad. Dooley waited to see what he would say next, which turned out to be something practical:

"Did anyone see you?"

"Are you kidding?" Dooley said. The sharp look his uncle gave him made him regret his words. "I was afraid if the husband saw me, he'd call the cops and accuse me of something just to get me busted."

"That didn't tell you something?" his uncle said, still angry.

"Yeah, well, maybe it was dumb—"

"*Maybe*?"

"—but you know what? If that dog hadn't come at me, I wouldn't have been anywhere near Mark Everley when he died. I would have been fifteen, maybe twenty minutes away. I wouldn't even have seen him go off that bridge. That kid on the bike would have found him, not me."

"Dog?" his uncle said, perking up. "What dog?"

"Just some dog," Dooley said. "It came out of nowhere." It had scared the shit out of him. "When that dog came at me, I hopped a fence into the next yard and got out of there—fast."

"Describe it," his uncle said.

"I didn't get that good a look at it. It was dark, and it was a dark-colored dog. All I saw were teeth." He remembered thinking that those teeth looked sharp.

"Was it a big dog? Small dog?"

"Medium-sized, I guess," Dooley said. "It came at me fast. Some of those medium-sized dogs can be scary." For example, pit bulls were medium-sized dogs.

"Medium-sized, dark-colored dog," his uncle said. "And where exactly were you at the time?"

"In the backyard."

"Did anyone come out to investigate?"

"Maybe," Dooley said. "I didn't stick around to find out."

"You didn't see anyone?"

Dooley shook his head.

"That doesn't mean no one saw you," his uncle said. "Tell me exactly what time this happened."

Dooley told him as close as he could remember.

"Did Graff ask you where you were that night?"

Dooley nodded.

"And?"

"And what?"

"What did you tell him?"

"Nothing. Annette said not to answer."

"Well, if he gets around to asking you again, tell him what you just told me," his uncle said.

"What for?" Dooley said. "He won't believe me." Especially if he asked Dooley what he'd been doing up there in the first place. Double-especially if Dooley told him. "Besides, no one saw me."

"Just do it, Ryan. Be straight with the man. In the meantime, I'll look into it. That dog belongs to someone. Maybe someone will remember it barking when you say it did. It's something," his uncle said. He looked less worried now and more focused, which unsettled Dooley. The last thing he wanted to believe was that he needed an alibi for the night Mark Everley died.

■ ■ ■

He should have expected it, but he didn't. He made his way to school, wishing he could drink something or swallow something that would make him numb all over and knowing, instead, that if he was going to make it, he was going to have to get used to feelings like the ones that were eating at him now, feelings of shame and dread. He told himself he didn't care, that he'd made a career out of not caring, but the truth was that he hadn't cared before because before he had novocained himself into a state of insensibility. Now he was clean and sober and, in his opinion, a pretty good argument for why booze worked, why pills worked, and why drugs worked.

So off to school—which he tolerated but did not enjoy—where he was still a freak, just like he'd been at every school he had ever attended and, boy, there had been a lot of them. Lorraine had moved around a lot, mostly getting kicked out of places because she never paid the rent on time or because of the men who went in and out of the place all night every night, or the so-called boyfriends who were assholes and who, to a man, drank too much or smoked too much. He'd seen it change, too, from poor little Ryan, he's falling behind, he looks like he hasn't had a home-cooked meal in weeks (try ever), he's wearing sneakers in the bitter cold and slush of January and February, by March his sneakers are falling apart, his reading skills are below grade average, his homework is mostly never done . . . to, that Ryan, he doesn't care, he never bothers to do his homework, he doesn't even take his textbooks home, his grades are abysmal, what's a kid with such poor reading, writing, and math skills even doing in junior high . . . to, Ryan Dooley, hard case, one more incident like that, mister, and you're out of here, do you understand me, one more tardy, one more assignment not completed, one more incident of swearing at a teacher, one more fight in the school yard, don't even think about it, Dooley, or I'll have the cops here so fast it will make your head spin . . .

To now, when vice principals like Rektor went out of their way to let Dooley know they had his number, they knew exactly the kind of person he was and they made sure he knew that he was there by their sufferance only (you know what that means, Ryan, or do you want me to spell it out for you?); when teachers, the old burned-out ones, the new inexperienced ones, the female ones, never called on him, never expected anything from him, never even looked at him except for times like now, when kids were dead and cops had been called and lawyers summoned and paid for and everyone knew—believed—wasn't surprised by the fact—that Ryan Dooley was at the center of it all.

That much he expected.

But he didn't expect what actually happened, which was that Beth was standing in front of his school, her head moving this way and that, looking for something. Looking for someone. Looking for Dooley, it turned out, because the minute she spotted him, *boom*, she was like a sprinter coming off her blocks, hurtling herself at him like he was the finish line and there was a medal waiting for her when she crossed it. Her eyes burned with—name that emotion—anger? Stronger. Rage? Fury? More personal. Hatred? Yeah, that was it. Pure and very personal hatred. She thrust her hands out in front of her like weapons and kept coming, kept coming, until, *umph*, her palms slammed into Dooley's chest and, what do you know, she wasn't big, but, boy, she made an impact. Dooley staggered backward.

"Hey," he said.

"You lied to me," she said. "Did you kill my brother too?"

Yeah, he should have expected that.

"You had his backpack," she said. "What did you do? Did you steal it off his dead body?" She was hammering at him with her fists now and her voice, which normally was deep for a girl, which made it kind of sexy, was loud and screechy and attracting a lot of attention. "I asked you about it. I told you it was important to me. And you had it the whole time. You had it the whole time!"

"No, I—"

"Now the cops have it and they won't give it back to me. They say it's evidence. They think someone pushed Mark."

Mr. Rektor had come out the front door and was walking toward them now, grim-faced, waving his arms as he approached to shoo staring students into the building. A woman scurried after him, her legs moving twice as fast as his, so that she looked like a little kid scrambling to keep up with her daddy. Dooley recognized her as one of the secretaries from the school office. The crowd parted to let them through and then closed up again. Hardly anyone went inside. Dooley saw Rhodes. Landers and Bracey were with him. He saw Warren, too. Geeze, Warren, who had Everley's flash drive.

"You lied to me," Beth said. "You killed my brother. You lied to me. You killed my brother." She sounded as enraged by the first accusation as by the second.

Mr. Rektor laid a hand on her arm. She spun around, fists up.

"Ms Patel will take you inside, Beth," Mr. Rektor said, his voice gentle, but phoney gentle, like it was something he'd learned in vice principal school: How to Calm Students 101. "You can phone your mother and ask her to come and pick you up. Or, if you'd prefer, Ms Patel can call you a cab."

She didn't want to go. She turned back to Dooley, tears

burning in her eyes.

"What did you do to him?" she said. "What did you do to my brother?"

"Nothing," Dooley said. "I didn't even know him."

Ms Patel took her by the arm and began to peel her gently away from the scene, the way a mother might peel a Band-aid off a small child, slowly, slowly, working hard to minimize the pain. Beth didn't want to go, but Ms Patel urged her along. As they nudged through the crowd, Rhodes approached her. She stopped and looked up at him. Her whole body shook and her hands went up to her face to cover her eyes. Rhodes stepped closer to her and put his arms around her. He held her, rubbing her back to soothe her. It was Rhodes who walked her inside. Ms Patel seemed relieved by his intervention.

Dooley looked at Mr. Rektor, whose face was hard now. But all he said to Dooley was, "You're going to be late for home form."

Dooley was in history class, second period, when he heard his name over the intercom: "Ryan Dooley, report to the office." Everyone in the class turned to look at him, Everyone watched him walk from the room.

Dooley knew why he'd been summoned even before he opened the office door because there was his uncle's voice, barking at someone. Dooley bet it was Rektor. Ms Patel glanced up from her computer.

"Mr. Rektor's office," she said. She looked glad to be behind the counter, out of his reach. Dooley wondered what she knew about him and exactly what she was afraid of.

He followed the sound of his uncle's voice, rapped on Mr. Rektor's closed door, and opened it before anyone invited him in. Mr. Rektor was sitting behind his desk. Dooley's uncle was standing in front of it, leaning over it so that his face was as close to Rektor's as it could get, given the desk between them. Rektor had tilted his chair back a little, maybe to avoid the spit that sometimes flew out of Dooley's uncle's mouth when he was mad and talking loud both at the same time. Dooley could see his uncle was on a roll, talking to Rektor the way he talked to Dooley when Dooley had done something phenomenally stupid.

"So let me get this straight," he was saying to Mr. Rektor, always Dooley's first clue when his uncle was talking to him that he was going to lay out just how screwed up his logic was or how foolish or ill-advised his actions had been, or both. "You're telling me that as a result of the police coming here and asking you about my nephew, you think *my nephew* would be more comfortable attending another school. Is that about the size of it?"

Rektor leaned back a little farther still. His voice was measured and calm when he said, "I am sure all of this is difficult enough for Ryan. I merely thought that under the circumstances he might appreciate being in a more . . . anonymous environment." He smiled blandly up at Dooley's uncle, which Dooley knew was a big mistake.

"Think again," Dooley's uncle said. "Ryan stays. If you or anyone else harasses him, I'll file a complaint. I'll sue this school, the school board, and you personally. You got that?" Rektor opened his mouth to speak. He shut it again when

Dooley's uncle went on. "I know for a fact that this is not the first time a student at this school has ever been questioned by the police. I know because I used to be a police officer and I questioned a few of them myself." Rektor wilted a little. Dooley guessed he didn't know that Dooley's uncle used to be a cop. All this time he'd been thinking: drycleaner. How intimidated is anyone going to be by a drycleaner? "Questioned means just that—questioned," his uncle said. "He hasn't been charged with anything. He hasn't been arrested. And even if he was, we have a principle here—innocent until proven guilty. Maybe you heard of it. So lay off."

He backed up and for the first time seemed to notice that Dooley was in the room.

"Get back to class," he said.

Dooley didn't move. The truth was, he was on Rektor's side on this one. He didn't want to be here. He felt like a freak the way everyone was always staring at him.

"What did I just say?" his uncle barked. He scowled at Rektor as if it was his fault that Dooley wasn't hotfooting it back to whatever class he was supposed to be in.

Rektor nodded at him: *Go on, get out of here before I decide to give you a detention.*

Dooley said to his uncle, "Can I talk to you for a minute?"

Dooley's uncle backed away from the desk. Rektor straightened his chair and his tie. He looked relieved. Dooley's uncle glowered at him, holding Rektor's eyes with his own, making it clear that the only reason he was leaving was that he had said his piece. He walked out of the office without a word. Dooley chased after him. His uncle glanced at him as he strode toward the front door. He waited until he was outside the school and had checked to see that there was no one within earshot—there was no one around at all before he said to Dooley, "What's up? You going to tell me you want to cave to that jerk-off, is that it?"

It was exactly what Dooley had been going to tell him. It always brought Dooley up short his uncle could read him that way.

"Well, forget it," his uncle said. "You're enrolled here. You've been doing the work here. You *have* been doing the work, haven't you, Ryan?"

"Yeah, sure—"

"You have rights, Ryan. Pricks like Rectal would love to screw you out of them, but that's not going to happen. You're going to go back in there and you're going to focus on your studies." He poked Dooley on the chest. "You're going to keep your nose clean." Another poke. "You aren't going to piss anyone off." Another poke. Even though he had checked first to see if anyone was around, like what he had to say to Dooley was personal and private, he was shouting the words at him. "You got that? Do you, Ryan?"

Yeah, well his uncle wasn't the only one who wasn't pleased with how things were shaking out.

"You know what it's like in there?" Dooley said. "They all think I'm some kind of psychopath. Everyone either hates me or is afraid of me. Even the teachers. They never give me a chance."

His uncle shook his head.

"After what you've been through, Ryan, you need to make your own chances. You need to prove to people that you've changed."

"I show up regular. I never skip. I do my homework, for Christ's sake. I do it all on time—"

"Cry me a river," his uncle said, so sarcastic that Dooley wanted to slug him. "You've got two ways to go, Ryan. It's always the same two ways. You can act like a baby and have a temper tantrum because people aren't treating you the way you think you deserve to be treated. Or you can be a man, suck it up, keep on paying your dues, keep focused on the things you can do something about—which is how you conduct your life, *your* life Ryan, not everyone else's life—and forget about the stuff that's out of your control, which is how other people choose to see you. You think of another way to handle it, you let me know. But you won't. You know why? Because there is no other way. You can only get through this minute and the next one and the one after that. You can't fast-forward, skip all the bullshit and the commercials, and end up with a nice, happy ending. Life isn't like that. Life's more like rehab, Ryan. One day at a time. I know you know what I'm talking about."

It was the longest speech his uncle had ever made, which was how Dooley knew that his uncle was serious about what he was saying and that he considered it vital that Dooley not walk away, that he go back in there and take whatever was coming. It was like walking into a fire so you could show everyone you were fireproof, even though you knew—and they knew—that you weren't. What was the point?

His uncle put a hand on Dooley's shoulder.

"I'm not saying it's easy." He was looking Dooley squarely in the eyes and talking softly. Dooley felt the warmth and strength of his hand. It wasn't something he was used to. "I'm just saying it's what you have to do. And for what it's worth, I've got your back."

Dooley was surprised to realize that it was worth more than almost anything else he could think of. His uncle nodded at him and turned to go. Dooley watched him climb into his car. As he pulled away from the curb, Dooley tracked him—and was startled to find that Beth hadn't been picked up by her mother or tucked into a cab by Ms Patel. No, she was standing outside the eastern-most exit to the school listening intently (it looked like) to the person who was talking to her. Dooley's heart burned when he saw who it was. Warren.

Jesus.

He watched for a moment, waiting to see if he could gauge Beth's reaction to whatever Warren was telling her, waiting to see if Warren was going to hand over the flash drive Dooley had left with him. They didn't part ways until the next bell rang. Warren went inside. Beth walked away. Dooley turned and looked up at the school. He didn't want to go back. He didn't want any more eyes on him or any more conversations dying the second he rounded a corner or stepped into a classroom. But what you want and what you get are never the same thing, are they? ■

Twenty-Three

arren was waiting at Dooley's locker after school. He looked around to make sure no one was close enough to hear and then he said, "I haven't had any luck with that thing."

"You still have it?" Dooley said, surprised.

"Yeah," Warren said, sounding even more surprised than Dooley. "Why? You want it back?"

"You were talking to Beth."

Warren fixed on something behind Dooley and looked down at the ground. Dooley glanced over his shoulder. A couple of guys were coming toward them. Dooley opened his locker and jammed his homework books into his backpack. The two guys stared at him as they passed. Dooley stared right back, dead-eyed. The guys moved a little faster and disappeared around a corner.

"You were talking to Beth," he said to Warren again after the guys were gone. "You know her?"

"Are you kidding?" Warren said.

"Why would I be kidding?"

"First of all," Warren said, "do I look like the kind of guy who would know a girl who looks like that? Second, before Everley died, I never set eyes on her. She was like this big secret. The way Everley used to talk about her, I thought maybe she was like my sister, which is why I was so mad when I heard he'd given her a hard time."

"What do you mean?" Dooley said, confused.

"Well, she doesn't go to school here. The way I heard it, Everley told people she went to a special school."

"She goes to a private school," Dooley said. "It's not that special."

"It *turns out* it's a private school," Warren said. "But that was never what Everley said. He always said a *special* school. *My* sister goes to a special school. I thought he meant his sister did, too, you know, because she had special problems."

Dooley remembered something Bracey had said about Beth at the party: *She is definitely not as advertised.*

"Why would he say something like that if it's not true?" Dooley said.

"How would I know? I told you. The guy was a jerk. You'd have to be to lie about your sister like that."

Dooley got the feeling that Warren never lied about his sister.

"So what were you talking to her about?" he said.

"I wanted to tell her I was sorry about Mark."

Dooley gave him a look.

"Yeah, well, somebody loses somebody who's close to them and a lot of times they want to talk about that person.

But you know what usually happens? No one wants to say anything because they're afraid it's going to upset you. So everyone you know, even people you thought were your friends, they all pretend that the person never existed. They tell themselves they don't want to upset you when the truth is they don't want to upset themselves."

Warren was talking so fast, so loud, and so angrily that little drops of spit flew from his lips. Dooley was surprised how spirited he could be, considering how used he was to being harassed and even beat up. He thought about what Warren had said about his mother, that she baked and decorated cakes to bring in extra money.

"Your father?" Dooley said.

"Yeah."

"I'm sorry," Dooley said.

Warren just shrugged. "I figured she might like to talk about her brother," he said.

"Did you tell her about that flash drive?"

Warren shook his head.

"You going to tell the cops?" Dooley said.

"What for?"

"You heard what they're saying about me. You know the cops questioned me, right?"

"Yeah. So? You ever hear what people say about me?"

Dooley had to admit that he didn't. "I bet they don't say the cops talked to you concerning a couple of deaths," he said.

"Did you kill anyone?" Warren said.

"No."

"Okay then," Warren said. "But you still want to know

what's on Mark Everley's flash drive, right?"

Dooley hesitated. Then, what the hell: "What I really want to know is if he took any pictures right before he died."

Warren shook his head. "Even supposing he did," he said. "There's no guarantee he'd have backed them up onto the flash drive right away. They'd probably still be in the camera."

Dooley hadn't thought about that.

"But you never know," Warren said. "Maybe he was one of those totally anal people who back everything up."

Maybe? Dooley didn't like maybes.

"His sister told me his favorite TV programs, his favorite bands, his favorite songs, his favorite things to eat, the pets he had when he was a kid, stuff like that."

Dooley looked blankly at him. He didn't get Warren. He hardly ever said what you expected him to say.

"Favorites and familiar things," he said now. "You want a password you're not going to accidentally forget, you go with personal favorites or things you're not likely to forget, like Skip, the puppy you got for your fifth birthday."

Oh.

"Are you working tonight or are you going to be at home?" he said. "In case I get anything."

"I'm working until midnight," Dooley said. "After that, I'll be home." He dug around in his backpack for a scrap of paper and scrawled out the store's phone number and his uncle's phone number for Warren. Also his pager number, telling Warren: "Just in case."

■ ■ ■

Dooley saw that something was wrong as soon as he got home. His uncle was pacing up and down on the porch, but stopped and came down the front walk as soon as he saw Dooley. Dooley felt his insides go liquid. Now what?

"Is it Graff?" he said. "Is he looking for me again?"

"No," his uncle said. "It's Jeannie's mother. She had a bad fall. She's in the hospital."

"Is she going to be okay?" Dooley said. He didn't understand why his uncle was so agitated. Maybe he had met Jeannie's mother. Maybe she was a terrific person, although by Dooley's calculation, she had to be up there, definitely in her late sixties, probably a lot older.

"Jeannie doesn't know," his uncle said. "All she knows is, it was bad and her mother is unconscious in the hospital. She lives up in Timmins. She asked me if I could drive her up there. She's pretty upset. I don't see her making the drive alone."

"Okay," Dooley said slowly. The way his uncle was acting, this was some kind of problem, but Dooley didn't see why.

"I'd like to take her," his uncle said. "But—" Here it came. His uncle looked him in the eye.

"I'll be fine," Dooley said.

"Graff could come after you anytime. Maybe soon. Maybe not for a couple of weeks or a couple of months, depending on how he's working the case. Hey, look on the bright side, maybe never."

"I didn't do anything," Dooley said.

"You know about tunnel vision, right, Ryan?" his uncle said, more serious than Dooley had seen him in months.

"I have the lawyer's phone number," Dooley said, meaning Annette Girondin. "And you're going to have your cell phone, right?" His uncle nodded. "I'll be fine," Dooley said. "If anything happens, I have the right to contact my lawyer and she can contact you."

His uncle's nod was almost imperceptible. Finally he said, "If they want to talk to you again or if, God forbid, they arrest you—"

Jesus, did his uncle really think there was a chance of that?

"—you don't say a word, Ryan, you got me? You say you want to contact your lawyer and then you keep your mouth shut—and I mean *glued* shut—until you've not only talked to Annette but she's right there beside you. You got that? Because if you decide to volunteer information, they can use it."

"I know that," Dooley said.

"Some people, they think they're smarter than the cops. But you know what? Ninety-nine times out of one hundred, they're wrong. Guys like Graff have questioned hundreds, maybe even thousands, of people. How many cops have you talked to, Ryan? More to the point, how many have you outsmarted?"

None, Dooley thought.

"When do you think you'll be back?" Dooley said.

"It depends how Jeannie's mom is. Maybe we'll be gone

the whole weekend. I'll have to be back for Monday for sure, no matter what Jeannie does."

"I'll be fine," Dooley said again, even though the idea of another encounter with Graff was making his stomach churn. "I'm working tonight and Sunday night. I have a ton of homework. You can call me or, if you want, I can check in with you regularly. You just tell me when."

"Maybe I should stay here," Dooley's uncle said. Boy, it was spooking Dooley how his uncle still seemed so reluctant to go. "I think Jeannie would understand if I couldn't make it." It seemed to Dooley that his uncle was trying to convince himself of this. "After all, she knows what the situation is with you."

Dooley was surprised to hear that. He knew his uncle well enough to know that he didn't go around discussing his personal affairs with just anyone. If his uncle had discussed his situation with Jeannie, then Jeannie had to be more important to his uncle than Dooley had thought.

His uncle finally phoned Jeannie and told her he'd be by in thirty minutes to pick her up. Then he went upstairs to pack a bag. He pressed some twenties into Dooley's hand "just in case" before he left.

Dooley got changed, grabbed a bite to eat, and went to work. He didn't hear from Warren that night. He hadn't expected to. But, boy, he got an earful from Kevin.

"The police were here," he said. "They questioned me. About you and that bum who showed up here."

To Kevin, this appeared to be a source of irritation. To Dooley, it was a source of relief.

"Did you describe the guy to them?" he said.

"I described how he smelled."

"I mean, what he looked like. And that backpack he was carrying."

"What backpack?" Kevin said.

Great.

"He had a backpack he'd found. He gave it to me. I brought it back into the store with me."

Kevin stared at him. "You brought some piece of garbage some homeless guy found into *my* store?"

Terrific. Kevin hadn't noticed that, either.

"What did you tell the cops?" Dooley said.

"That some bum showed up here and that you got rid of him. What else is there to tell?"

Just terrific.

■ ■ ■

He hadn't expected Warren to appear at the door first thing the next morning, either, but that's exactly what happened.

Dooley was sleeping on the couch. He was wearing the same clothes that he'd worn to work. He had come home, opened the fridge to get some milk for his cereal, and stood there for five full minutes, staring at the half dozen or so bottles of imported beer chilling on the second shelf. Then he'd opened the cupboard to get a box of cereal and had spent another five minutes staring at a bottle of scotch and another one of vodka. He tried to tell himself that no one would notice if he took one drink, especially if he poured an equal amount of water into the bottle to replace what he'd taken. But he didn't think he could stand to disappoint his uncle, not now when all of a sudden he was running up legal bills and Dooley's problems were making him think twice about doing the things he wanted to do, the things that he'd do automatically if Dooley didn't happen to be living with him. So he poured himself some cereal, carried it into the living room, and dropped onto the couch in front of the TV to eat it.

It was nearly one in the morning by the time he finished eating, and he knew that he should go to bed. What he had told his uncle was true; he had a ton of homework. And he had to work again tonight. But he couldn't make himself get up and go to his room. For one thing, he couldn't remember the last time that he'd been able to just sit and channel-surf into the wee hours without someone (his uncle) appearing and ordering him to get to bed, usually grousing what was the matter with him, didn't he know he had to get up in the morning to go to school, do chores, do homework, go to work, whatever.

But that wasn't the main reason he stayed on the couch.

No, the main reason was the feeling in his gut, the one that made everything churn, even milk and cereal, the feeling that in the old days he would have warded off with booze or pills or weed or whatever was handy. It was the same feeling that used to creep over him when he was a kid and all alone in a dark room, listening for noises out in the hall (doors opening, footsteps approaching, hammering on the door) or in his mother's room next to his. It was the feeling that came on him when he got called on in school and he didn't know the answer and kids would look at him like he was stupid. It was the feeling that however bad things were now, they were about to get worse. When he felt like that, he usually reacted in one of two ways: he got blasted or he blasted someone (or something)—either one did the trick, which was to stop him for thinking too much about what was going to happen. To make the gut clenching disappear. To either dull pain or add a whole new dimension to it—it didn't matter which.

But he couldn't do that now. Not unless he wanted to end up back in the pit he'd been trying so hard to stay out of the past few months.

So there he was, staring at the TV but not really watching it, while Graff filled his mind. Geeze, the guy was scary. He had a stare that Dooley bet could penetrate a brick wall—or, at least, he bet Graff liked to think it could. And he had a cool certainty about him, like, *of course*, Dooley had killed Gillette and, what's more, he had probably killed Everley, too, even though at first everyone was saying that one was an accident. Now all that remained was for Graff to nail down the details and see Dooley's sorry ass in lockup. Dooley bet he'd push hard for an adult sentence, too. And then, he had no idea when, he must have fallen asleep. What woke him up was the doorbell.

He staggered to his feet and went into the front hall so that he could see through the glass in the door.

Warren was standing out on the porch, his hand out to ring the bell again.

Dooley opened the door.

"Hey," Warren said, grinning at him until he saw the

messed-up, only-half-awake look on Dooley's face. "Hey," he said, subdued now. "I must have pressed the bell ten times. I was beginning to think there was no one home."

"Ten times?" Dooley said. Dooley only ever rang a doorbell twice, three times at the most. If no one answered by then, he assumed no one was home.

"Well, I wanted to make sure the bell wasn't broken," Warren said, and he grinned again, just a little, like he couldn't help himself. That's when Dooley noticed that he had an envelope in his hand. "Is it okay if I come in?" he said.

"Yeah, I guess," Dooley said. He stepped aside to let Warren pass. It didn't occur to him to ask until after he closed the door. "How do you know where I live?"

"You gave me your phone number," Warren said, as if that explained anything.

Dooley decided to let it pass. He watched as Warren's eyes swept the place, checking out the front hall, the living room, the dining room, the doorway to the kitchen, everything neat, the tile on the kitchen floor gleaming. He wondered what Warren had expected. For sure it wasn't what he was looking at because his mouth hung open a little and there was a trace of awe in his voice when he said, "Nice place."

"What's up?" Dooley said.

Warren grinned again and tossed him the flash drive.

"You did it?" Dooley said.

Warren nodded. He handed Dooley the envelope.

"I got into the locked files," he said. "Turns out the password is the name of the hamster he had in second grade.

I printed out the pictures for you. Some go back a few months. Others are more recent. And I gotta tell you, some of them are totally weird." He stood there in the front hall, rocking back and forth, heel to toe, heel to toe, while Dooley opened the envelope and pulled out some photographs. He flipped through them. Most, but not all, were photographs of a girl. There was even one of Everley with the girl, which, Dooley guessed, Everley must have taken with some kind of delay on his camera. "You know her?" Warren said.

"Yeah," Dooley said. But by now he was looking at one of the non-girl photos. It looked like a skull of some kind. There were several more just like it, all kind of the same, but kind of different, too. Draped over one of them was a gold heart on a chain. "What are these?" he said to Warren.

"Some kind of animal, I think. Dogs maybe. Or cats."

"Why would Everley take pictures of animal skulls?" Dooley said. More to the point: "Why did he lock them with a password?"

"'Cause he's fucked up," Warren said. "They're kind of creepy, huh?"

"The guy wrote stories," Dooley said. "Lots of them. They were kind of creepy, too. Lots of gore and violence, stuff like that." Dooley squinted at another photo. "What are those? Newspapers?" There were a couple of them, each one neatly folded with something sitting next to it. Dooley looked closer. One was next to what looked like a ratty pair of old gloves; the other was next to a grimy looking hat.

"They're from last year," Warren said. "When I enlarged the pictures on-screen, I could read the dates. You can make them out on those with a magnifying glass. ”

Dooley shuffled to another photograph—it was a close-up of the skull with the heart and chain.

“Weird stuff to password-protect, huh?” Warren said.

“I hardly knew the guy,” Dooley said. It was possible that Everley did stuff like that all the time. There was no way of knowing.

Or maybe there was.

Dooley shuffled through the pictures again. He thought about telling Warren the cops’ latest theory on Mark Everley’s death. But if he did tell him and if the cops ever talked to Warren, maybe they’d try to scare him somehow, tell him that he was an accessory after the fact, something like that. Dooley could see Warren pissing his pants over that. Probably it was better not to tell Warren anything, and, if it came to it, let him tell the cops how Ryan Dooley had pulled a fast one on him.

“That day out in the schoolyard,” he said instead, “when Landers was giving you a hard time—what was that about?”

“The first rule of comedy,” Warren said.

“What?”

“The first rule of comedy—the biggest laughs come from someone else’s pain,” Warren said.

This was news to Dooley, and he didn’t see how it was relevant, but boy, if it were true, then all his life needed was a laugh track.

“I was sitting outside reading,” Warren said. “My back-pack was on the ground and Landers and them walked by and Landers’ foot got caught in one of the straps and he tripped. His arms started flailing in the air, like he was looking for something to hang onto, and then, boom, he went down. It was like watching a guy slip on a banana peel. You see it—you know chances are excellent the guy's going to fall, he might even hurt himself, but you can't help it, it's funny, so you laugh at the guy's pain. The first rule of comedy."

"I'm guessing Landers didn't find it funny." Landers seemed like the kind of guy who would only embrace the first rule of comedy if he was the guy watching and someone else was the guy slipping.

"I knew it was a mistake to laugh," Warren said. "But I couldn't help it. He's a big guy—well, bigger than me—and big guys are just naturally funny when they fall. The harder they fall, right? He hit hard. I laughed. And the next thing I knew, he was on his feet again, like he'd bounced up, like he had springs on his feet or something. And he reached down and grabbed the collar of my shirt and yanked me to my feet and that's when I knew I was fucked. It was like falling down a long flight of stairs. You know it's going to hurt every bump of the way, but there's no way you can stop it. The most you can hope for is that you'll still be alive when you hit bottom."

Dooley looked at Warren. He was slight and scrawny and, as far as Dooley could tell, had no physical confidence. Half the time he seemed to be asking for it. But he had a wry way of looking at things, and he was smart.

"I should have stepped in," Dooley said. "I could have made him stop."

"Well, you slowed him down," Warren said. He didn't sound angry or resentful. "I should have thanked Everley's sister. It was her showing up that did it. That's why Rhodes came to my rescue."

"To impress her, you mean?"

"Yeah," Warren said.

It figured. Dooley wished he had thought of it first.

"He sure didn't do it because he likes me," Warren said. "He told Landers, look who's here, and then he said, you can have your fun some other time. Landers didn't want to let me go."

Dooley remembered how angry Landers had been when Rhodes intervened.

"If she hadn't walked by, I'd have probably ended up in the hospital," Warren said.

Dooley didn't know what to tell him: learn to control your laughter or learn to fight. One or the other was probably a good idea if Warren was going to survive high school.

"Hey, Warren, if there's ever anything I can do—"

"Forget it," Warren said. "You already did it." ■

Twenty-Four

Dooley sat on the couch after Warren had left, fingering the flash drive and staring at the pictures. Everley had photographed small animal skulls, one of them with a gold heart draped over it. He had photographed old newspapers.

And he had taken lots of pictures of Esperanza. Esperanza, smiling into the camera, her face radiant in every picture, but who had been crying on Gillette's shoulder the night of the party. Esperanza who had been afraid that Landers might tell on her—but tell about what?

Everley had locked all of those pictures in password-protected files.

Why would he do something like that?

■ ■ ■

Dooley phoned Rhodes's house. He believed it was Esperanza who answered. She had a soft Spanish accent and a softer voice, and she told him that Rhodes—she called him Mr. Winston—was out and wasn't expected back until later in the day. She asked Dooley if he wanted to leave a message. Dooley said, "No, thank you."

Dooley looked at the flash drive and the envelope of photographs. He should have given them back to Warren for safekeeping, but he hadn't. He wondered what the cops would make of them if they came looking for him again. He shoved the pictures and the flash drive in his pocket, thinking he'd drop them off at Warren's later. Then he took the bus up to Rhodes's house.

He pressed the bell and Esperanza answered.

"You remember me?" Dooley said. "I was at Winston's party, the one to raise money for Mark's scholarship."

She had big brown eyes and a small, heart-shaped face. "Mr. Winston is not here," she said.

"I don't want to talk to him," Dooley said. "I want to talk to you."

That seemed to confuse her. She looked over her shoulder.

"I want to talk to you about Mark," he said. "You were good friends with him, weren't you? Maybe more than friends."

She recoiled a little at that and glanced over her shoulder again.

"I just want to ask you a few questions about him," Dooley said.

She took a step backwards.

"Questions?" she said.

"About Mark," Dooley said, talking to her the way he might to a frightened child, trying to reassure her. "About what happened to him."

She was shaking her head before Dooley finished speaking.

"Esperanza," a voice called. It was a man's voice, but not Rhodes's. "Esperanza, where are my shirts? Did the cleaners drop them off?" A man appeared on the divided staircase behind her. He peered at Dooley and then shifted his gaze to Esperanza. "I need my shirts, Esperanza. And I can't find my black loafers. I need them, too. The airport limousine is picking Mrs. Rhodes and me up at noon."

"I have to go," Esperanza said softly.

The man—Rhodes's father; Dooley would have bet his life on it—descended a few more stairs, his eyes locked on Dooley again.

"Can I help you with something?" he said.

Dooley shook his head. "No, it's okay," he said. He glanced at Esperanza, but she refused to meet his eyes. As she started to swing the door shut, Dooley heard the man say, "You know the rules, Esperanza. No visitors during work hours. No exceptions."

She was afraid of something, Dooley thought. Maybe just of being caught talking to someone when she was supposed to be working. Or maybe it was something else.

Dooley reached out, caught the door, and pushed it open again. The man turned toward it, surprised.

"Actually," Dooley said, "I was looking for Win. I'm a friend of his from school."

"Oh," the man said. He looked Dooley over again. "He's out for the day. But you can probably chase him down on his cell."

"I'll do that," Dooley said. "Thanks."

Esperanza dared a glance at him as she pushed the door shut again. This time she looked grateful.

■ ■ ■

Two houses away from his uncle's place, Dooley's heart slammed to a stop in his chest. Beth was sitting on his uncle's porch steps. She looked fine in jeans and a pale blue sweater with a jacket over top. She stood up when she saw Dooley. Dooley hesitated. Was she going to yell at him again? Was she going to get all the elderly neighbors outside, the ones who were home all day and who had nothing to do but look out the window or sit on their porches and watch what was going on, which was usually nothing, which meant that a girl screaming at a guy right out there where everyone could see would be a real attention-getter.

She stood so still there on the steps that it seemed to Dooley that she wasn't even breathing. He walked toward her, his insides churning, his breath coming so fast it was keeping time with his heart, which had started pounding in his ears, boy, it was beating double-time. He turned and headed up the walk, and now he could smell her, all soapy and fresh, her long hair gleaming in the sunlight.

She said, "Why didn't you tell me what the fight was about?"

"What fight?" Dooley said.

"When you hit my brother."

Now it was hit. Before it had been attack.

"That friend of yours told me. I didn't believe him. I told

him so. He said I could ask at the video store. He said one of the clerks saw it, a girl, Linelle. She told me what you did and why you did it."

Good old Linelle. Dooley owed her another one and wondered how he was going to pay her back.

"I'm sorry Mark did that," she said. "I thought he was getting better."

Getting better? What did she mean by that?

"You didn't push him off that bridge, did you?" she said, her tone telling him she had already made up her mind.

"I hardly knew him," Dooley said. The more he said it, the gladder he was that it was true.

"They're saying now their pretty sure he *was* pushed."

"I know." He looked into her big, sad eyes. "If you want me to, I'll get hypnotized." There was no reason not to anymore. He had told his uncle the truth. Maybe he'd get into trouble for where he'd been that night, but that would be nothing compared to the trouble Graff could make for him. "But I'm pretty sure I didn't see anyone up there with him."

"I don't understand why anyone would push Mark off a bridge," she said. Her eyes were filling up with tears, but her voice was firm. "I know you probably don't have the best impression of him." That was putting it mildly. "I know he could be difficult. But it's not his fault—and he tries to deal with it. Well, most of the time he tries to deal with it. Tried. And he can be so sweet. He participated in this special program at his school last year. He spent all of this past January in Guatemala, helping to build a school in a small village. He loved it there. And people liked him." Dooley wondered where Esperanza was from. "He was like a different person when he came back. He was relaxed. For a while, anyway" She showed him the whisper of a smile. Then her eyes clouded again and she said, "I don't understand what you were doing with his backpack."

He looked at her and wished he could put his arms around her. He wished he could hold her and feel how warm she was. Instead he said, "You want to come into the house?" He said it not because he expected her to say yes but because the old lady across the street had come onto her porch and was standing there, a dust rag in her hand, like she'd come outside to shake it. But she wasn't shaking it; no, she was just standing there, looking across the street at Dooley. Dooley knew that the old woman knew her uncle, who said good morning or good evening to her when he saw her and sometimes went across the street and stood on the sidewalk and chatted with her. Dooley wondered if his uncle had asked her to keep an eye on things. It was possible.

"Okay," Beth said, following his gaze across the street. "Sure."

Dooley led the way up the steps and unlocked the front door. He went in first and held the door for her. She stepped in behind him and stood there in the hall, looking around, listening, probably wondering if anyone else was home.

"I live with my uncle," Dooley said. "He's not here right now."

He waited to see if she would change her mind, but she didn't. She closed the door behind herself.

"Can I get you anything?" Dooley said. "Maybe something

to drink? A soda? Water? I can make you some tea if you want."

"I'm fine," she said.

They stood in the hall. Dooley didn't know how she felt, but he felt awkward. Here was this beautiful girl in his house—well, in his uncle's house—not sure about him, but here and, for a change, not yelling at him.

"You want to sit down?" He nodded toward the living room.

She went in, looking all around her the way Warren had, the same half-surprised look on her face that made Dooley wonder exactly what people had been saying about him and what impressions they had formed based on what they had heard. She took a seat on one of the armchairs. He sat across from her, on the sofa.

"How did you get his backpack?" she said.

So he explained how he had gone looking for it, how he had asked around and passed the word, and how a homeless guy had finally showed up at the store with it.

"I was going to give it to you," he said. "But the cops got hold of it first."

"They won't let me have it," she said. "They say it's evidence."

"I'm sorry."

"Detective Graff won't say, but I get the feeling he thinks you had something to do with it. But you didn't, did you?"

"No."

He fingered the envelope of photographs in his jacket pocket and considered showing them to her. But he hesitated.

Finding her brother's backpack was one thing. What would she think if she knew that he had gone through her brother's personal things and had broken into his locked files?

"I really am sorry," he said, apologizing for that even though she didn't know about it. "At first I thought if I could find out where he was between the time he left home that day and the time I saw . . . the time he died . . . I wanted to do something, you know." Boy, he bet he sounded lame. "I thought if you knew that, it might help you find out what happened that night."

"At first?"

"When the cops found the backpack . . ." He hesitated. "You're right. I think they're looking at me as a suspect. I thought as long as I'm still out and walking around—" He broke off. She was giving him that look again, the one that told him although she lived just across town, she might as well live on the other side of the world. She had no idea what he was talking about. Probably the most trouble she'd ever been in was being late for school. Probably the only time she had ever talked to a cop before her brother died was if one had come to her school to talk about safety or the hazards of doing drugs. "Beth, was your brother seeing anyone?"

"Seeing anyone?" The idea seemed to surprise her. "You mean, did he have a girlfriend?"

Dooley nodded.

"No."

Dooley remembered the pictures of Esperanza that Everley had taken close up. You could see the joy in Esperanza's eyes. You could see how smooth and clear her skin was and you could imagine how it felt to touch it, especially in the ones where she was lounging against something, not wearing much, staring into that camera like she was staring into her lover's eyes. Dooley would have bet everything he had that she was. When he'd seen her crying on Gillette's shoulder the night of the party at Rhodes' house, he had assumed it was because Landers had been hassling her. Now it looked like there was another reason for her tears. But Beth didn't know about her. He thought about the party at Rhodes' house. All of Everley's friends had been there, but not Esperanza, at least, not in the same way as everyone else. She'd only been there because she was working. Rhodes and the rest of them hadn't paid any attention to her at all other than to make sure she brought in the snacks and answered the door—well, except Landers who had hassled her and Gillette who had comforted her when she was crying. He wondered now . . . yeah, that had to be it. For some reason, Everley and Esperanza had kept their relationship a secret. That would explain Esperanza's tears and the way she was treated at the party, like the maid instead of Everley's grieving girlfriend. It would explain why Everley had locked her pictures on the flash drive. The cops had talked to all of Everley's friends, but had they talked to Esperanza? If no one knew about her and Everley, maybe they hadn't.

But if Esperanza had been in love with Everley, why hadn't she spoken to the police on her own? Maybe for the same reason she and Everley had kept their relationship a secret. But what reason was that? Maybe it had to do with Rhodes' parents. She had seemed nervous enough when Dooley was at the door.

He looked at Beth and said, “Are Rhodes’ parents funny about the hired help?”

“What do you mean?”

“You know, like, are they strict with their maid? Do they have a lot of rules she has to follow?”

“How would I know that?” Beth said, the look on her face telling him that there was a part two to her question: *What does that have to do with anything*?

“Well, you know them. Rhodes and his parents, I mean. You know more than me what they’re like.”

“No, I don’t.”

“Okay, so maybe you don’t know everything about them. But you’ve probably seen what they’re like with the help—”

“I’ve never met Win’s parents,” Beth said. “In fact, I only met Win about a week before . . .” Her throat seemed to close up on her. It looked to Dooley like she was fighting for breath for a few seconds. “I was in this club with some of my friends about a week before Mark died.” Her chin trembled a little. “Mark came in with Win and Peter. He was really surprised to see me there.”

“Win was?”

“No, Mark.” She frowned. “He acted kind of weird that night.”

“What do you mean?”

“When he came into the club, at first he pretended like he didn’t see me. Then it looked like he suddenly changed his mind and was trying to get Win and Peter to leave with him. So I went up to him and said, ‘Aren’t you going to introduce me to your friends?' I could see he didn't want to, which made me mad, you know? So I introduced myself. Win and Peter laughed. They thought I was kidding. They thought it was some kind of joke, you know, like Mark had brought them there to pull one over on them. They kept saying, *sure* I was his sister, like they didn't believe it, like Mark had put me up to telling them I was."

"So you'd never even met any of his friends before that?"

She shook her head.

No wonder Bracey had said what he had at the party. Anyone who had formed an impression of Beth based on the knowledge that she went to a special school and then met her in person would be more than a little surprised.

"You don't think that's strange?" Dooley said.

She shook her head slowly. "Mark worried about me all the time. I used to tell him he was being over-protective."

Dooley wanted to ask what Everley had been protecting her from, but he decided to wait and let her tell it her way.

"I asked him a couple of times why he didn't bring his friends over to the house. He always said they weren't my kind of people. I thought he meant because some of them were rough, you know? Maybe that was part of it. You saw how Peter was in the schoolyard that time, and at the party? His girlfriend told me he has a real temper. He gets into a lot of fights. I heard stuff about Eddy, too. Win told me how he met him. Mark probably didn't want me around people like that. He was probably afraid how I'd react."

Dooley didn't understand. She looked down at the floor for a moment and was quiet, as if she were lost in her private thoughts. Finally she said, "When I was ten and Mark was eleven, we went down to the States with our father. He was a writer, scripts and stuff. Mostly he wrote things that never got produced. This time, he had just sold a script to one of the big studios and he took Mark and me to L.A. with him. He had a bunch of meetings to go to, but he had lots of time to show us the sights. It was really exciting, you know? We even met some movie stars."

She had her hands clasped in her lap. It seemed to Dooley as if she were trying to tame them, but she wasn't having much success. She kept fidgeting while she talked.

"We were on the freeway one night, on our way to a restaurant where my dad said all the celebrities ate. My father was so happy. He'd been trying to make it for a long time and this was a really big deal for him. He was taking us out to celebrate and . . ." Her voice trailed off. Her chest heaved as she drew in a deep breath and looked at Dooley. "We were car-jacked. Can you believe it? I was riding up front with my father and we pulled up at a light and this guy came at the car with a gun. He made my dad open the door and he told him to get out. My father tried to tell him that he had kids in the car, but that just made the guy angry. He yanked my father out of the car and started hitting him and kicking him. Then he shot him." She was looking at Dooley, but Dooley knew that she was seeing something else, something from the past. "My father was shot and the guy was screaming at me to get out of the car. But I didn't. I couldn't move. I knew he was terrified he was going to shoot me if I didn't get out, but I just couldn't make myself do it. I felt like

I'd turned to stone."

She drew in another breath. Dooley could see that she was struggling to stay calm—well, as calm as she could, which, in fact, wasn't all that calm. Her eyes were glistening now. Dooley knew it was just a matter of time before tears started dribbling down her cheeks. He felt bad for her.

"Mark was in the back seat, and the car windows were tinted. So I don't think the car-jacker saw him. At least, that's what Mark always said." She frowned when she said it, almost as if she didn't believe it. "I was sitting up front, staring at the guy. Mark burst out of the back seat and he grabbed the gun. I remember screaming. The man had already shot my father. I was sure he was going to shoot Mark and then he was going to shoot me and all I could think of was some police officer ringing the doorbell back home and telling my mother that both her kids and her ex-husband had been shot dead."

There they were, those tears. They streaked down her cheeks, pooled at her jaw line, and fell like plump raindrops into her lap. She didn't seem to notice.

"But it didn't turn out that way. Mark jumped out of the car and he grabbed the guy's gun. Do you believe it? He was eleven years old—well, almost twelve. It was two weeks before his twelfth birthday. Anyway, I guess the guy was taken by surprise or something because the next thing I knew the gun went off again, only this time it was the car-jacker who was shot, not Mark. The guy fell down and Mark started kicking him. The guy was lying there on the ground—I don't know if he was dead of not. I couldn't take my eyes off Mark. He was kicking him and kicking him and kicking him. You can't believe the sound it made." She shuddered, as if she were hearing it right that second. "He was still kicking the guy when the police got there. He didn't even check to see how my dad was. Neither of us did. Can you believe it? We didn't even check. He could have been alive and we wouldn't have known it. By the time the police and the ambulance got there, though, he was dead. That's what the ambulance guys said. Mark was a mess. He kicked the guy until he couldn't stand up anymore. And I was screaming. That's what Mark said. He said I was screaming and he was yelling at me to stop, but I wouldn't. He said that scared him worse than anything."

Jesus, Dooley thought. He didn't know what to say. He got up, grabbed a box of tissues from an end table, and handed it to her. She pulled out a tissue and wiped her eyes and her cheeks.

"Anyway," she said, "I guess you could say we both had problems after that." Dooley just bet they did—Everley especially. He wondered how much Beth knew about her brother and what he'd been up to. "I'd get scared," she said. "Strange people, sudden moves, loud noises, that kind of thing. My mom took me out of public school and sent me to a small private school. Mark had different problems. He used to get so angry. But never with me. He never got angry with me. He always looked after me."

And that, Dooley guessed he was supposed to assume, was why Mark Everley told his friends that his sister went to a special school. To protect her. But what did he expect her to do with her life? Become a nun?

She blew her nose delicately and looked at Dooley.

"I thought that was why he didn't want to introduce me to his friends."

It sounded like a good reason not to introduce her to Landers. But what about Rhodes?

"Later that night, Mark told me it was also because of the way his friends were with girls. He said they were never serious, that they were only interested in one thing."

Dooley flashed on an image of Landers at the party, pushing himself on Esperanza. Yeah, he could see how a guy wouldn't want to introduce his own sister to someone like that.

"Win, though, he's different," Beth said. "He called me the next night and we talked for an hour." A smile played across her mouth. Dooley tried to imagine what it must be like to be the guy who could make her glow like that. "He's kind of shy, you know? He called me four or five times before he finally asked me out." Dooley wished he could ask her out. He wished that there was even a ghost of a chance that if he did, she would say yes. "It didn't work out, though, because then Mark died and Win . . . I guess he thinks I need some time. He's been great. He calls all the time to see how I am. He threw that party to raise money for the scholarship. He even came over one time and talked to my mother—told her all kinds of nice things about Mark. It meant a lot to her." Her eyes were moist now and Dooley was afraid she was going to start crying again. There was no way he could even consider showing her the other pictures.

If it ever came to it, he sure didn't want to be the one to show her how fucked up her brother really was. "Why do you want to know how Win's parents are with their servants?"

Dooley shrugged.

"Curiosity, I guess," he said. "I never saw a place like theirs before. I never knew anyone with a maid. I was just wondering."

She nodded and they sat there for a few moments, Dooley wishing he could think of something to say and wishing even more than that that he was in the same league as Rhodes so that at least he'd have a fighting chance, and Beth, well, Dooley guessed she was thinking either about her brother or about Rhodes, and why not?

"Well," she said, breaking the silence. "I just wanted to apologize."

"No problem," Dooley said, jumping to his feet when he saw she was getting up.

She stood opposite him, looking at him. He wanted to reach out and touch her. He wanted to pull her close against him so that he could feel her all over. He wanted to kiss her and taste her and . . .

She turned and started for the door. Dooley stumbled behind her. They both reached for the doorknob at the same time, their hands making contact, then they both pulled their hands back at the same time as if they had each touched an open flame which, in truth, was exactly how Dooley felt. Finally Dooley opened the door and she said a soft good-bye as she stepped out onto the porch. Dooley closed the door quickly behind her so that he didn't look like a complete loser, but he stood there, looking out the little diamond-shaped window, watching her cross the porch, descend the steps, walk down the path to the sidewalk, and, finally, disappear from sight. Only after she had vanished did he think again about Esperanza.

Esperanza with her soft sweet Spanish accent.

Esperanza who was afraid of something.

Esperanza with her secret.

Then he was ran up to his room, taking the stairs two at a time, praying that his uncle hadn't done one of his circuits of the house with a big trash bag, emptying all the wastepaper baskets.

And . . .

No. It was still there where Dooley had left it. He scooped it out now—the business card he had found in Everley's backpack—Bryce Someone-or-other, who had something to do with immigrants and refugees, together with the scraps of paper that had fallen out of the notebook along with the card. He glanced at the scraps. Everley had photocopied something—it looked like something from the newspaper—and then had torn it up. Dooley threw them back into the wastepaper basket. He read the address on the business card and then stuck it into his pocket. ■

Twenty-Five

The address turned out to be a large office above a hardware store. The place was open-concept. Just inside the door, facing what Dooley took to be a reception desk, were a couple of rows of chairs where people—all kinds of people from, it looked like, all over the world—were waiting with, in some cases, what looked like their whole families. Beyond that were dividers that, as far as Dooley could see, marked off little cubicles where still more people sat at desks piled high with file folders while they talked to still other people.

Dooley went up to the woman at the reception desk, who was having a conversation with a man in gray flannel pants and a sports jacket. When the receptionist finally turned to Dooley, he asked to see the man whose name was printed on the business card.

"I'm Bryce Weathers," the man in the gray flannel pants said. "What can I do for you?"

Dooley had given this some thought on the way over. There were two ways to go: tell the truth or bend the truth.

He chose the latter.

"A friend of mine was in here a while ago," Dooley said. "Mark Everley."

Bryce Weathers frowned. "The name doesn't ring a bell," he said. "What was the issue?"

"It was about his girlfriend."

"Can you be more specific?"

"Mark died a few weeks ago. His girlfriend gave me the card you gave Mark. She asked me to talk to you."

Dooley fished the card out of his pocket. Bryce Weathers looked at it and handed it back to Dooley.

"Oh," he said. "He saw Sara, not me. Sara is always running out of business cards. When she does, she grabs one of mine and scribbles her name on it." He went up on tiptoe so that he could look over the tops of the dividers. "Down that aisle, fourth cubicle on the left."

Dooley followed his directions and found himself looking into a cluttered cubicle at a young black woman who was talking on the phone. She looked up and waved him into a chair, putting up a finger to signal that she'd be just a minute.

Dooley sat down and waited a couple of minutes before she finally hung up the phone.

"What can I do for you?" she said.

"I'm here because of my friend Mark Everley," Dooley said. "He came to see you about his girlfriend Esperanza."

Sara didn't say anything. If Dooley had been forced to name the expression on her face, he would have said it was suspicion. Dooley put the business card on the desk in front of her. She glanced at it and then looked at him.

"Mark died a few weeks ago," Dooley said.

That made her sit up straight.

"What happened?" she said.

"He fell off a bridge. It was in the papers."

"The papers," she said. "I don't have time to read the papers. I feel like I don't have time for anything anymore. Was it an accident?"

"Yeah," Dooley said. If she didn't read the papers, what was the harm?

She let out a sigh. "Well, thank goodness for that."

Dooley looked at her.

"I'm sorry," she said. "He was your friend. It's just that when he was here . . ." She broke off. "I'm sorry. I really can't discuss my conversation with Mark. We guarantee confidentiality."

"But Esperanza asked me to come," Dooley said.

"With all due respect, how do I know that you're telling me the truth?" Sara said. "You could be anyone. You could be with the immigration department."

"I'm seventeen years old," Dooley said, pulling out his ID to prove it. "I went to school with Mark. I know Esperanza. She needs help."

She looked at his ID, including his student card. Then she studied him for a moment. Dooley let her think it through. If she wasn't going to tell him, she wasn't going to tell him.

"I'm afraid I can't tell you anything that I didn't already tell Mark. Esperanza's visitor's visa expired over a year ago. She could have applied to extend it, but she didn't and now it's too late. She's in the country illegally. The only hope for her being able to get status here is to leave the country and then to apply through the regular channels. And there are no guarantees she would be accepted, especially since she extended her stay illegally in the first place."

Well, that explained why Mark had the business card.

"As for her employment conditions," Sara continued. Employment conditions? Dooley wondered what Sara was talking about. "There's really nothing that she can do about that, either, except leave her job and try to find another one. But the reality is that it's very difficult for undocumented workers to find decent employment. First of all, anyone who hires them knowing of their status is breaking the law. Second, without documentation, there are very few honest people who are willing to hire them. As I understand it, Esperanza got her present employment through a friend of her family's who is also in the country legally. Her employers are fully aware of her situation. From what Mark says, it sounds as though they think they're doing her a favor—saving her from a terrible life back home. It doesn't matter. They are still breaking the law. So is Esperanza."

Dooley wondered how much of a favor Rhodes' parents were doing. Judging by how nervous she was around Rhodes' father, he wouldn't be surprised to find out that Rhodes's father was taking advantage of her situation.

"I'm sorry about Mark," Sara said. "And I'm sorry for Esperanza. But there really isn't much I can do except offer to go with her to immigration."

Dooley thanked her for her time. He got up. As he was leaving her cubicle, he said, "Why thank goodness?"

She looked at him.

"You looked relieved when I said his death was an accident,' Dooley said.

She offered him a wan smile. "I was probably being overdramatic," she said. "But . . ." She hesitated again. "I gave him nothing but bad news when he was here. Just before he left, he said he had one more question." She hesitated again. Dooley bided hid time. "He wanted to know, if anyone Esperanza knew got into serious trouble with the police and the police questioned her and found out she was here illegally, what would happen to her?"

"What would happen?" Dooley said.

"Well, at the moment the police have a don't-ask, don't-tell policy. They wouldn't ask her about her immigration status unless it were relevant. But if someone else were to tell them, she'd be taken into custody, handed over to immigration officials, and deported."

He felt bad for Esperanza, too, but not too bad. Maybe she didn't know it, but she was better off without Mark Everley. He also felt confident that, knowing what he did, he could get her to tell him whatever she knew about the pictures Everley had taken and what he had been up to the night he had died.

■ ■ ■

Esperanza didn't answer the door at the Rhodes residence. Rhodes did.

"Hey, Dooley," he said, smiling, pleasantly surprised.

"My dad called me from the airport. He said you came by. What's up?"

Going through Dooley's head at that exact moment were two words: think fast.

Then it occurred to him: why not just play it straight—well, as straight as he could without blowing things for Esperanza before he had a chance to speak to her.

"I wanted to talk to you about Mark," he said.

Rhodes looked surprised.

"What about him?" he said.

"You heard what happened at school yesterday," Dooley said. Of course he had. Rhodes had been right there. Dooley had seen him put his arm around Beth and lead her inside. "So you probably know that the cops think maybe I pushed him off that bridge."

Rhodes' cheeks turned pink. "I heard," he said, peering at Dooley from behind the lenses of his glasses. "Did you?"

"No," Dooley said.

Rhodes hesitated before opening the door wider.

"Come on in," he said. He led Dooley down the hall to the games room where the party for Everley's scholarship had been held. "You want something to drink?" he said.

"Ginger ale," Dooley said.

Rhodes went behind the bar and pulled a can of soda and a beer from the fridge.

"You sure you don't want something else?" he said. He held up the beer can. "Something with a little more kick? We got it all."

"Ginger ale is fine," Dooley said.

Rhodes shrugged and tossed him the can of ginger ale. He twisted the cap off a beer for himself and waved Dooley over to a couch.

"You knew Mark pretty well, didn't you?" Dooley said.

"Sure. As well as anyone, I guess. Why?"

"He ever strike you as . . . odd?"

"Odd?"

"Strange," Dooley said, trying to clarify without getting into too much detail. "For example, he sure seemed to like to pick a fight."

"Mark had issues," Rhodes said. "Something about what happened to him when he was a kid."

"Did he tell you about that?"

"Not much," Rhodes said. "Just that his father was murdered. He didn't go into details. But my mom used to be a social worker, so I know all about stuff like that. Mark's father was killed right in front of him. Mark had problems with that. People see something like that . . ." His voice trailed off and he shook his head again.

"Did he ever say anything to you about other stuff he might have done? Weird stuff?"

"Weird stuff? Like what?"

"He never mentioned anything about, say, animals?"

"Animals?" Rhodes looked completely baffled. "What are you talking about, Dooley?"

Yeah, Dooley, what *are* you talking about? What kind of person would collect small animal skulls? A sick person, that's what kind. And how likely do you think that person would be to discuss that collection with his pals? He decided to try another tack, feel things out a little.

"Do you know if Mark was seeing anyone?"

"You mean, did he have a girlfriend? Why?"

"If he was, maybe I could talk to her. Maybe—"

Dooley's pager vibrated. He dug it out of his pocket and looked at it. Wouldn't you know it?

"Everything okay?" Rhodes said.

"I have to make a call," Dooley said, looking around.

Rhodes looked at him as if he'd just dropped down from Mars.

"You don't have a cell phone?"

Dooley shook his head. He was definitely going to have to do something about that.

"You can use that phone," Rhodes said, nodding to the one on the end of the bar.

Dooley thought about what his uncle, who had just paged him, would say if he found out that Dooley was at Winston Rhodes' house after everything that had happened and after his uncle had warned him to stay away from Rhodes and the rest of them.

"I think I'm going to have to find a pay phone," he said.

Rhodes thought for a moment. "I think the closest one is . . . well, to be honest, I have no idea where the closest one is. But there must be one in the neighborhood somewhere."

Shit.

"My uncle," Dooley said, feeling as lame as he no doubt sounded. "After what happened at your party . . ."

Rhodes understood immediately.

"You can use the phone here," he said. "We're not listed.

The read-out says Private Number. You could tell him you're at a friend's house."

Dooley supposed he could, if he thought his uncle would believe for one minute that he even had a friend.

"Or maybe you borrowed someone's cell phone," Rhodes said. "You know, someone who wants to keep it private."

Someone, Dooley thought, like Linelle.

"If you need some privacy, there's a phone in the kitchen," Rhodes said.

Dooley went into the kitchen and punched in his uncle's cell number.

"How's Jeannie's mother?" Dooley said as soon as his uncle answered.

"It's too soon to tell," his uncle said. "What's up with you? Graff hasn't come at you again, has he?"

Dooley told him no. He asked, "How's Jeannie? Is she okay?"

"She's worried," Dooley's uncle said. "What about you, Ryan?"

"I'm fine. Linelle and I are having lunch."

"Linelle?"

"From work. She's the one who usually answers the phone when you call the store."

"Linelle," Dooley's uncle said again. "The one who told me you were in the can when you were really at the party? That Linelle?"

"She was just doing me a favor," Dooley said. "You want me to put her on so she can apologize to you?"

There was a pause on the other end of the phone, and Dooley was afraid his uncle would say, sure, go ahead. Instead, he said, "You working tonight?"

"Tomorrow night."

"So I can get you at home later if I need to."

"Yeah," Dooley said.

"And you'll call me or get Annette to call me if anything happens?"

"Yeah," Dooley said. "You still planning to be back in town tomorrow night?"

"Why? You got another party planned?"

Jesus, the guy never let up

"Yeah, probably tomorrow night," his uncle. "If anything changes, I'll call you."

"Tell Jeannie I said I hope her mom's going to be okay," Dooley said before he hung up.

When Dooley went back to the games room, Rhodes was sitting in the same place, nursing the same beer.

"Everything okay?" he said.

"My uncle's a hard-ass," Dooley said. "He checks up on me all the time."

"My dad's like that sometimes," Rhodes said. "What were you saying about Mark? What weird stuff?"

Jesus, and didn't his pager vibrate again? He checked the read-out.

"Not your uncle again, I hope?" Rhodes said.

"He's giving me a hard time, that's for sure," Dooley said. "Do you mind?"

Rhodes gave him a sympathetic look.

Dooley hesitated.

"I don't suppose there's another phone I could use. Maybe a little more private."

"Sure," Rhodes said. "My dad's study is down the hall from the kitchen. There's a phone in there." He grinned at Dooley. "Don't tell me . . . it's a girl, right?"

"I won't be long," Dooley said.

He had no trouble finding the study. He'd used the phone in there the night of the party. He dialled the number on his pager.

Warren answered on the first ring.

"I went to the library and checked out those newspaper pages that were in those pictures," he said as soon as he knew it was Dooley. "And guess what?"

He was really buzzing, talking fast and talking loud. Dooley bet his face was flushed.

"They're from different dates," Warren said. "But they're both from last winter, one in January, one in March."

January and March. Dooley remembered the scraps of photocopies that he'd found in Everley's backpack. He'd seen partial dates on them—January and March.

"And you know what else, Dooley?" Warren said.

Dooley humored him. "What?"

"On both of them there are stories about homeless guys who were killed."

"Killed? What do you mean, killed?"

"The paper said homicide," Warren said. "I checked all the newspapers that came after, all the way up until yesterday, and as far as I can tell, the cops never found out who killed those guys. No one saw anything. They didn't find any evidence they could use—at least, that's what it sounded like in the paper. But you know cops. There's plenty of stuff they don't tell regular people."

Yeah, Dooley knew cops.

"You get it, right, Dooley?" Warren said. "First there's the animal skulls—maybe from animals that he tortured and killed. You know what they say about people who kill small animals, don't you? Guys who torture cats and puppies, they're the ones that grow up to be serial killers."

"Tell me those dates again," Dooley said. When Warren told him, he said, "You mean *last* January, Warren?"

"I mean, just this past January," Warren said. "I told you Mark Everley was fucked up. I told you."

On the basis of what Beth had told him, Dooley had to agree.

"You want me to call the cops?" Warren said.

"No," Dooley said. He thought again about what Beth had said. He thought about how she would react. He thought about Rhodes comforting her. "No, it's okay," he said. Sometimes, the less people knew, the better. "I've got the stuff with me. I'll take care of it, Warren." He was already making a plan. Step one, go home and call his uncle. Step two, call Annette Girondin—his uncle would tell him to do it—and get her to go with him to the police. No way was he going on his own. "Do you have copies of those pictures, Warren?"

"I printed them out and gave them to you."

"All of them?"

"Yeah."

"You don't have copies on your computer?"

"No," Warren said. "I printed them off the flash drive and I gave the drive back to you."

Dooley patted his pocket, reassuring himself that the drive was still there.

"Okay," he said. "Don't do anything. I'll take care of it. I'll let you know, okay?" He was about to hang up when he remembered another question he wanted to ask. "Hey, Warren? You know those locked files? You said some were older than others. Do you remember which ones were the most recent?"

"Sure," Warren said. "The weirdest ones—the ones of the skulls and the dead homeless guys. Everley locked those almost exactly a month ago."

Dooley glanced at the calendar on the desk. A month ago was two days before Everley died.

"Thanks, Warren," he said.

He hung up the phone and started to turn around, glancing as he did at the family portrait in the silver frame at the edge of the desk, then at one of the smaller single portraits beside it. He picked it up and looked closely at it. He fumbled in his pocket for the pictures Warren had printed. What were the chances? He looked at them both again and then put the pictures and the small framed portrait into his pocket. Then he turned toward the door, and jumped—involuntarily—when he saw Landers leaning against the doorframe. Dooley wondered how long he had been there. He put a blank look on his face and pushed past Landers, but felt him behind him all the way back to the games room.

"Everything okay?" Rhodes said. He wasn't on the couch where Dooley had left him, but was over by the bar now.

"Yeah," Dooley said. "That was my uncle again. Look, I gotta go."

Landers was right beside him now, crowding him.

"I thought you wanted to ask me something about Mark," Rhodes said. "And about his girlfriend? That's why you came over here, isn't it?"

"It's going to have to wait," Dooley said. "If I don't get home, my uncle is going to bust me. If you ever met him, you'd know what I mean."

"At least finish your drink," Rhodes said. "What's a couple of minutes? It's not like your uncle's going to know, right?"

Huh?

"He's out of town until tomorrow night, isn't that what you said?"

He sure hadn't said it to Rhodes.

So much for privacy in the kitchen. Dooley was glad he'd made his second call from the den.

"That doesn't mean he can't check up on me," Dooley said. "He calls me where I'm supposed to be and then freaks out if I'm not there. And today I'm supposed to be home. I really have to go."

"He took a picture from your dad's desk," Landers said.

Shit. What was Landers even doing here?

"A picture?" Rhodes said.

"One of the framed ones," Landers said. "I saw him put it in his pocket."

Rhodes looked almost disappointed. He reached out a hand. Dooley took the framed picture from his pocket and handed it to him.

Rhodes glanced at it and set it on the bar.

"Eddy told me you used to steal things,"he said. "But he never told me that you stole from friends."

Dooley shrugged apologetically. He muttered that he was sorry and headed for the door. For sure Rhodes would want him out of there, and Dooley was only to happy to oblige. Landers blocked his way.

"He was talking to someone named Warren," Landers said. "I think it was that dweeb from school. I told you I saw them leaving school together the other day. Hanging with the losers, huh, Dooley? Guess it takes one to know one." He glanced at Rhodes. "They were talking about pictures."

Rhodes didn't ask what pictures. He didn't even look surprised that that's what Dooley had been talking about. He just nodded. That's when Dooley saw exactly where Rhodes was sitting—on a stool at the end of the bar, right beside the phone.

Dooley started again for the door. Rhodes nodded at Landers. Landers shoved him back hard.

"Hand them over," Rhodes said, sliding off the bar stool and coming toward Dooley.

"I don't know what you're talking about."

"The photos and the flash drive. Hand them over."

So he knew about the flash drive. That meant he'd been listening. Dooley shoved Landers out of his way. Landers shoved him back and, Jesus, the guy was strong. Dooley would have bet everything he had that Landers worked out. Regularly. When Dooley tried again to get past him, Landers took a shot at him. Dooley made a move to strike back, but Rhodes grabbed him from behind and pinned his arms. Dooley struggled to free himself. Rhodes's parents were out of town. Dooley had no idea where Esperanza was. He had to get out of there—*now*. But Rhodes turned out to be as strong as Landers. He held Dooley while Landers punched him, hard, in the head—bam, ***bam***, ***bam***, Jesus—almost knocking him out. Dooley sank to his knees, then to all fours. His head was ringing.

"Empty his pockets," Rhodes said.

Dooley felt hands on him, thrusting into his jacket pockets, his pants pockets, pulling out stuff, his wallet, his keys, the envelope of pictures, the flash drive. Rhodes kept a firm grip on him the whole time.

"There's a utility bin under the sink at the bar," Rhodes said. "There's some duct tape in it. Get it."

Landers went for it. When he returned, Rhodes held Dooley and Landers taped Dooley's hands behind his back. Once Dooley was secured, Rhodes picked up the envelope and flicked through the photos.

"What's in them?" Landers said, glancing at Rhodes but mostly keeping a close eye on Dooley, ready to hit him again if he had to. Maybe eager to hit him again. Dooley's head pounded. He wished he had his baseball bat and free hands to use it.

"He knows," Rhodes said. "Eddy must have told him."

Dooley looked at him, surprised.

Landers turned pale. "Jesus, Win, what are we—"

"Relax," Rhodes said.

"Yeah, but—"

"It's okay, Peter," Rhodes said. "The cops already think Dooley killed Eddy." He set the photos on the bar. "What do you think they'd do, Dooley, if they found out the whole story about you and Eddy?"

So Gillette hadn't kept his mouth shut about that. Dooley supposed that figured.

"They also have their suspicions about you and Mark," Rhodes said. "What if someone told them that you'd made threats against Mark? Peter was there when you had that fight. He could tell the police that you and Mark had words the next day. Maybe Mark tried to get even with you and you didn't like that. Maybe you decided to deal with him once and for all. With your history and your record, not to mention your temper—what do you think would happen then? After all, they found you with his backpack."

Dooley tried not to panic. What was Rhodes going to do? Call the cops on him and frame him for murder? Well, good luck. That wasn't going to stop Dooley from telling what he knew. He was surprised that a guy as smart as Rhodes didn't realize that. Besides, Warren had seen the pictures, even if he hadn't kept copies of them. Warren could back him up. Well, except Warren thought the photos were about Everley. Even if they were, they weren't *just* about Everley.

Rhodes was leaning calmly against the bar now, looking relaxed. He came across like a smart guy. Preppy, with a good-guy likeability about him, happy to welcome people into his house. But he wasn't anything like he seemed. He went behind the bar and fiddled with something. When he came back around the bar, he had a glass in his hand.

"Have a drink, Dooley," he said, extending a glass.

"No, thanks," Dooley said.

Rhodes grabbed a handful of Dooley's hair and jerked his head up. Dooley turned his head aside.

"Hold his nose, Peter," Rhodes said.

Landers hesitated. Dooley tried to get up. Rhodes pushed him down again.

"Do it, Peter."

Landers pinched Dooley's nose shut. Dooley held his breath as long as he could, but finally he had to open his mouth. Rhodes jerked his head back further and started pouring the drink down his throat. Dooley resisted, tried to spit it out, and almost choked instead.

"Good boy," Rhodes said, getting up and taking the glass back behind the bar where he washed it and dried it and set it back on a shelf. "Watch him," he said. He left the room.

Dooley turned to Landers.

"Win's right," he said. "I know. I know what you did." He was guessing Landers was involved—look at the way he'd reacted when Rhodes had said it must have been Gillette who told Dooley. "What you *and* Rhodes did," Dooley said. "And Mark." He saw right away from Landers' face that he was wrong there. Everley hadn't been involved. So where did he fit in? He must have found out somehow. Found out and taken those pictures. "I bet it was Rhodes who instigated it, am I right, Peter?" Dooley thought about the little framed picture he had taken from the desk in the den. He thought about how Everley could have known. "You know what I would do if I were you, Peter? I'd go to the cops. I'd get there first, before Rhodes can say anything, and I'd tell them he made you do it. You cooperate and they could go easy on you."

Landers just stared at him, but Dooley knew he was right. He remembered what Warren had told him. When Rhodes got Landers to back off, he'd told him he could have his fun some other time. Rhodes was the leader. Landers was the follower. And Rhodes had befriended Gillette, of all people. He had described the circumstances. Dooley had a pretty good idea how Everley had ended up as a friend, too. Rhodes probably thought the two of them had a lot in common.

"I've known a lot of guys who did a lot of shit, Peter," Dooley said. "I've done a lot of shit myself. And I'll tell you what—you think you're never going to get caught, but eventually you do. Mark found out what you and Rhodes did. I found out. You think someone else won't?"

"Mark?" Landers said. He looked surprised. Maybe too surprised.

"That's why you and Rhodes killed him," Dooley said, watching Landers' face and realizing with alarm that the room was starting to move around him. There had been days, plenty of days, when he would have welcomed the feeling, would have sought it out if no one had offered it. But not today. Not now. "You killed those homeless guys and Mark found out, is that it? Did he tell you he was going to the police? Or did you and Rhodes find out about the pictures

Mark had taken? Is that it?"

"What are you talking about?" Landers said. "Mark fell. Nobody killed him. The cops said it was an accident." Either he was an outstanding actor or he really believed what he was saying.

"You didn't hear?" Dooley said. "The cops think someone pushed Mark off that bridge."

"They think *you* pushed him," Rhodes said, coming back into the room, carrying something in his hand. "They also think you killed Eddy. And then you came over here because you know that I can tell the police what Eddy told me—the night of my party when you got into it with Eddy, you told him if he wasn't careful, he was going to end up just like Mark Everley. Isn't that what you said, Dooley? Oh, no, wait a minute—your excuse is that you don't remember what you did that night. I bet the police are really buying that."

"At first I thought it was Mark," Dooley said, looking at Landers, not Rhodes, working to keep Landers in focus. "I thought that was his stuff. From what Beth told me, he seemed fucked up enough. I thought those were his pictures. His trophies."

"Trophies?" Landers said. "What are you talking about?"

"But they aren't," Dooley said. "Mark wasn't even in the country last January."

Landers shot Rhodes a look.

"Did he tell you he had the pictures?" Dooley said. "Did he threaten you with them? Was he trying to help Esperanza?" Dooley could see a guy like Everley thinking he could pull that off. "Or did you find out he had taken the pictures? Is that it? You found out he'd stumbled onto your secret and he'd photographed it."

"*What* pictures?" Landers said again, angry now. "Pictures of what?"

Dooley thought about what the woman at the immigration place had told him. He turned to Rhodes. "You know what I think?" he said. "I think Mark was here the night he died. I think he came to get Esperanza. I think he wanted to make sure she was safe before he took those pictures to the police. Isn't that right?" It made sense now. Everley had wanted to get Esperanza out of there. Dooley bet Rhodes knew about the two of them and Everley didn't want Rhodes to try to get back at him by having Esperanza deported.

Landers looked confused. "What's he talking about, Win? *What* pictures?"

"You killed Mark," Dooley said. "He knew how fucked up you are and he didn't want any part of it, so you killed him."

"As I told the police," Rhodes said. "I didn't leave the house the night Mark died. Esperanza has verified that. She told the police that she was here all night and so was I."

"You sure she's going to stick to that story?" Dooley said. He caught a flicker of something in Rhodes's face. Doubt?

"Will someone please tell me what the hell is going on?" Landers said.

"He's right," Rhodes said quietly. "Mark knew. He was going to the police."

"What?" Landers stared at him incredulously.

"He was going to turn us in, Peter. I tried to talk to him. I tried to stop him. That's all that happened. I tried to stop him and he fell."

"Fell?" Landers said.

"The cops say he was pushed," Dooley said.

"He fell," Rhodes said again, his voice hard. "And if you stay calm, Peter, everything will be okay."

"First you killed those homeless guys," Dooley said. "Then you killed Mark. You know what I bet, Rhodes? I bet you have something of his in your treasure chest along with whatever stuff you took from those homeless guys. Am I right?" Another flicker.

'What stuff?" Landers said. "What does he keep talking about homeless *guys*?"

Rhodes' eyes flicked in Landers' direction. "The less said, the better, Peter."

"But why Gillette?" Dooley said, except the words weren't coming out smoothly anymore. He had trouble shaping them around all that cotton in his mouth. "He wasn't in on it. He didn't even know you last year. Why did you kill him?" It didn't make sense. Unless— "You knew Beth wanted me to get hypnotized. You were afraid I'd remember seeing you up there, shoving Mark off that bridge, weren't you? You sent Gillette to ask me about it." That had to be why Gillette had approached Dooley at school and asked him what he had seen and whether he thought Everley had been pushed. Gillette was a lot of things, but he wasn't stupid. He'd probably wondered why Rhodes was so interested.

He'd been tight with Esperanza at the party. Maybe she'd said something that got him thinking. "That's why you invited me to your party. You put something in my drink, and the next thing I know, I'm a suspect in a smash-and-grab—"

"The electronics store was Eddy's idea," Rhodes said mildly. "He didn't like you much, Dooley. If you ask me, he was afraid of you." The idea seemed to amuse Rhodes.

"The smash-and-grab would have got me out of the way, if that's all you wanted," Dooley said. "Why did you kill him?"

"I didn't kill him. I didn't kill Mark and I didn't kill Eddy," Rhodes said, and Dooley had to hand it to him, he was calm. "I have an alibi for both times. Esperanza told the police exactly where I was the night Mark died. And I have half a dozen witnesses for the night Eddy died—we partied pretty late that night, Dooley."

Dooley glanced at Landers.

"How about you, Peter? What's *your* alibi for the night Gillette died? You dropped Megan off at her house, but you didn't stay with her. Where did you go? What's your plan, Peter? Are you going to get Megan to lie for you the way Rhodes gets Esperanza to lie for him? What if she won't? What if her parents were up when she got home or woke up and saw she was there alone? What's your plan B?"

Landers looked nervously at Rhodes.

"That's enough," Rhodes said.

"Look at the pictures, Peter," Dooley said. "Right there on the bar. Look at them."

Landers turned to look at the envelope on the bar. Slowly, he walked toward it and picked it up.

"You knew Mark. You knew how he was always taking pictures. Well, he took some pictures a couple of days before he died. They're in that envelope. Open it. Go ahead. Take a look."

Landers hesitated but finally opened the envelope. He studied the pictures, looking from them to Dooley and back again, and frowned. Finally he said, "What *is* this?"

"I figure they're mementos," Dooley said. "Those newspapers you see? They both have articles about those homeless guys who were killed." Landers looked up, confused.

"Guys," he said. "You keep saying guys."

"Don't listen to him, Peter," Rhodes said.

"Yeah, guys," Dooley said. "Two of them. One in January, one in March. The animal skulls . . . well—" He glanced at Rhodes. "I figure Rhodes has had those for a long time. If you look closely, you'll see a pair of gloves and a hat. I'll bet you anything they're from the homeless guys." But Dooley was watching Landers now, not Rhodes. More than anything, Landers looked bewildered. "See that skull with the gold chain and gold heart around it. Now look at the other picture on the bar, the one in the frame. That's Rhodes' sister. Look at what she's wearing around her neck, Peter."

Landers picked up the framed photograph and stared at it. Then he looked at one of Mark Everley's photos. Finally he glanced at Rhodes.

"You know what I think, Peter?" Dooley said. "I think your pal Rhodes got started torturing small animals. Then he moved onto something just as helpless—his kid sister. Maybe that held him for a while, but he had a taste of it. I've met a few guys like that, Peter. They're scary. Once they get a taste, they get off on it. They want more. So he moved up to a couple of homeless guys—I bet you thought no one would care, right, Rhodes? I bet you thought you could get your thrills and no one was even going to notice."

Landers was still holding the photos. He shook his head. "You keep saying guys, but you've got it wrong. It was only one guy and it didn't happen the way you think."

"Shut up, Peter," Rhodes said.

"We were downtown one night," Landers said. "We'd been out at a movie and then we fooled around and we were on our way home when this old guy came up to us and started to harass us—"

"Peter, shut up," Rhodes said again.

"He's got it all wrong," Landers said. "The guy was in our face. He was hassling us. He was drunk or high or something and he stank. He got aggressive, so Win pushed him away. But the guy kept coming back and coming back. So we—"

"Peter, shut the fuck up."

"When he was down, we kicked him. I just wanted to make sure he didn't get up again, he didn't hassle us anymore, you know?" Landers looked almost sorry. "We didn't even know the guy was dead until the next day. And then—" He shrugged helplessly. "Nobody knew. Nobody saw us. The cops didn't have any leads." He looked at Rhodes.

"Be smart for a change, Peter," Dooley said. The room was starting to spin. His head pounded. "If you're telling the truth, undo me, Peter. Undo me and come to the police with me and tell them everything you know. They can make it easy on you, if you were only involved in that one, if you had nothing to do with the second one, and if you cooperate."

Landers didn't move. "The second one?" he said to Rhodes. "You killed another guy?"

"The first one probably got him all worked up," Dooley said. "He probably couldn't wait to do it again."

Landers stared at Rhodes. "*Two* guys?"

"Don't listen to him, Peter. He doesn't know what he's talking about."

"Look at the pictures, Peter," Dooley said.

Landers was staring at them, first one, then another, then another.

"You said Eddy found out. Eddy, not Mark. You said that's why we . . . "

Dooley had been fishing when he'd asked if Landers had killed Gillette. But, Jesus, if he really had . . .

"I don't know what he told you, Peter. But if you think you're going to get away with it, if you think somehow all of this . . . " he nodded around the room, "if you think all this is going to protect you, if you think *he*'s going to protect you, you're wrong. He killed Mark—your *friend* Mark. Look at the pictures, Peter. He killed his own sister."

Rhodes tensed.

"What are you talking about?" Landers said.

"The animal skulls, the newspapers, the gloves, the hat—they're trophies. Mementos. He probably takes them out and looks at them the way most people look at their vacation souvenirs. He relives the thrill. Why do you think he's got his sister's necklace in there with all that stuff?"

Landers stared at Rhodes.

"My sister drowned," Rhodes said calmly. "It was an accident."

"But these pictures—"

"Forget the pictures. We got bigger things to worry about, Peter."

"What if someone else has seen them?" Landers said.

Rhodes and Landers both turned to Dooley. Dooley couldn't help smiling just a little.

"That dweeb Warren has seen them, but he thinks they belong to Mark. And he doesn't have copies," Rhodes said. "We have everything right here. If the cops ask him about them or if he talks to the cops, that's what he'll say. That the stuff belonged to Mark and that Dooley here had the only copies. And he—" he nodded at Dooley "– he hasn't shown them to the cops yet. He hasn't shown them to anyone yet, have you, Dooley?"

Dooley was sweating now. He had to work hard to stay focused on Rhodes, on his face and on what he was saying.

"Gillette didn't know about the homeless guys," he said. "He couldn't have. But he knew about Mark. Isn't that right, Rhodes? You sent him to talk to me about what I saw that night. And he knew Mark was here the night he died—Esperanza told him, didn't she? And then you asked him to help set me up—to get me out of the way. He knew something was up, didn't he? Did he threaten you or blackmail you?" The room was spinning faster and faster. "Or did you think if Gillette turned up dead, I'd be the natural suspect?"

Landers looked at Rhodes, completely lost now. "What's he talking about, Win? Mark fell, right? That's what you said, right?"

"Shut up, Peter," Rhodes said wearily. He came out from behind the bar. He had a gun in his hand.

Landers' eyes got big staring at it. "What the fuck?" he said. "You're not going to—"

Rhodes crossed to the fireplace, took a brass poker from a stand on the hearth, walked back to where Landers was standing, and handed Landers the gun. Landers stared down at it, like he couldn't believe he was holding it.

"Is this loaded?" he said.

Rhodes didn't answer.

"Win, you're not going to—"

"Mark was one sick guy, Peter," Rhodes said, his voice eerily calm, even soothing. "He told me what he did. He told me everything. I'm pretty sure that's why he jumped. I didn't want to say anything—his family has already been through a lot."

"I don't get it," Landers said. He seemed to be struggling now to keep up. "I thought you said—"

Rhodes raised the poker and brought it down hard on Landers' head. A look of surprise flickered across Landers' face before he crumpled. Rhodes raised the poker and hit him again, harder this time, it seemed to Dooley, the poker making a sickening sound when it made contact with Landers' skull. Rhodes hit him a third time and then straightened up and turned to Dooley. He seemed perfectly calm, one hundred percent in control.

"You came here," Rhodes said to him. "You were completely out of it. I think he must have been on drugs, officer," he said, as if he were talking to the cops now. "He burst into the house, he was completely crazy, he was making crazy accusations. He threatened Peter. It wasn't the first time. He and Peter and Mark Everley were in a street fight in the summer. And then he attacked Peter at my party—you can ask anyone who was there. The next thing I knew, he grabbed a poker from the fireplace and he attacked Peter with it. It was awful. He kept hitting him and hitting him. I didn't know what to do. He was killing Peter. He was doing it right before my eyes. So I ran and got one of my father's guns—yes, officer, I know it shouldn't have been loaded, but, my God, if it hadn't been, I'd be dead by now. I tried to stop him. Honest I did. But after he finished with Peter, he came after me with that poker and I knew he was going to kill me. I had to do it. I had to shoot him." Rhodes bent to pick up the gun that Landers had dropped.

Dooley staggered to his feet. His knees were jelly, but he managed to stay upright. He charged Rhodes as he was straightening up and heard something—it sounded like an explosion—in the split second before his head made contact with Rhodes' belly. Dooley went down. ■

Twenty-Six

"You're not listening, are you?" Warren said.

"What?" Dooley said, turning away from the window because, really, what was the point of looking out anyway? He couldn't see the street, much less the entrance to the hospital. And even if he could, what good would it do? If she hadn't showed up by now, she wasn't going to.

"That's okay," Warren said. "I really just came to drop off the card." The card was enormous. It was made out of construction paper and decorated all over with marking pens and cut-out red hearts. It was from Warren's sister. "She wanted to come with me, but my mother didn't think it was a good idea. Don't ask me why."

Dooley had a pretty good idea. He had seen the newspaper. Rhodes, who was eighteen, was named in the article. So was Landers, seventeen, dead. Also mentioned were two murders (Mark Everley and Edward Gillette) and that the police were looking into additional criminal acts in conjunction with Rhodes and one of the unnamed youths. Dooley imagined there weren't a lot of mothers who wanted their daughters visiting someone who had been involved in all that, especially when it was far from clear what "all that" involved.

"Does it hurt?" Warren said, nodding at Dooley's arm.

"Like a bitch," Dooley said. Rhodes had shot just before Dooley's head plowed into Rhodes' abdomen and just as Dooley was starting to feel that he was losing it. He was pretty sure that Rhodes would have finished him off if his head hadn't made contact with the granite hearth of the fireplace. "But I'm getting discharged first thing tomorrow, so I guess that means it's not serious." He looked at the card that Warren had propped up on the bedside table. "Tell Alicia thanks," he said.

"Sure thing," Warren said.

He and Dooley both turned toward the door in response to a rap on the doorframe, and Dooley lost his breath and his heart in that one instant.

Beth was standing there. She was dressed casually—jeans and a soft blue sweater—but to Dooley she sparkled as if she were wearing jewels. She smiled shyly at him.

"Can I come in?"

Dooley started to say, "Of course," but his mouth was so dry he couldn't get the words out. In the end, he just nodded.

Warren wasn't much better. He stared open-mouthed at Beth for a few moments before he finally stuttered a hello. He told Dooley he had to go, whirled around to leave, and tripped on the chair that was standing beside the bed. He grabbed the back of the chair to steady himself, but the chair started to tip over. If Beth hadn't grabbed an arm to steady him, he would have ended up on the floor. As it was, his face turned crimson, he stammered an apology to Beth—Dooley didn't know why he was apologizing, but he did understand why Warren was acting the way he was—and stumbled out of the room. After he had gone, Beth turned back to Dooley, her head slightly bowed as if she were afraid to look him in the eye.

"I was going to come sooner," she said, "but I wasn't sure you'd want to see me."

Dooley couldn't think of a single reason that he wouldn't want to see her.

"You know," she said, "because of all those things I said about you and thought about you. And because—" She looked down at the floor for a moment. "They said you were shot. That wouldn't have happened if it wasn't for Mark. I'm sorry."

Dooley started to shrug, but the pain caught him and he winced. Beth looked even more upset.

"It's okay," Dooley said. "I'm being discharged tomorrow. The doctor said it was just a flesh wound—it didn't hit any bone or anything. Believe me, I've been hurt worse." He said the last part to make her feel better and remembered too late how she felt about people hurting people and people getting hurt by other people. Jesus, he never said the right thing when she was around.

"I brought you something," she said. She reached into her purse, brought out a plastic bag from a bookstore, and handed it to him. It was a book—Irvine Welsh. "Your uncle said you like him. It's his latest. I hope you haven't read it."

He thanked her.

"How about you?" he said. "How are you doing?"

She shrugged. Her head was bowed again.

"I feel like I'm mad at everyone," she said. "I feel like I want to hurt everyone—Win for what he did to Mark. Peter, for doing what he did. Both of them, pretending to be Mark's friends. Win's maid." She shook her head. "I know Mark loved her, but none of this would have happened if it wasn't for her."

When she looked up at him again, there were tears in her eyes. She wiped them fiercely away.

"I know you didn't like Mark," she said.

"I didn't know him," Dooley reminded her.

"But he was trying to do the right thing," she said. "That's what the police say. The maid—"

"Esperanza," Dooley said quietly. "Her name is Esperanza."

"Esperanza," she said, trying it out but not liking it. "She told the police that Mark called her and told her she should pack her things, he was coming to get her and take her out of there."

Dooley nodded. "He wanted to get her out of the house before he called the police. He didn't want her to get caught up in anything. He was afraid she was going to get deported. He loved her, Beth."

She looked at him, her brown eyes glistening.

"I should go," she said.

He wanted to tell her, no. No, she shouldn't go. She should stay. She should stay forever. But why would she do that? Why would she want to be anywhere near him ever again? Forever and always, he was associated with the death of her brother.

She stood there for a moment longer. Then she was gone.

■ ■ ■

Dooley's uncle came by first thing the next morning. He had an overnight bag with him, which he dropped onto the end of Dooley's bed. He waited out in the hall while Dooley got dressed. He signed the discharge papers and listened closely while the doctor who had seen Dooley explained about wound treatment. He carried the overnight bag for Dooley when they left the hospital. When they got to the car, he said, "You feel good enough to go out for breakfast, or do you want to go straight home?"

After two days of hospital food, it was a no-brainer.

"Breakfast sounds good," Dooley said.

They went to a little place that Dooley's uncle said had the best breakfast in town and did a pretty good steak, too. Dooley ordered the three-egg special, over easy, with sausages, home fries, toast, and juice. His uncle went for a cheese omelet. After they had eaten, his uncle said, "They found the trunk."

"Trunk?

"That kid, Rhodes, he kept all that stuff in a trunk. They found it in the basement, but they said it looked like he'd just put it there recently. They found Mark Everley's camera in it."

Boy, just like Dooley had guessed.

"It had the pictures in it—the same ones as on the flash

drive. They think they can match the hat and the gloves to the two homeless guys who were killed," his uncle said. "That kid is one sick fuck. Jesus, Ryan, he could have killed you."

He almost did, Dooley thought. And he had killed Landers. But he didn't say it. His uncle was getting worked up enough as it was.

"He's still in the hospital," his uncle said. "What I heard, he hit his head pretty hard. They don't know the damage yet."

"What about Esperanza?" Dooley said.

Dooley's uncle shook his head. "She gave a statement. She said she was in love with Everley. He used to come over to the house when no one was there. Apparently her employers—" He spat the word out like a bad taste, telling Dooley exactly what he thought about Rhodes' parents. "She said the father forced himself on her. More than once. And they didn't like her having company in their house. She'd sneak Everley in when no one else was there. She said he liked to wander around the house—go exploring, is how she put it." He looked at Dooley. "I guess that's some house, huh?"

"You could put a dozen of your place in it," Dooley said.

"Yeah, and all that money, where does it get you, huh?" his uncle said. He took a sip of his coffee.

"Esperanza," Dooley said after a moment, nudging his uncle back to his story.

"Esperanza," his uncle said. "Nice name."

Dooley waited. His uncle took another sip of coffee.

"She said one night after she and Everley made love, she fell asleep. Everley woke her up. He said he had to get out of the house fast, that Rhodes was there. She said he was upset—more upset than she thought he should be. He got her to call him the next day when the coast was clear and she let him back in the house. She says he didn't tell her what he was doing, but he went into Rhodes' room with his camera."

"Warren says the files those photos were in were dated two days before he died," Dooley said. "That must be when he took those pictures.

"Could be," his uncle said. "Day after that, he called her up and told her to get ready, he was coming to get her. She still didn't know what was going on—just that he said she had to leave the house and never go back. When he got there to get her, he wanted to leave right away, but—" He shook his head. "Kids. They fooled around again. Rhodes caught them at it. She said she had the feeling maybe he watched them."

"Everley had his backpack with him. He always had it with him," Dooley said. "You think maybe Rhodes looked at his camera? It's digital. He could have seen the pictures."

"Maybe," Dooley's uncle said. "Anyway, she said Rhodes was friendly. Said he wouldn't tell his parents Everley was there, that kind of thing. He invited Everley to play pool with him. She thinks Everley went along with it so Rhodes wouldn't think anything was wrong. The maid fell asleep—"

"I bet he put something in her drink."

"Maybe," Dooley's uncle said again, a real cop, always with the maybes until he knew for sure. "When she woke up, Everley was gone and Rhodes was in bed—she checked.

Then Everley turns up dead and Rhodes is telling her that he and Everley both got drunk and stoned, if his parents find out Everley was here and they were doing stuff like that, they'd mess him up, and if they did that, maybe some stuff would go missing around the place and maybe someone would think she did it and the cops will come and the next thing you know, she'll be on a plane back home."

"So she just kept her mouth shut," Dooley said.

"She thought it was an accident. Everyone did. She had no idea what he'd stumbled across."

"What are they going to do to her?" Dooley said. "Are they going to deport her?"

Dooley's uncle said he didn't know.

He fished in his pocket. Dooley thought he was going for his wallet to pay for breakfast, but, no, he pulled out something else and dropped it onto the table in front of Dooley. His grandfather's ring.

Dooley stared at it.

"You going to ask me where I got it?" his uncle said.

Dooley looked across the table at him.

"That house you were at the night Everley died—the guy thought he heard a prowler. He's jumpy, on account of what happened. He called the cops. They took a report. Then he was out doing some yard work last week, and he found that."

Dooley swallowed hard.

"He turned it in," his uncle said. "He thought either someone had lost it or the prowler had dropped it. When I started asking around, a guy I know showed it to me."

Dooley reached for ring, then pulled his hand back.

Maybe his uncle was just showing it to him, not giving it back.

"Go ahead," his uncle said. "You didn't commit any crime, Ryan. This time."

Dooley hesitated. He looked at his uncle. He had told Dooley he would look into it, and he had. He'd said he had Dooley's back. It looked like he meant it.

"Go on, pick it up," his uncle said. "And do us both a favor, okay? Take it in and get it sized properly." ■

Twenty-Seven

"You're sure about this?" Dooley's uncle said a few days later. He had asked the same question the night before. He had asked it at breakfast when he'd told Dooley he would swing by the house around four and pick him up and drive him over there if that's what he wanted. He had asked it when Dooley got into the car. And now here he was asking it again as Dooley got out.

"Yeah," Dooley said. "I'm sure. I've been thinking about it a lot."

He got out, shut the car door, and looked around. The place should have been familiar, but it wasn't. He wouldn't have recognized it without the address. Of course, it was daytime now and the last two times he'd been here—once a couple of years ago, with Gillette, and once the night Mark Everley had died—it had been night, not to mention the first time, he'd been completely out of it. Still, this was the place that had changed his life. He would have thought it would be burned in his memory. It wasn't.

A little to his left, a guy came down a driveway with a giant-sized brown paper bag full of yard waste. He glanced at Dooley, probably wondering what he was doing just standing there. Dooley tried to block him out. But the man had stopped and was standing there at the edge of his drive, looking at Dooley like maybe he'd seen him some place before but wasn't sure where. Dooley wondered if he had been in court, but he didn't want to turn and look at him just in case he had been.

Okay, one foot in front of the other, that's all it takes to get you from point A to point B. Off the sidewalk onto the pavement, across the pavement and up onto the sidewalk on the other side of the street. Don't stop now. Keep walking, up the path, up the steps onto the porch. He glanced back over his shoulder as he rang the bell. His uncle, behind the wheel of his car, nodded at him. The man was still standing at the end of his driveway, still staring at Dooley, but with a different look on his face, not recognition, but indifference. He turned and headed back up to his house. Dooley turned back to the door. It seemed quiet inside. Maybe no one was home.

A face appeared. A man peered out over half-moon glasses at Dooley. His eyes were dull and gray. The door opened.

"Yes?" the man said, saying the polite thing but looking with suspicion at Dooley.

"I was wondering," Dooley said. He hadn't felt this dry even when he was in rehab. "Mrs. Lytton. Is she home?"

The man was about the same height as Dooley, but he bowed his head when he looked at Dooley so that he would see over the top of his reading glasses.

"Who are you?" the man said. Then his eyes widened a

little, and the suspicion changed slowly from *you-look-familiar* to *no-it-can't-be-you* to *what-the-hell-kind-of-nerve-would-make-you-think-you'd-be-welcome-here*. "You're that boy," the man said. "You're the one who put her in that chair."

Dooley had been in this scene a million times. He'd lain awake nights imagining it, well, imagining running into the man accidentally, usually in a crowd, and the man recognizing him and saying pretty much what he was saying now, but yelling it so that the whole crowd would turn to look at Dooley as if he were some kind of monster. He'd dreamed it, same dream. He'd stood in front of a mirror and practiced what he would say in response. Or what he would say if he ever got up the courage to do what he was trying to do now. He'd spent even more time telling himself: what's the point? Nothing you say now will change anything.

"I was wondering," Dooley said, "if I could speak to her."

"Speak to her?" the man said. He ripped the reading glasses off his face. "You want to speak to her?" He was up close to Dooley now, his voice high, his face twisted. Dooley had to fight the urge to step back, turn, and flee from the porch, down the path, out into the street.

"I wanted to apologize," he said. "For what happ—for what I did."

"You want to apologize?" the man said, his voice full of venom and disdain.

"Look, I'm sorry," Dooley said. "I really am. And I know it won't change things, but I just thought—"

"Oh, you *thought*," the man said. "That must have been a new experience for you because as I recall from the trial, what you said is, you didn't think. *Couldn't* think, as I recall. You were too high. Have I got that right?"

"I just—"

"Just what?" The man stepped closer to Dooley, forcing him back a half-step. "Get out of here," he said. "You might as well have killed her, the way she is now. At least she'd be out of her misery and I could have moved on. It wouldn't have made a jot of difference to how long they kept you locked up, but at least she wouldn't be suffering and neither would I. Get out of here." His voice got louder with every word. Dooley glanced over his shoulder and saw that the man across the street, the one that had been carrying out bags of yard waste, was outside again, looking over at where Dooley was standing. He strode to the end of his driveway and stood there, listening, watching, then calling, "Walt, everything okay?" Dooley's uncle got out of his car and stood there, his eyes wary.

"Get off my porch," the man, Mr. Lytton, said, pushing the words out one at a time with a space between each one. "Get off my porch."

"I'm sorry," Dooley said. "Tell her I'm sorry." And then there was nothing he could do except turn and walk away, feeling the man's eyes on his back, aware of the man across the street watching. His uncle got back into the car. He leaned across the passenger seat and pushed the door open for Dooley. After Dooley buckled his seatbelt, his uncle said, "You can't blame the guy."

Dooley knew it was true, but, boy, he wished things were different.

■ ■ ■

The next Friday night, his arm still in a sling, Dooley was back at work, taking over the cash from Linelle, when Beth came into the store. She hovered near the door for a moment, then pulled herself up straight and marched over to where he was standing.

"Hi," she said.

"Hi."

She glanced at Linelle, who said, "Why don't you take a break, Dooley?"

He was about to ask her what was wrong with her, he'd only just come back from his break, when she gave him a little shove, propelling him through the opening in the counter.

"Yeah," he said. "Sure." His knees were weak and his mouth dry as he looked at Beth.

"There's a coffee place just down the block," she said.

They walked there in silence. When they got there, she said he should grab a table, she'd get the coffees. He protested. She looked pointedly at his sling.

She came back with two coffees and settled in the chair opposite him.

"I went to your school, to tell them we'd changed our minds about the scholarship," she said. "My mother's afraid what people will associate it with. She's afraid no one will apply for it."

Dooley could see that. He felt bad about it, though.

"I ran into Marcus Bracey. He told me he heard that

Win's going to be okay," she said. "He said the doctors say he's lucky."

"Yeah?" Dooley said. "I bet if you talked to the cops, they'd think they were lucky they get to make a case against him."

"I talked to the police," she said. She took a sip of her coffee. "Esperanza's disappeared."

"You mean, something happened to her?"

"They think she went underground. But they have her statement. They have the trunk. They have the pictures and the flash drive. And they have you and what you saw. So they're pretty sure it's going to be okay."

He looked into the blackness of his own coffee for a moment and then up again into her coffee-colored eyes.

"Can I tell you something?" he said.

She nodded.

"It could be hard to hear," he warned her.

"Is it about Mark?"

"It's about me."

She said she wanted to hear it, whatever it was. He started talking, slowly at first, but not stopping, telling her everything, the whole story, even though it took longer than any reasonable break time, even though Kevin was probably going to have a freak-out when he finally got back to the store. As long as she was willing to listen, he was going to talk. He was going to tell it all, every word of it, so that she'd know, she'd be able to make an informed decision when he finally got up the nerve to ask her what he'd been aching to tell her from the very first time she had walked into the store. ■

About the Author

Norah McClintock is the author of more than thirty novels for young adults. She is a five-time winner of the Crime Writers of Canada's Arthur Ellis Award. Her books have been translated into more than a dozen languages. She lives in Toronto with her family.